THE HUNCHBACK OF NOTRE DAME

VOLUME ONE OF TWO

The Hunchback of Notre Dame
Hugo, Victor 1802 – 1885
First Published by Gosselin in 1831

Text set in 18 point Helvetica.
Chapter headings set in Helvetica Neue.

ISBN: 978-1-83412-391-2 Volume One
ISBN: 978-1-83412-392-9 Volume Two

THE HUNCHBACK OF NOTRE DAME

VOLUME ONE OF TWO

VICTOR HUGO

GRAND TYPE CLASSICS

CONTENTS

VOLUME TWO

Book Seventh

Preface

A FEW YEARS AGO, while visiting or, rather, rummaging about Notre-Dame, the author of this book found, in an obscure nook of one of the towers, the following word, engraved by hand upon the wall:–

ʼΑΝБΓΚΗ.

These Greek capitals, black with age, and quite deeply graven in the stone, with I know not what signs peculiar to Gothic caligraphy imprinted upon their forms and upon their attitudes, as though with the purpose of revealing that it had been a hand of the Middle

Ages which had inscribed them there, and especially the fatal and melancholy meaning contained in them, struck the author deeply.

He questioned himself; he sought to divine who could have been that soul in torment which had not been willing to quit this world without leaving this stigma of crime or unhappiness upon the brow of the ancient church.

Afterwards, the wall was whitewashed or scraped down, I know not which, and the inscription disappeared. For it is thus that people have been in the habit of proceeding with the marvellous churches of the Middle Ages for the last two hundred years. Mutilations come to them from every quarter, from within as well as from without. The priest whitewashes them, the archdeacon scrapes them down; then the populace arrives and demolishes them.

Thus, with the exception of the fragile memory which the author of this book here consecrates to it, there remains to-day nothing whatever of the mysterious word engraved within the gloomy tower of Notre-Dame,–nothing of the destiny which it so sadly summed up. The man who wrote that word upon the wall disappeared from the midst of the generations of man many centuries ago; the word, in its turn, has been effaced from the wall of the church; the church will, perhaps, itself soon disappear from the face of the earth.

It is upon this word that this book is founded.

March, 1831.

VOLUME ONE

BOOK FIRST

CHAPTER ONE

The Grand Hall

THREE HUNDRED and forty-eight years, six months, and nineteen days ago to-day, the Parisians awoke to the sound of all the bells in the triple circuit of the city, the university, and the town ringing a full peal.

The sixth of January, 1482, is not, however,

a day of which history has preserved the memory. There was nothing notable in the event which thus set the bells and the **bourgeois** of Paris in a ferment from early morning. It was neither an assault by the Picards nor the Burgundians, nor a hunt led along in procession, nor a revolt of scholars in the town of Laas, nor an entry of "our much dread lord, monsieur the king," nor even a pretty hanging of male and female thieves by the courts of Paris. Neither was it the arrival, so frequent in the fifteenth century, of some plumed and bedizened embassy. It was barely two days since the last cavalcade of that nature, that of the Flemish ambassadors charged with concluding the marriage between the dauphin and Marguerite of Flanders, had made its entry into Paris, to the great annoyance of M. le Cardinal de Bourbon, who, for the sake of pleasing the king, had been obliged to assume an amiable mien towards this whole rustic rabble of Flemish burgomasters, and to regale them at his Hôtel de Bourbon, with a very "pretty morality, allegorical satire, and farce," while a driving rain drenched the magnificent tapestries at his door.

What put the "whole population of Paris in commotion," as Jehan de Troyes expresses it, on the sixth of January, was the double solemnity, united from time immemorial, of the Epiphany and the Feast of Fools.

On that day, there was to be a bonfire on the Place de Grève, a maypole at the Chapelle de Braque, and a mystery at the Palais de Justice. It had been cried, to the sound of the trumpet, the preceding evening at all the cross roads, by the provost's men, clad in handsome, short, sleeveless coats of violet camelot, with large white crosses upon their breasts.

So the crowd of citizens, male and female, having closed their houses and shops, thronged from every direction, at early morn, towards some one of the three spots designated.

Each had made his choice; one, the bonfire; another, the maypole; another, the mystery play. It must be stated, in honor of the good sense of the loungers of Paris, that the greater part of this crowd directed their steps towards the bonfire, which was quite in season, or towards the mystery play, which was to be presented in the grand hall of the Palais de Justice (the courts of law), which was well roofed and walled; and that the curious left the poor, scantily flowered maypole to shiver all alone beneath the sky of January, in the cemetery of the Chapel of Braque.

The populace thronged the avenues of the law courts in particular, because they knew that the Flemish ambassadors, who had arrived two days previously, intended to be present at the representation of the mystery, and at the election of the Pope of the Fools, which was also to take place in the grand hall.

It was no easy matter on that day, to force

one's way into that grand hall, although it was then reputed to be the largest covered enclosure in the world (it is true that Sauval had not yet measured the grand hall of the Château of Montargis). The palace place, encumbered with people, offered to the curious gazers at the windows the aspect of a sea; into which five or six streets, like so many mouths of rivers, discharged every moment fresh floods of heads. The waves of this crowd, augmented incessantly, dashed against the angles of the houses which projected here and there, like so many promontories, into the irregular basin of the place. In the centre of the lofty Gothic[1]

1 The word Gothic, in the sense in which it is generally employed, is wholly unsuitable, but wholly consecrated. Hence we accept it and we adopt it, like all the rest of the world, to characterize the architecture of the second half of the Middle Ages, where the ogive is the principle which succeeds the architecture of the first period, of which the semi-circle is the father.

façade of the palace, the grand staircase, incessantly ascended and descended by a double current, which, after parting on the intermediate landing-place, flowed in broad waves along its lateral slopes,–the grand staircase, I say, trickled incessantly into the place, like a cascade into a lake. The cries, the laughter, the trampling of those thousands of feet, produced a great noise and a great clamor. From time to time, this noise and clamor redoubled; the current which drove the crowd towards the grand staircase flowed backwards, became troubled, formed whirlpools. This was produced by the buffet of an archer, or the horse of one of the provost's sergeants, which kicked to restore order; an admirable tradition which the provostship has bequeathed to the constablery, the constablery to the **maréchaussée**, the **maréchaussée** to our **gendarmeri** of Paris.

Thousands of good, calm, **bourgeois** faces thronged the windows, the doors, the dormer windows, the roofs, gazing at the palace, gazing at the populace, and asking nothing more; for many Parisians content themselves with the spectacle of the spectators, and a wall behind which something is going on becomes at once, for us, a very curious thing indeed.

If it could be granted to us, the men of 1830, to mingle in thought with those Parisians of the fifteenth century, and to enter with them, jostled, elbowed, pulled about, into that immense hall of the palace, which was so cramped on that sixth of January, 1482, the spectacle would not be devoid of either interest or charm, and we should have about us only things that were so old that they would seem new.

With the reader's consent, we will endeavor to retrace in thought, the impression which he would have experienced in company with us on crossing the threshold of that grand hall, in the midst of that tumultuous crowd in surcoats, short, sleeveless jackets, and doublets.

And, first of all, there is a buzzing in the ears, a dazzlement in the eyes. Above our heads is a double ogive vault, panelled with wood carving, painted azure, and sown with golden fleurs-de-lis; beneath our feet a pavement of black and white marble, alternating. A few paces distant, an enormous pillar, then another, then another; seven pillars in all, down the length of the hall, sustaining the spring of the arches of the double vault, in the centre of its width. Around four of the pillars, stalls of merchants, all sparkling with glass and tinsel; around the last three, benches of oak, worn and polished by the trunk hose of the litigants, and the robes of the attorneys. Around the hall, along the lofty wall, between the doors, between the windows, between the pillars, the interminable row of all the kings of France, from Pharamond down: the lazy kings, with pendent arms and downcast eyes; the valiant and combative kings, with heads and arms raised boldly heavenward. Then in the long, pointed windows, glass of a thousand hues; at the wide entrances to the hall, rich doors, finely sculptured; and all, the vaults, pillars, walls, jambs, panelling, doors, statues, covered from top to bottom with a splendid blue and gold illumination, which, a trifle tarnished at the epoch when we behold it, had almost entirely disappeared beneath dust and spiders in the year of grace, 1549, when du Breul still admired it from tradition.

Let the reader picture to himself now, this immense, oblong hall, illuminated by the pallid light of a January day, invaded by a motley and noisy throng which drifts along the walls, and eddies round the seven pillars, and he will have a confused idea of the whole effect of the picture, whose curious details we shall make an effort to indicate with more precision.

It is certain, that if Ravaillac had not assassinated Henri IV., there would have been no documents in the trial of Ravaillac deposited in the clerk's office of the Palais de Justice, no accomplices interested in causing the said documents to disappear; hence, no incendiaries obliged, for lack of better means, to burn the clerk's office in order to burn the documents, and to burn the Palais de Justice in order to burn the clerk's office; consequently, in short, no conflagration in 1618. The old Palais would be standing still, with its ancient grand hall; I should be able to say to the reader, "Go and look at it," and we should thus both escape the necessity,–I of making, and he of reading, a description of it, such as it is. Which demonstrates a new truth: that great events have incalculable results.

It is true that it may be quite possible, in the first place, that Ravaillac had no accomplices; and in the second, that if he had any, they were in no way connected with the fire of 1618. Two other very plausible explanations exist: First, the great flaming star, a foot broad, and a cubit high, which fell from heaven, as every one knows, upon the law courts, after midnight on the seventh of March; second, Théophile's quatrain,–

"Sure, 'twas but a sorry game
When at Paris, Dame Justice,
Through having eaten too much spice,
Set the palace all aflame."

Whatever may be thought of this triple explanation, political, physical, and poetical, of the burning of the law courts in 1618, the unfortunate fact of the fire is certain. Very little to-day remains, thanks to this catastrophe,–thanks, above all, to the successive restorations which have completed what it spared,–very little remains of that first dwelling of the kings of France,–of that elder palace of the Louvre, already so old in the time of Philip the Handsome, that they sought there for the traces of the magnificent buildings erected by King Robert and described by Helgaldus. Nearly everything has disappeared. What has become of the chamber of the chancellery, where Saint Louis consummated his marriage? the garden where he administered justice, “clad in a coat of camelot, a surcoat of linsey-woolsey, without sleeves, and a sur-mantle of black sandal, as he lay upon the carpet with Joinville?” Where is the chamber of the Emperor Sigismond? and that of Charles IV.? that of Jean the Landless? Where is the staircase, from which Charles VI. promulgated his edict of pardon? the slab where Marcel cut the throats of Robert de Clermont and the Marshal of Champagne, in the presence of the dauphin? the wicket where the bulls of Pope Benedict were torn, and whence those who had brought them departed decked out, in derision, in copes and mitres, and making an apology through all Paris? and the grand hall, with its gilding, its azure, its statues, its pointed arches, its pillars, its immense vault, all fretted with carvings? and the gilded chamber? and the stone lion, which stood at the door, with lowered head and tail between his legs, like the lions on the throne of Solomon, in the humiliated attitude which befits force in the presence of justice? and the beautiful doors? and the stained glass? and the chased ironwork, which drove Biscornette to despair? and the delicate woodwork of Hancy? What has time, what have men done with these marvels? What have they given us in return for all this Gallic history, for all this Gothic art? The heavy flattened arches of M. de Brosse, that awkward architect of the Saint-Gervais portal. So much for art; and, as for history, we have the gossiping reminiscences of the great pillar, still ringing with the tattle of the Patru.

It is not much. Let us return to the veritable grand hall of the veritable old palace. The two extremities of this gigantic parallelogram were occupied, the one by the famous marble table, so long, so broad, and so thick that, as the ancient land rolls–in a style that would have given Gargantua an appetite–say, "such a slice of marble as was never beheld in the world"; the other by the chapel where Louis XI. had himself sculptured on his knees before the Virgin, and whither he caused to be brought, without heeding the two gaps thus made in the row of royal statues, the statues of Charlemagne and of Saint Louis, two saints whom he supposed to be great in favor in heaven, as kings of France. This chapel, quite new, having been built only six years, was entirely in that charming taste of delicate architecture, of marvellous sculpture, of fine and deep chasing, which marks with us the end of the Gothic era, and which is perpetuated to about the middle of the sixteenth century in the fairylike fancies of the Renaissance. The little open-work rose window, pierced above the portal, was, in particular, a masterpiece of lightness and grace; one would have pronounced it a star of lace.

In the middle of the hall, opposite the great door, a platform of gold brocade, placed against the wall, a special entrance to which had been effected through a window in the corridor of the gold chamber, had been erected for the Flemish emissaries and the other great personages invited to the presentation of the mystery play.

It was upon the marble table that the mystery was to be enacted, as usual. It had been arranged for the purpose, early in the morning; its rich slabs of marble, all scratched by the heels of law clerks, supported a cage of carpenter's work of considerable height, the upper surface of which, within view of the whole hall, was to serve as the theatre, and whose interior, masked by tapestries, was to take the place of dressing-rooms for the personages of the piece. A ladder, naively placed on the outside, was to serve as means of communication between the dressing-room and the stage, and lend its rude rungs to entrances as well as to exits. There was no personage, however unexpected, no sudden change, no theatrical effect, which was not obliged to mount that ladder. Innocent and venerable infancy of art and contrivances!

Four of the bailiff of the palace's sergeants, perfunctory guardians of all the pleasures of the people, on days of festival as well as on days of execution, stood at the four corners of the marble table.

The piece was only to begin with the twelfth stroke of the great palace clock sounding midday. It was very late, no doubt, for a theatrical representation, but they had been obliged to fix the hour to suit the convenience of the ambassadors.

Now, this whole multitude had been waiting since morning. A goodly number of curious, good people had been shivering since daybreak before the grand staircase of the palace; some even affirmed that they had passed the night across the threshold of the great door, in order to make sure that they should be the first to pass in. The crowd grew more dense every moment, and, like water, which rises above its normal level, began to mount along the walls, to swell around the pillars, to spread out on the entablatures, on the cornices, on the window-sills, on all the salient points of the architecture, on all the reliefs of the sculpture. Hence, discomfort, impatience, weariness, the liberty of a day of cynicism and folly, the quarrels which break forth for all sorts of causes–a pointed elbow, an iron-shod shoe, the fatigue of long waiting–had already, long before the hour appointed for the arrival of the ambassadors, imparted a harsh and bitter accent to the clamor of these people who were shut in, fitted into each other, pressed, trampled upon, stifled. Nothing was to be heard but imprecations on the Flemish, the provost of the merchants, the Cardinal de Bourbon, the bailiff of the courts, Madame Marguerite of Austria, the sergeants with their rods, the cold, the heat, the bad weather, the Bishop of Paris, the Pope of the Fools, the pillars, the statues, that closed door, that open window; all to the vast amusement of a band of scholars and lackeys scattered through the mass, who mingled with all this discontent their teasing remarks, and their malicious suggestions, and pricked the general bad temper with a pin, so to speak.

Among the rest there was a group of those merry imps, who, after smashing the glass in a window, had seated themselves hardily on the entablature, and from that point despatched their gaze and their railleries both within and without, upon the throng in the hall, and the throng upon the Place. It was easy to see, from their parodied gestures, their ringing laughter, the bantering appeals which they exchanged with their comrades, from one end of the hall to the other, that these young clerks did not share the weariness and fatigue of the rest of the spectators, and that they understood very well the art of extracting, for their own private diversion from that which they had under their eyes, a spectacle which made them await the other with patience.

"Upon my soul, so it's you, 'Joannes Frollo de Molendino!'" cried one of them, to a sort of little, light-haired imp, with a well-favored and malign countenance, clinging to the acanthus leaves of a capital; "you are well named John of the Mill, for your two arms and your two legs have the air of four wings fluttering on the breeze. How long have you been here?"

"By the mercy of the devil," retorted Joannes Frollo, "these four hours and more; and I hope that they will be reckoned to my credit in purgatory. I heard the eight singers of the King of Sicily intone the first verse of seven o'clock mass in the Sainte-Chapelle."

"Fine singers!" replied the other, "with voices even more pointed than their caps! Before founding a mass for Monsieur Saint John, the king should have inquired whether Monsieur Saint John likes Latin droned out in a Provençal accent."

"He did it for the sake of employing those

accursed singers of the King of Sicily!" cried an old woman sharply from among the crowd beneath the window. "I just put it to you! A thousand **livres parisi** for a mass! and out of the tax on sea fish in the markets of Paris, to boot!"

"Peace, old crone," said a tall, grave person, stopping up his nose on the side towards the fishwife; "a mass had to be founded. Would you wish the king to fall ill again?"

"Bravely spoken, Sire Gilles Lecornu, master furrier of king's robes!" cried the little student, clinging to the capital.

A shout of laughter from all the students greeted the unlucky name of the poor furrier of the king's robes.

"Lecornu! Gilles Lecornu!" said some.

"**Cornutus et hirsutus**, horned and hairy," another went on.

"He! of course," continued the small imp on the capital, "What are they laughing at? An honorable man is Gilles Lecornu, brother of Master Jehan Lecornu, provost of the king's house, son of Master Mahiet Lecornu, first porter of the Bois de Vincennes,–all **bourgeois** of Paris, all married, from father to son."

The gayety redoubled. The big furrier, without uttering a word in reply, tried to escape all the eyes riveted upon him from all sides; but he perspired and panted in vain; like a wedge entering the wood, his efforts served only to bury still more deeply in the shoulders of his neighbors, his large, apoplectic face, purple with spite and rage.

At length one of these, as fat, short, and venerable as himself, came to his rescue.

"Abomination! scholars addressing a **bourgeois** in that fashion in my day would have been flogged with a fagot, which would have afterwards been used to burn them."

The whole band burst into laughter.

"Holà hé! who is scolding so? Who is that screech owl of evil fortune?"

"Hold, I know him" said one of them; "'tis Master Andry Musnier."

"Because he is one of the four sworn booksellers of the university!" said the other.

"Everything goes by fours in that shop," cried a third; "the four nations, the four faculties, the four feasts, the four procurators, the four electors, the four booksellers."

"Well," began Jean Frollo once more, "we must play the devil with them."[2]

"Musnier, we'll burn your books."

"Musnier, we'll beat your lackeys."

"Musnier, we'll kiss your wife."

"That fine, big Mademoiselle Oudarde."

"Who is as fresh and as gay as though she were a widow."

"Devil take you!" growled Master Andry Musnier.

"Master Andry," pursued Jean Jehan, still clinging to his capital, "hold your tongue, or I'll drop on your head!"

---

2 Faire le diable à quatre.

Master Andry raised his eyes, seemed to measure in an instant the height of the pillar, the weight of the scamp, mentally multiplied that weight by the square of the velocity and remained silent.

Jehan, master of the field of battle, pursued triumphantly:

"That's what I'll do, even if I am the brother of an archdeacon!"

"Fine gentry are our people of the university, not to have caused our privileges to be respected on such a day as this! However, there is a maypole and a bonfire in the town; a mystery, Pope of the Fools, and Flemish ambassadors in the city; and, at the university, nothing!"

"Nevertheless, the Place Maubert is sufficiently large!" interposed one of the clerks established on the window-sill.

"Down with the rector, the electors, and the procurators!" cried Joannes.

"We must have a bonfire this evening in the Champ-Gaillard," went on the other, "made of Master Andry's books."

"And the desks of the scribes!" added his neighbor.

"And the beadles' wands!"

"And the spittoons of the deans!"

"And the cupboards of the procurators!"

"And the hutches of the electors!"

"And the stools of the rector!"

"Down with them!" put in little Jehan, as counterpoint; "down with Master Andry, the beadles and the scribes; the theologians, the doctors and the decretists; the procurators, the electors and the rector!"

"The end of the world has come!" muttered Master Andry, stopping up his ears.

"By the way, there's the rector! see, he is passing through the Place," cried one of those in the window.

Each rivalled his neighbor in his haste to turn towards the Place.

"Is it really our venerable rector, Master Thibaut?" demanded Jehan Frollo du Moulin, who, as he was clinging to one of the inner pillars, could not see what was going on outside.

"Yes, yes," replied all the others, "it is really he, Master Thibaut, the rector."

It was, in fact, the rector and all the dignitaries of the university, who were marching in procession in front of the embassy, and at that moment traversing the Place. The students crowded into the window, saluted them as they passed with sarcasms and ironical applause. The rector, who was walking at the head of his company, had to support the first broadside; it was severe.

"Good day, monsieur le recteur! Holà hé! good day there!"

"How does he manage to be here, the old gambler? Has he abandoned his dice?"

"How he trots along on his mule! her ears are not so long as his!"

"Holà hé! good day, monsieur le recteur Thibaut! **Tybalde aleator**! Old fool! old gambler!"

"God preserve you! Did you throw double six often last night?"

"Oh! what a decrepit face, livid and haggard and drawn with the love of gambling and of dice!"

"Where are you bound for in that fashion, Thibaut, **Tybalde ad dados**, with your back turned to the university, and trotting towards the town?"

"He is on his way, no doubt, to seek a lodging in the Rue Thibautodé?"[3] cried Jehan du M. Moulin.

The entire band repeated this quip in a voice of thunder, clapping their hands furiously.

"You are going to seek a lodging in the Rue Thibautodé, are you not, monsieur le recteur, gamester on the side of the devil?"

Then came the turns of the other dignitaries.

"Down with the beadles! down with the mace-bearers!"

---

3 Thibaut au des,—Thibaut of the dice.

"Tell me, Robin Pouissepain, who is that yonder?"

"He is Gilbert de Suilly, **Gilbertus de Soliaco**, the chancellor of the College of Autun."

"Hold on, here's my shoe; you are better placed than I, fling it in his face."

"**Saturnalitias mittimus ecce nuces**."

"Down with the six theologians, with their white surplices!"

"Are those the theologians? I thought they were the white geese given by Sainte-Geneviève to the city, for the fief of Roogny."

"Down with the doctors!"

"Down with the cardinal disputations, and quibblers!"

"My cap to you, Chancellor of Sainte-Geneviève! You have done me a wrong. 'Tis true; he gave my place in the nation of Normandy to little Ascanio Falzapada, who comes from the province of Bourges, since he is an Italian."

"That is an injustice," said all the scholars.

"Down with the Chancellor of Sainte-Geneviève!"

"Ho hé! Master Joachim de Ladehors! Ho hé! Louis Dahuille! Ho hé Lambert Hoctement!"

"May the devil stifle the procurator of the German nation!"

"And the chaplains of the Sainte-Chapelle, with their gray **amices; cum tunices grisis**!"

"**Seu de pellibus grisis fourratis**!"

"Holà hé! Masters of Arts! All the beautiful black copes! all the fine red copes!"

"They make a fine tail for the rector."

"One would say that he was a Doge of Venice on his way to his bridal with the sea."

"Say, Jehan! here are the canons of Sainte-Geneviève!"

"To the deuce with the whole set of canons!"

"Abbé Claude Choart! Doctor Claude Choart! Are you in search of Marie la Giffarde?"

"She is in the Rue de Glatigny."

"She is making the bed of the king of the

debauchees."

"She is paying her four deniers[4] **quatuor denarios**."

"**Aut unum bombum**."

"Would you like to have her pay you in the face?"

"Comrades! Master Simon Sanguin, the Elector of Picardy, with his wife on the crupper!"

"**Post equitem sedet atra cura**–behind the horseman sits black care."

"Courage, Master Simon!"

"Good day, Mister Elector!"

"Good night, Madame Electress!"

"How happy they are to see all that!" sighed Joannes de Molendino, still perched in the foliage of his capital.

Meanwhile, the sworn bookseller of the university, Master Andry Musnier, was inclining his ear to the furrier of the king's robes, Master Gilles Lecornu.

---

4 An old French coin, equal to the two hundred and fortieth part of a pound.

"I tell you, sir, that the end of the world has come. No one has ever beheld such outbreaks among the students! It is the accursed inventions of this century that are ruining everything,–artilleries, bombards, and, above all, printing, that other German pest. No more manuscripts, no more books! printing will kill bookselling. It is the end of the world that is drawing nigh."

"I see that plainly, from the progress of velvet stuffs," said the fur-merchant.

At this moment, midday sounded.

"Ha!" exclaimed the entire crowd, in one voice.

The scholars held their peace. Then a great hurly-burly ensued; a vast movement of feet, hands, and heads; a general outbreak of coughs and handkerchiefs; each one arranged himself, assumed his post, raised himself up, and grouped himself. Then came a great silence; all necks remained outstretched, all mouths remained open, all glances were directed towards the marble table. Nothing made its appearance there. The bailiff's four sergeants were still there, stiff, motionless, as painted statues. All eyes turned to the estrade reserved for the Flemish envoys. The door remained closed, the platform empty. This crowd had been waiting since daybreak for three things: noonday, the embassy from Flanders, the mystery play. Noonday alone had arrived on time.

On this occasion, it was too much.

They waited one, two, three, five minutes, a quarter of an hour; nothing came. The dais remained empty, the theatre dumb. In the meantime, wrath had succeeded to impatience. Irritated words circulated in a low tone, still, it is true. "The mystery! the mystery!" they murmured, in hollow voices. Heads began to ferment. A tempest, which was only rumbling in the distance as yet, was floating on the surface of this crowd. It was Jehan du Moulin who struck the first spark from it.

"The mystery, and to the devil with the Flemings!" he exclaimed at the full force of his lungs, twining like a serpent around his pillar.

The crowd clapped their hands.

"The mystery!" it repeated, "and may all the devils take Flanders!"

"We must have the mystery instantly," resumed the student; "or else, my advice is that we should hang the bailiff of the courts, by way of a morality and a comedy."

"Well said," cried the people, "and let us begin the hanging with his sergeants."

A grand acclamation followed. The four poor fellows began to turn pale, and to exchange glances. The crowd hurled itself towards them, and they already beheld the frail wooden railing, which separated them from it, giving way and bending before the pressure of the throng.

It was a critical moment.

"To the sack, to the sack!" rose the cry on all sides.

At that moment, the tapestry of the dressing-room, which we have described above, was raised, and afforded passage to a personage, the mere sight of whom suddenly stopped the crowd, and changed its wrath into curiosity as by enchantment.

"Silence! silence!"

The personage, but little reassured, and trembling in every limb, advanced to the edge of the marble table with a vast amount of bows, which, in proportion as he drew nearer, more and more resembled genuflections.

In the meanwhile, tranquillity had gradually been restored. All that remained was that slight murmur which always rises above the silence of a crowd.

"Messieurs the **bourgeois**," said he, "and mesdemoiselles the **bourgeoises**, we shall have the honor of declaiming and representing, before his eminence, monsieur the cardinal, a very beautiful morality which has for its title, 'The Good Judgment of

Madame the Virgin Mary.' I am to play Jupiter. His eminence is, at this moment, escorting the very honorable embassy of the Duke of Austria; which is detained, at present, listening to the harangue of monsieur the rector of the university, at the gate Baudets. As soon as his illustrious eminence, the cardinal, arrives, we will begin."

It is certain, that nothing less than the intervention of Jupiter was required to save the four unfortunate sergeants of the bailiff of the courts. If we had the happiness of having invented this very veracious tale, and of being, in consequence, responsible for it before our Lady Criticism, it is not against us that the classic precept, **Nec deus intersit**, could be invoked. Moreover, the costume of Seigneur Jupiter, was very handsome, and contributed not a little towards calming the crowd, by attracting all its attention. Jupiter was clad in a coat of mail, covered with black velvet, with gilt nails; and had it not been for the rouge, and the huge red beard, each of which covered one-half of his face,–had it not been for the roll of gilded cardboard, spangled, and all bristling with strips of tinsel, which he held in his hand, and in which the eyes of the initiated easily recognized thunderbolts,–had not his feet been flesh-colored, and banded with ribbons in Greek fashion, he might have borne comparison, so far as the severity of his mien was concerned, with a Breton archer from the guard of Monsieur de Berry.

CHAPTER TWO

Pierre Gringoire

NEVERTHELESS, AS BE harangued them, the satisfaction and admiration unanimously excited by his costume were dissipated by his words; and when he reached that untoward conclusion: "As soon as his illustrious eminence, the cardinal, arrives, we will begin," his voice was drowned in a thunder of hooting.

"Begin instantly! The mystery! the mystery

immediately!" shrieked the people. And above all the voices, that of Johannes de Molendino was audible, piercing the uproar like the fife's derisive serenade: "Commence instantly!" yelped the scholar.

"Down with Jupiter and the Cardinal de Bourbon!" vociferated Robin Poussepain and the other clerks perched in the window.

"The morality this very instant!" repeated the crowd; "this very instant! the sack and the rope for the comedians, and the cardinal!"

Poor Jupiter, haggard, frightened, pale beneath his rouge, dropped his thunderbolt, took his cap in his hand; then he bowed and trembled and stammered: "His eminence–the ambassadors–Madame Marguerite of Flanders–." He did not know what to say. In truth, he was afraid of being hung.

Hung by the populace for waiting, hung by the cardinal for not having waited, he saw between the two dilemmas only an abyss; that is to say, a gallows.

Luckily, some one came to rescue him

from his embarrassment, and assume the responsibility.

An individual who was standing beyond the railing, in the free space around the marble table, and whom no one had yet caught sight of, since his long, thin body was completely sheltered from every visual ray by the diameter of the pillar against which he was leaning; this individual, we say, tall, gaunt, pallid, blond, still young, although already wrinkled about the brow and cheeks, with brilliant eyes and a smiling mouth, clad in garments of black serge, worn and shining with age, approached the marble table, and made a sign to the poor sufferer. But the other was so confused that he did not see him. The new comer advanced another step.

"Jupiter," said he, "my dear Jupiter!"

The other did not hear.

At last, the tall blond, driven out of patience, shrieked almost in his face,–

"Michel Giborne!"

"Who calls me?" said Jupiter, as though

awakened with a start.

"I," replied the person clad in black.

"Ah!" said Jupiter.

"Begin at once," went on the other. "Satisfy the populace; I undertake to appease the bailiff, who will appease monsieur the cardinal."

Jupiter breathed once more.

"Messeigneurs the **bourgeois**," he cried, at the top of his lungs to the crowd, which continued to hoot him, "we are going to begin at once."

"**Evoe Jupiter! Plaudite cives**! All hail, Jupiter! Applaud, citizens!" shouted the scholars.

"Noël! Noël! good, good," shouted the people.

The hand clapping was deafening, and Jupiter had already withdrawn under his tapestry, while the hall still trembled with acclamations.

In the meanwhile, the personage who had so magically turned the tempest into dead calm, as our old and dear Corneille puts it, had modestly retreated to the half-shadow of his pillar, and would, no doubt, have remained invisible there, motionless, and mute as before, had he not been plucked by the sleeve by two young women, who, standing in the front row of the spectators, had noticed his colloquy with Michel Giborne-Jupiter.

"Master," said one of them, making him a sign to approach.

"Hold your tongue, my dear Liénarde," said her neighbor, pretty, fresh, and very brave, in consequence of being dressed up in her best attire. "He is not a clerk, he is a layman; you must not say master to him, but messire."

"Messire," said Liénarde.

The stranger approached the railing.

"What would you have of me, damsels?" he asked, with alacrity.

"Oh! nothing," replied Liénarde, in great confusion; "it is my neighbor, Gisquette la Gencienne, who wishes to speak with you."

"Not so," replied Gisquette, blushing; "it was Liénarde who called you master; I only told her to say messire."

The two young girls dropped their eyes. The man, who asked nothing better than to enter into conversation, looked at them with a smile.

"So you have nothing to say to me, damsels?"

"Oh! nothing at all," replied Gisquette.

"Nothing," said Liénarde.

The tall, light-haired young man retreated a step; but the two curious maidens had no mind to let slip their prize.

"Messire," said Gisquette, with the impetuosity of an open sluice, or of a woman who has made up her mind, "do you know that soldier who is to play the part of Madame the Virgin in the mystery?"

"You mean the part of Jupiter?" replied the stranger.

"Hé! yes," said Liénarde, "isn't she stupid? So you know Jupiter?"

"Michel Giborne?" replied the unknown; "yes, madam."

"He has a fine beard!" said Liénarde.

"Will what they are about to say here be fine?" inquired Gisquette, timidly.

"Very fine, mademoiselle," replied the unknown, without the slightest hesitation.

"What is it to be?" said Liénarde.

"'The Good Judgment of Madame the Virgin,'–a morality, if you please, damsel."

"Ah! that makes a difference," responded Liénarde.

A brief silence ensued–broken by the stranger.

"It is a perfectly new morality, and one which has never yet been played."

"Then it is not the same one," said Gisquette, "that was given two years ago, on the day of the entrance of monsieur the legate, and where three handsome maids played the parts–"

"Of sirens," said Liénarde.

"And all naked," added the young man.

Liénarde lowered her eyes modestly. Gisquette glanced at her and did the same. He continued, with a smile,–

"It was a very pleasant thing to see. To-day it is a morality made expressly for Madame the Demoiselle of Flanders."

"Will they sing shepherd songs?" inquired Gisquette.

"Fie!" said the stranger, "in a morality? you must not confound styles. If it were a farce, well and good."

"That is a pity," resumed Gisquette. "That day, at the Ponceau Fountain, there were wild men and women, who fought and assumed many aspects, as they sang little motets and bergerettes."

"That which is suitable for a legate," returned the stranger, with a good deal of dryness, "is not suitable for a princess."

"And beside them," resumed Liénarde, "played many brass instruments, making great melodies."

"And for the refreshment of the passers-by," continued Gisquette, "the fountain spouted through three mouths, wine, milk, and hippocrass, of which every one drank who wished."

"And a little below the Ponceau, at the Trinity," pursued Liénarde, "there was a passion performed, and without any speaking."

"How well I remember that!" exclaimed Gisquette; "God on the cross, and the two thieves on the right and the left." Here the young gossips, growing warm at the memory of the entrance of monsieur the legate, both began to talk at once.

"And, further on, at the Painters' Gate, there were other personages, very richly clad."

"And at the fountain of Saint-Innocent, that huntsman, who was chasing a hind with great clamor of dogs and hunting-horns."

"And, at the Paris slaughter-houses, stages, representing the fortress of Dieppe!"

"And when the legate passed, you remember, Gisquette? they made the assault, and the English all had their throats cut."

"And against the gate of the Châtelet, there were very fine personages!"

"And on the Port au Change, which was all draped above!"

"And when the legate passed, they let fly on the bridge more than two hundred sorts of birds; wasn't it beautiful, Liénarde?"

"It will be better to-day," finally resumed their interlocutor, who seemed to listen to them with impatience.

"Do you promise us that this mystery will be fine?" said Gisquette.

"Without doubt," he replied; then he added, with a certain emphasis,–"I am the author of it, damsels."

"Truly?" said the young girls, quite taken aback.

"Truly!" replied the poet, bridling a little; "that is, to say, there are two of us; Jehan Marchand, who has sawed the planks and erected the framework of the theatre and the woodwork; and I, who have made the piece. My name is Pierre Gringoire."

The author of the "Cid" could not have said "Pierre Corneille" with more pride.

Our readers have been able to observe, that a certain amount of time must have already elapsed from the moment when Jupiter had retired beneath the tapestry to the instant when the author of the new morality had thus abruptly revealed himself to the innocent admiration of Gisquette and Liénarde. Remarkable fact: that whole crowd, so tumultuous but a few moments before, now waited amiably on the word of the comedian; which proves the eternal truth, still experienced every day in our theatres, that the best means of making the public wait patiently is to assure them that one is about to begin instantly.

However, scholar Johannes had not fallen asleep.

"Holà hé!" he shouted suddenly, in the midst of the peaceable waiting which had followed the tumult. "Jupiter, Madame the Virgin, buffoons of the devil! are you jeering at us? The piece! the piece! commence or we will commence again!"

This was all that was needed.

The music of high and low instruments immediately became audible from the interior of the stage; the tapestry was raised; four personages, in motley attire and painted faces, emerged from it, climbed the steep ladder of the theatre, and, arrived upon the upper platform, arranged themselves in a line before the public, whom they saluted with profound reverences; then the symphony ceased.

The mystery was about to begin.

The four personages, after having reaped a rich reward of applause for their reverences, began, in the midst of profound silence, a prologue, which we gladly spare the reader. Moreover, as happens in our own day, the public was more occupied with the costumes that the actors wore than with the roles that they were enacting; and, in truth, they were right. All four were dressed in parti-colored robes of yellow and white, which were distinguished from each other only by the nature of the stuff; the first was of gold and silver brocade; the second, of silk; the third, of wool; the fourth, of linen. The first of these personages carried in his right hand a sword; the second, two golden keys; the third, a pair of scales; the fourth, a spade: and, in order to aid sluggish minds which would not have seen clearly through the transparency of these attributes, there was to be read, in large, black letters, on the hem of the robe of brocade, MY NAME IS NOBILITY; on the hem of the silken robe, MY NAME IS CLERGY; on the hem of the woolen robe, MY NAME IS MERCHANDISE; on the hem of the linen robe, MY NAME IS LABOR. The sex of the two male characters was briefly indicated to every judicious spectator, by their shorter robes, and by the cap which they wore on their heads; while the two female characters, less briefly clad, were covered with hoods.

Much ill-will would also have been required, not to comprehend, through the medium of the poetry of the prologue, that Labor was wedded to Merchandise, and Clergy to Nobility, and that the two happy couples possessed in common a magnificent golden dolphin, which they desired to adjudge to the fairest only. So they were roaming about the world seeking and searching for this beauty, and, after having successively rejected the Queen of Golconda, the Princess of Trebizonde, the daughter of the Grand Khan of Tartary, etc., Labor and Clergy, Nobility and Merchandise, had come to rest upon the marble table of the Palais de Justice, and to utter, in the presence of the honest audience, as many sentences and maxims as could then be dispensed at the Faculty of Arts, at examinations, sophisms, determinances, figures, and acts, where the masters took their degrees.

All this was, in fact, very fine.

Nevertheless, in that throng, upon which the four allegories vied with each other in pouring out floods of metaphors, there was no ear more attentive, no heart that palpitated more, not an eye was more haggard, no neck more outstretched, than the eye, the ear, the neck, and the heart of the author, of the poet, of that brave Pierre Gringoire, who had not been able to resist, a moment before, the joy of telling his name to two pretty girls. He had retreated a few paces from them, behind his pillar, and there he listened, looked, enjoyed. The amiable applause which had greeted the beginning of his prologue was still echoing in his bosom, and he was completely absorbed in that species of ecstatic contemplation with which an author beholds his ideas fall, one by one, from the mouth of the actor into the vast silence of the audience. Worthy Pierre Gringoire!

It pains us to say it, but this first ecstasy was speedily disturbed. Hardly had Gringoire raised this intoxicating cup of joy and triumph to his lips, when a drop of bitterness was mingled with it.

A tattered mendicant, who could not collect any coins, lost as he was in the midst of the crowd, and who had not probably found sufficient indemnity in the pockets of his neighbors, had hit upon the idea of perching himself upon some conspicuous point, in order to attract looks and alms. He had, accordingly, hoisted himself, during the first verses of the prologue, with the aid of the pillars of the reserve gallery, to the cornice which ran round the balustrade at its lower edge; and there he had seated himself, soliciting the attention and the pity of the multitude, with his rags and a hideous sore which covered his right arm. However, he uttered not a word.

The silence which he preserved allowed the prologue to proceed without hindrance, and no perceptible disorder would have ensued, if ill-luck had not willed that the scholar Joannes should catch sight, from the heights of his pillar, of the mendicant and his grimaces. A wild fit of laughter took possession of the young scamp, who, without caring that he was interrupting the spectacle, and disturbing the universal composure, shouted boldly,–

"Look! see that sickly creature asking alms!"

Any one who has thrown a stone into a frog pond, or fired a shot into a covey of birds, can form an idea of the effect produced by these incongruous words, in the midst of the general attention. It made Gringoire shudder as though it had been an electric shock. The prologue stopped short, and all heads turned tumultuously towards the beggar, who, far from being disconcerted by this, saw, in this incident, a good opportunity for reaping his harvest, and who began to whine in a doleful way, half closing his eyes the while,–"Charity, please!"

"Well–upon my soul," resumed Joannes,

"it's Clopin Trouillefou! Holà hé, my friend, did your sore bother you on the leg, that you have transferred it to your arm?" So saying, with the dexterity of a monkey, he flung a bit of silver into the gray felt hat which the beggar held in his ailing arm. The mendicant received both the alms and the sarcasm without wincing, and continued, in lamentable tones,–

"Charity, please!"

This episode considerably distracted the attention of the audience; and a goodly number of spectators, among them Robin Poussepain, and all the clerks at their head, gayly applauded this eccentric duet, which the scholar, with his shrill voice, and the mendicant had just improvised in the middle of the prologue.

Gringoire was highly displeased. On recovering from his first stupefaction, he bestirred himself to shout, to the four personages on the stage, "Go on! What the devil!–go on!"–without even deigning to cast a glance of disdain upon the two interrupters.

At that moment, he felt some one pluck at the hem of his surtout; he turned round, and not without ill-humor, and found considerable difficulty in smiling; but he was obliged to do so, nevertheless. It was the pretty arm of Gisquette la Gencienne, which, passed through the railing, was soliciting his attention in this manner.

"Monsieur," said the young girl, "are they going to continue?"

"Of course," replied Gringoire, a good deal shocked by the question.

"In that case, messire," she resumed, "would you have the courtesy to explain to me–"

"What they are about to say?" interrupted Gringoire. "Well, listen."

"No," said Gisquette, "but what they have said so far."

Gringoire started, like a man whose wound has been probed to the quick.

"A plague on the stupid and dull-witted

little girl!" he muttered, between his teeth.

From that moment forth, Gisquette was nothing to him.

In the meantime, the actors had obeyed his injunction, and the public, seeing that they were beginning to speak again, began once more to listen, not without having lost many beauties in the sort of soldered joint which was formed between the two portions of the piece thus abruptly cut short. Gringoire commented on it bitterly to himself. Nevertheless, tranquillity was gradually restored, the scholar held his peace, the mendicant counted over some coins in his hat, and the piece resumed the upper hand.

It was, in fact, a very fine work, and one which, as it seems to us, might be put to use to-day, by the aid of a little rearrangement. The exposition, rather long and rather empty, that is to say, according to the rules, was simple; and Gringoire, in the candid sanctuary of his own conscience, admired its clearness. As the reader may surmise, the four allegorical personages were somewhat weary with having traversed the three sections of the world, without having found suitable opportunity for getting rid of their golden dolphin. Thereupon a eulogy of the marvellous fish, with a thousand delicate allusions to the young betrothed of Marguerite of Flanders, then sadly cloistered in at Amboise, and without a suspicion that Labor and Clergy, Nobility and Merchandise had just made the circuit of the world in his behalf. The said dauphin was then young, was handsome, was stout, and, above all (magnificent origin of all royal virtues), he was the son of the Lion of France. I declare that this bold metaphor is admirable, and that the natural history of the theatre, on a day of allegory and royal marriage songs, is not in the least startled by a dolphin who is the son of a lion. It is precisely these rare and Pindaric mixtures which prove the poet's enthusiasm. Nevertheless, in order to play the part of critic also, the poet might have developed this beautiful idea in something less than two hundred lines. It is true that the mystery was to last from noon until four o'clock, in accordance with the orders of monsieur the provost, and that it was necessary to say something. Besides, the people listened patiently.

All at once, in the very middle of a quarrel between Mademoiselle Merchandise and Madame Nobility, at the moment when Monsieur Labor was giving utterance to this wonderful line,–

In forest ne'er was seen a more triumphant beast;

the door of the reserved gallery which had hitherto remained so inopportunely closed, opened still more inopportunely; and the ringing voice of the usher announced abruptly, "His eminence, Monseigneur the Cardinal de Bourbon."

CHAPTER THREE

Monsieur the Cardinal

POOR GRINGOIRE! THE din of all the great double petards of the Saint-Jean, the discharge of twenty arquebuses on supports, the detonation of that famous serpentine of the Tower of Billy, which, during the siege of Paris, on Sunday, the twenty-sixth of September, 1465, killed seven Burgundians at one blow, the explosion of all the powder stored at the gate of the Temple, would have rent his ears less rudely at that solemn and dramatic moment, than these few words, which fell from the lips of the usher, "His eminence, Monseigneur the Cardinal de Bourbon."

It is not that Pierre Gringoire either feared or disdained monsieur the cardinal. He had neither the weakness nor the audacity for that. A true eclectic, as it would be expressed nowadays, Gringoire was one of those firm and lofty, moderate and calm spirits, which always know how to bear themselves amid all circumstances (**stare in dimidio rerum**), and who are full of reason and of liberal philosophy, while still setting store by cardinals. A rare, precious, and never interrupted race of philosophers to whom wisdom, like another Ariadne, seems to have given a clew of thread which they have been walking along unwinding since the beginning of the world, through the labyrinth of human affairs. One finds them in all ages, ever the same; that is to say, always according to all times. And, without reckoning our Pierre Gringoire, who may represent them in the fifteenth century if we succeed in bestowing upon him the distinction which he deserves, it certainly was their spirit which animated Father du Breul, when he wrote, in the sixteenth, these naively sublime words, worthy of all centuries: "I am a Parisian by nation, and a Parrhisian in language, for **parrhisia** in Greek signifies liberty of speech; of which I have made use even towards messeigneurs the cardinals, uncle and brother to Monsieur the Prince de Conty, always with respect to their greatness, and without offending any one of their suite, which is much to say."

There was then neither hatred for the cardinal, nor disdain for his presence, in the disagreeable impression produced upon Pierre Gringoire. Quite the contrary; our poet had too much good sense and too threadbare a coat, not to attach particular importance to having the numerous allusions in his prologue, and, in particular, the glorification of the dauphin, son of the Lion of France, fall upon the most eminent ear. But it is not interest which predominates in the noble nature of poets. I suppose that the entity of the poet may be represented by the number ten; it is certain that a chemist on analyzing and pharmacopolizing it, as Rabelais says, would find it composed of one part interest to nine parts of self-esteem.

Now, at the moment when the door had opened to admit the cardinal, the nine parts of self-esteem in Gringoire, swollen and expanded by the breath of popular admiration, were in a state of prodigious augmentation, beneath which disappeared, as though stifled, that imperceptible molecule of which we have just remarked upon in the constitution of poets; a precious ingredient, by the way, a ballast of reality and humanity, without which they would not touch the earth.

Gringoire enjoyed seeing, feeling, fingering, so to speak an entire assembly (of knaves, it is true, but what matters that?) stupefied, petrified, and as though asphyxiated in the presence of the incommensurable tirades which welled up every instant from all parts of his bridal song. I affirm that he shared the general beatitude, and that, quite the reverse of La Fontaine, who, at the presentation of his comedy of the "Florentine," asked, "Who is the ill-bred lout who made that rhapsody?" Gringoire would gladly have inquired of his neighbor, "Whose masterpiece is this?"

The reader can now judge of the effect produced upon him by the abrupt and unseasonable arrival of the cardinal.

That which he had to fear was only too fully realized. The entrance of his eminence upset the audience. All heads turned towards the gallery. It was no longer possible to hear one's self. "The cardinal! The cardinal!" repeated all mouths. The unhappy prologue stopped short for the second time.

The cardinal halted for a moment on the threshold of the estrade. While he was sending a rather indifferent glance around the audience, the tumult redoubled. Each person wished to get a better view of him. Each man vied with the other in thrusting his head over his neighbor's shoulder.

He was, in fact, an exalted personage, the sight of whom was well worth any other comedy. Charles, Cardinal de Bourbon, Archbishop and Comte of Lyon, Primate of the Gauls, was allied both to Louis XI., through his brother, Pierre, Seigneur de Beaujeu, who had married the king's eldest daughter, and to Charles the Bold through his mother, Agnes of Burgundy. Now, the dominating trait, the peculiar and distinctive trait of the character of the Primate of the Gauls, was the spirit of the courtier, and devotion to the powers that be. The reader can form an idea of the numberless embarrassments which this double relationship had caused him, and of all the temporal reefs among which his spiritual bark had been forced to tack, in order not to suffer shipwreck on either Louis or Charles, that Scylla and that Charybdis which had devoured the Duc de Nemours and the Constable de Saint-Pol. Thanks to Heaven's mercy, he had made the voyage successfully, and had reached home without hindrance. But although he was in port, and precisely because he was in port, he never recalled without disquiet the varied haps of his political career, so long uneasy and laborious. Thus, he was in the habit of saying that the year 1476 had been "white and black" for him–meaning thereby, that in the course of that year he had lost his mother, the Duchesse de la Bourbonnais, and his cousin, the Duke of Burgundy, and that one grief had consoled him for the other.

Nevertheless, he was a fine man; he led a joyous cardinal's life, liked to enliven himself with the royal vintage of Challuau, did not hate Richarde la Garmoise and Thomasse la Saillarde, bestowed alms on pretty girls rather than on old women,–and for all these reasons was very agreeable to the **populace** of Paris. He never went about otherwise than surrounded by a small court of bishops and abbés of high lineage, gallant, jovial, and given to carousing on occasion; and more than once the good and devout women of Saint Germain d'Auxerre, when passing at night beneath the brightly illuminated windows of Bourbon, had been scandalized to hear the same voices which had intoned vespers for them during the day carolling, to the clinking of glasses, the bacchic proverb of Benedict XII., that pope who had added a third crown to the Tiara– **Bibamus papaliter**.

It was this justly acquired popularity, no doubt, which preserved him on his entrance from any bad reception at the hands of the mob, which had been so displeased but a moment before, and very little disposed to respect a cardinal on the very day when it was to elect a pope. But the Parisians cherish little rancor; and then, having forced the beginning of the play by their authority, the good **bourgeois** had got the upper hand of the cardinal, and this triumph was sufficient for them. Moreover, the Cardinal de Bourbon was a handsome man,–he wore a fine scarlet robe, which he carried off very well,–that is to say, he had all the women on his side, and, consequently, the best half of the audience. Assuredly, it would be injustice and bad taste to hoot a cardinal for having come late to the spectacle, when he is a handsome man, and when he wears his scarlet robe well.

He entered, then, bowed to those present with the hereditary smile of the great for the people, and directed his course slowly towards his scarlet velvet arm-chair, with the air of thinking of something quite different. His cortege–what we should nowadays call his staff–of bishops and abbés invaded the estrade in his train, not without causing redoubled tumult and curiosity among the audience. Each man vied with his neighbor in pointing them out and naming them, in seeing who should recognize at least one of them: this one, the Bishop of Marseilles (Alaudet, if my memory serves me right);– this one, the primicier of Saint-Denis;–this one, Robert de Lespinasse, Abbé of Saint-Germain des Prés, that libertine brother of a mistress of Louis XI.; all with many errors and absurdities. As for the scholars, they swore. This was their day, their feast of fools, their saturnalia, the annual orgy of the corporation of law clerks and of the school. There was no turpitude which was not sacred on that day. And then there were gay gossips in the crowd–Simone Quatrelivres, Agnès la Gadine, and Rabine Piédebou. Was it not the least that one could do to swear at one's ease and revile the name of God a little, on so fine a day, in such good company as dignitaries of the church and loose women? So they did not abstain; and, in the midst of the uproar, there was a frightful concert of blasphemies and enormities of all the unbridled tongues, the tongues of clerks and students restrained during the rest of the year, by the fear of the hot iron of Saint Louis. Poor Saint Louis! how they set him at defiance in his own court of law! Each one of them selected from the new-comers on the platform, a black, gray, white, or violet cassock as his target. Joannes Frollo de Molendin, in his quality of brother to an archdeacon, boldly attacked the scarlet; he sang in deafening tones, with his impudent eyes fastened on the cardinal, "**Cappa repleta mero**!"

All these details which we here lay bare for the edification of the reader, were so covered by the general uproar, that they were lost in it before reaching the reserved platforms; moreover, they would have moved the cardinal but little, so much a part of the customs were the liberties of that day. Moreover, he had another cause for solicitude, and his mien as wholly preoccupied with it, which entered the estrade the same time as himself; this was the embassy from Flanders.

Not that he was a profound politician, nor was he borrowing trouble about the possible consequences of the marriage of his cousin Marguerite de Bourgoyne to his cousin Charles, Dauphin de Vienne; nor as to how long the good understanding which had been patched up between the Duke of Austria and the King of France would last; nor how the King of England would take this disdain of his daughter. All that troubled him but little; and he gave a warm reception every evening to the wine of the royal vintage of Chaillot, without a suspicion that several flasks of that same wine (somewhat revised and corrected, it is true, by Doctor Coictier), cordially offered to Edward IV. by Louis XI., would, some fine morning, rid Louis XI. of Edward IV. "The much honored embassy of Monsieur the Duke of Austria," brought the cardinal none of these cares, but it troubled him in another direction. It was, in fact, somewhat hard, and we have already hinted at it on the second page of this book,–for him, Charles de Bourbon, to be obliged to feast and receive cordially no one knows what **bourgeois**;–for him, a cardinal, to receive aldermen;–for him, a Frenchman, and a jolly companion, to receive Flemish beer-drinkers,–and that in public! This was, certainly, one of the most irksome grimaces that he had ever executed for the good pleasure of the king.

So he turned toward the door, and with the best grace in the world (so well had he trained himself to it), when the usher announced, in a sonorous voice, "Messieurs the Envoys of Monsieur the Duke of Austria." It is useless to add that the whole hall did the same.

Then arrived, two by two, with a gravity which made a contrast in the midst of the frisky ecclesiastical escort of Charles de

Bourbon, the eight and forty ambassadors of Maximilian of Austria, having at their head the reverend Father in God, Jehan, Abbot of Saint-Bertin, Chancellor of the Golden Fleece, and Jacques de Goy, Sieur Dauby, Grand Bailiff of Ghent. A deep silence settled over the assembly, accompanied by stifled laughter at the preposterous names and all the **bourgeois** designations which each of these personages transmitted with imperturbable gravity to the usher, who then tossed names and titles pell-mell and mutilated to the crowd below. There were Master Loys Roelof, alderman of the city of Louvain; Messire Clays d'Etuelde, alderman of Brussels; Messire Paul de Baeust, Sieur de Voirmizelle, President of Flanders; Master Jehan Coleghens, burgomaster of the city of Antwerp; Master George de la Moere, first alderman of the kuere of the city of Ghent; Master Gheldolf van der Hage, first alderman of the **parchons** of the said town; and the Sieur de Bierbecque, and Jehan

Pinnock, and Jehan Dymaerzelle, etc., etc., etc.; bailiffs, aldermen, burgomasters; burgomasters, aldermen, bailiffs–all stiff, affectedly grave, formal, dressed out in velvet and damask, hooded with caps of black velvet, with great tufts of Cyprus gold thread; good Flemish heads, after all, severe and worthy faces, of the family which Rembrandt makes to stand out so strong and grave from the black background of his "Night Patrol"; personages all of whom bore, written on their brows, that Maximilian of Austria had done well in "trusting implicitly," as the manifest ran, "in their sense, valor, experience, loyalty, and good wisdom."

There was one exception, however. It was a subtle, intelligent, crafty-looking face, a sort of combined monkey and diplomat phiz, before whom the cardinal made three steps and a profound bow, and whose name, nevertheless, was only, "Guillaume Rym, counsellor and pensioner of the City of Ghent."

Few persons were then aware who Guillaume Rym was. A rare genius who in a time of revolution would have made a brilliant appearance on the surface of events, but who in the fifteenth century was reduced to cavernous intrigues, and to "living in mines," as the Duc de Saint-Simon expresses it. Nevertheless, he was appreciated by the "miner" of Europe; he plotted familiarly with Louis XI., and often lent a hand to the king's secret jobs. All which things were quite unknown to that throng, who were amazed at the cardinal's politeness to that frail figure of a Flemish bailiff.

CHAPTER FOUR

Master Jacques Coppenole

WHILE THE PENSIONER OF Ghent and his eminence were exchanging very low bows and a few words in voices still lower, a man of lofty stature, with a large face and broad shoulders, presented himself, in order to enter abreast with Guillaume Rym; one would have pronounced him a bull-dog by the side of a fox. His felt doublet and leather jerkin made a spot on the velvet and silk which surrounded him. Presuming that he was some groom who had stolen in, the usher stopped him.

"Hold, my friend, you cannot pass!"

The man in the leather jerkin shouldered him aside.

"What does this knave want with me?" said he, in stentorian tones, which rendered the entire hall attentive to this strange colloquy. "Don't you see that I am one of them?"

"Your name?" demanded the usher.

"Jacques Coppenole."

"Your titles?"

"Hosier at the sign of the 'Three Little Chains,' of Ghent."

The usher recoiled. One might bring one's self to announce aldermen and burgomasters, but a hosier was too much. The cardinal was on thorns. All the people were staring and listening. For two days his eminence had been exerting his utmost efforts to lick these Flemish bears into shape, and to render them a little more presentable to the public, and this freak was startling. But Guillaume Rym, with his polished smile, approached the usher.

"Announce Master Jacques Coppenole, clerk of the aldermen of the city of Ghent," he whispered, very low.

"Usher," interposed the cardinal, aloud, "announce Master Jacques Coppenole, clerk of the aldermen of the illustrious city of Ghent."

This was a mistake. Guillaume Rym alone might have conjured away the difficulty, but Coppenole had heard the cardinal.

"No, cross of God?" he exclaimed, in his voice of thunder, "Jacques Coppenole, hosier. Do you hear, usher? Nothing more, nothing less. Cross of God! hosier; that's fine enough. Monsieur the Archduke has more than once sought his **gant**[5] in my hose."

Laughter and applause burst forth. A

---

5 Got the first idea of a thing.

jest is always understood in Paris, and, consequently, always applauded.

Let us add that Coppenole was of the people, and that the auditors which surrounded him were also of the people. Thus the communication between him and them had been prompt, electric, and, so to speak, on a level. The haughty air of the Flemish hosier, by humiliating the courtiers, had touched in all these plebeian souls that latent sentiment of dignity still vague and indistinct in the fifteenth century.

This hosier was an equal, who had just held his own before monsieur the cardinal. A very sweet reflection to poor fellows habituated to respect and obedience towards the underlings of the sergeants of the bailiff of Sainte-Geneviève, the cardinal's train-bearer.

Coppenole proudly saluted his eminence, who returned the salute of the all-powerful **bourgeois** feared by Louis XI. Then, while Guillaume Rym, a "sage and malicious man," as Philippe de Comines puts it, watched them both with a smile of raillery and superiority, each sought his place, the cardinal quite abashed and troubled, Coppenole tranquil and haughty, and thinking, no doubt, that his title of hosier was as good as any other, after all, and that Marie of Burgundy, mother to that Marguerite whom Coppenole was to-day bestowing in marriage, would have been less afraid of the cardinal than of the hosier; for it is not a cardinal who would have stirred up a revolt among the men of Ghent against the favorites of the daughter of Charles the Bold; it is not a cardinal who could have fortified the populace with a word against her tears and prayers, when the Maid of Flanders came to supplicate her people in their behalf, even at the very foot of the scaffold; while the hosier had only to raise his leather elbow, in order to cause to fall your two heads, most illustrious seigneurs, Guy d'Hymbercourt and Chancellor Guillaume Hugonet.

Nevertheless, all was over for the poor cardinal, and he was obliged to quaff to the dregs the bitter cup of being in such bad company.

The reader has, probably, not forgotten the impudent beggar who had been clinging fast to the fringes of the cardinal's gallery ever since the beginning of the prologue. The arrival of the illustrious guests had by no means caused him to relax his hold, and, while the prelates and ambassadors were packing themselves into the stalls–like genuine Flemish herrings–he settled himself at his ease, and boldly crossed his legs on the architrave. The insolence of this proceeding was extraordinary, yet no one noticed it at first, the attention of all being directed elsewhere. He, on his side, perceived nothing that was going on in the hall; he wagged his head with the unconcern of a Neapolitan, repeating from time to time, amid the clamor, as from a mechanical habit, "Charity, please!" And, assuredly, he was, out of all those present, the only one who had not deigned to turn his head at the altercation between Coppenole and the usher. Now, chance ordained that the master hosier of Ghent, with whom the people were already in lively sympathy, and upon whom all eyes were riveted–should come and seat himself in the front row of the gallery, directly above the mendicant; and people were not a little amazed to see the Flemish ambassador, on concluding his inspection of the knave thus placed beneath his eyes, bestow a friendly tap on that ragged shoulder. The beggar turned round; there was surprise, recognition, a lighting up of the two countenances, and so forth; then, without paying the slightest heed in the world to the spectators, the hosier and the wretched being began to converse in a low tone, holding each other's hands, in the meantime, while the rags of Clopin Trouillefou, spread out upon the cloth of gold of the dais, produced the effect of a caterpillar on an orange.

The novelty of this singular scene excited such a murmur of mirth and gayety in the hall, that the cardinal was not slow to perceive it; he half bent forward, and, as from the point where he was placed he could catch only an imperfect view of Trouillerfou's ignominious doublet, he very naturally imagined that the mendicant was asking alms, and, disgusted with his audacity, he exclaimed: "Bailiff of the Courts, toss me that knave into the river!"

"Cross of God! monseigneur the cardinal," said Coppenole, without quitting Clopin's hand, "he's a friend of mine."

"Good! good!" shouted the populace. From that moment, Master Coppenole enjoyed in Paris as in Ghent, "great favor with the people; for men of that sort do enjoy it," says Philippe de Comines, "when they are thus disorderly." The cardinal bit his lips. He bent towards his neighbor, the Abbé of Sainte-Geneviève, and said to him in a low tone,– "Fine ambassadors monsieur the archduke sends here, to announce to us Madame Marguerite!"

"Your eminence," replied the abbé, "wastes your politeness on these Flemish swine. **Margaritas ante porcos**, pearls before swine."

"Say rather," retorted the cardinal, with a smile, "**Porcos ante Margaritam**, swine before the pearl."

The whole little court in cassocks went into ecstacies over this play upon words. The cardinal felt a little relieved; he was quits with Coppenole, he also had had his jest applauded.

Now, will those of our readers who possess the power of generalizing an image or an idea, as the expression runs in the style of to-day, permit us to ask them if they have formed a very clear conception of the spectacle presented at this moment, upon which we have arrested their attention, by the vast parallelogram of the grand hall of the palace.

In the middle of the hall, backed against the western wall, a large and magnificent gallery draped with cloth of gold, into which enter in procession, through a small, arched door, grave personages, announced successively by the shrill voice of an usher. On the front benches were already a number of venerable figures, muffled in ermine, velvet, and scarlet. Around the dais–which remains silent and dignified–below, opposite, everywhere, a great crowd and a great murmur. Thousands of glances directed by the people on each face upon the dais, a thousand whispers over each name. Certainly, the spectacle is curious, and well deserves the attention of the spectators. But yonder, quite at the end, what is that sort of trestle work with four motley puppets upon it, and more below? Who is that man beside the trestle, with a black doublet and a pale face? Alas! my dear reader, it is Pierre Gringoire and his prologue.

We have all forgotten him completely.

This is precisely what he feared.

From the moment of the cardinal's entrance, Gringoire had never ceased to tremble for the safety of his prologue. At first he had enjoined the actors, who had stopped in suspense, to continue, and to raise their voices; then, perceiving that no one was listening, he had stopped them; and, during the entire quarter of an hour that the interruption lasted, he had not ceased to stamp, to flounce about, to appeal to Gisquette and Liénarde, and to urge his neighbors to the continuance of the prologue; all in vain. No one quitted the cardinal, the embassy, and the gallery–sole centre of this vast circle of visual rays. We must also believe, and we say it with regret, that the prologue had begun slightly to weary the audience at the moment when his eminence had arrived, and created a diversion in so terrible a fashion. After all, on the gallery as well as on the marble table, the spectacle was the same: the conflict of Labor and Clergy, of Nobility and Merchandise. And many people preferred to see them alive, breathing, moving, elbowing each other in flesh and blood, in this Flemish embassy, in this Episcopal court, under the cardinal's robe, under Coppenole's jerkin, than painted, decked out, talking in verse, and, so to speak, stuffed beneath the yellow amid white tunics in which Gringoire had so ridiculously clothed them.

Nevertheless, when our poet beheld quiet reestablished to some extent, he devised a stratagem which might have redeemed all.

"Monsieur," he said, turning towards one of his neighbors, a fine, big man, with a patient face, "suppose we begin again."

"What?" said his neighbor.

"Hé! the Mystery," said Gringoire.

"As you like," returned his neighbor.

This semi-approbation sufficed for Gringoire, and, conducting his own affairs, he began to shout, confounding himself with the crowd as much as possible: "Begin the mystery again! begin again!"

"The devil!" said Joannes de Molendino, "what are they jabbering down yonder, at the end of the hall?" (for Gringoire was making noise enough for four.) "Say, comrades, isn't that mystery finished? They want to begin it all over again. That's not fair!"

"No, no!" shouted all the scholars. "Down with the mystery! Down with it!"

But Gringoire had multiplied himself, and only shouted the more vigorously: "Begin again! begin again!"

These clamors attracted the attention of the cardinal.

"Monsieur Bailiff of the Courts," said he to a tall, black man, placed a few paces from him, "are those knaves in a holy-water vessel, that they make such a hellish noise?"

The bailiff of the courts was a sort of amphibious magistrate, a sort of bat of the judicial order, related to both the rat and the bird, the judge and the soldier.

He approached his eminence, and not without a good deal of fear of the latter's displeasure, he awkwardly explained to him the seeming disrespect of the audience: that noonday had arrived before his eminence, and that the comedians had been forced to begin without waiting for his eminence.

The cardinal burst into a laugh.

"On my faith, the rector of the university ought to have done the same. What say you, Master Guillaume Rym?"

"Monseigneur," replied Guillaume Rym, "let us be content with having escaped half of the comedy. There is at least that much gained."

"Can these rascals continue their farce?" asked the bailiff.

"Continue, continue," said the cardinal, "it's all the same to me. I'll read my breviary in the meantime."

The bailiff advanced to the edge of the estrade, and cried, after having invoked silence by a wave of the hand,–

"**Bourgeois**, rustics, and citizens, in order to satisfy those who wish the play to begin again, and those who wish it to end, his eminence orders that it be continued."

Both parties were forced to resign themselves. But the public and the author long cherished a grudge against the cardinal.

So the personages on the stage took up their parts, and Gringoire hoped that the rest of his work, at least, would be listened to. This hope was speedily dispelled like his other illusions; silence had indeed, been restored in the audience, after a fashion; but Gringoire had not observed that at the moment when the cardinal gave the order to continue, the gallery was far from full, and that after the Flemish envoys there had arrived new personages forming part of the **cortège**, whose names and ranks, shouted out in the midst of his dialogue by the intermittent cry of the usher, produced considerable ravages in it. Let the reader imagine the effect in the midst of a theatrical piece, of the yelping of an usher, flinging in between two rhymes, and often in the middle of a line, parentheses like the following,–

"Master Jacques Charmolue, procurator to the king in the Ecclesiastical Courts!"

"Jehan de Harlay, equerry guardian of the office of chevalier of the night watch of the city of Paris!"

"Messire Galiot de Genoilhac, chevalier, seigneur de Brussac, master of the king's artillery!"

"Master Dreux-Raguier, surveyor of the woods and forests of the king our sovereign, in the land of France, Champagne and Brie!"

"Messire Louis de Graville, chevalier, councillor, and chamberlain of the king, admiral of France, keeper of the Forest of Vincennes!"

"Master Denis le Mercier, guardian of the house of the blind at Paris!" etc., etc., etc.

This was becoming unbearable.

This strange accompaniment, which rendered it difficult to follow the piece, made

Gringoire all the more indignant because he could not conceal from himself the fact that the interest was continually increasing, and that all his work required was a chance of being heard.

It was, in fact, difficult to imagine a more ingenious and more dramatic composition. The four personages of the prologue were bewailing themselves in their mortal embarrassment, when Venus in person, (**vera incessa patuit dea**) presented herself to them, clad in a fine robe bearing the heraldic device of the ship of the city of Paris. She had come herself to claim the dolphin promised to the most beautiful. Jupiter, whose thunder could be heard rumbling in the dressing-room, supported her claim, and Venus was on the point of carrying it off,–that is to say, without allegory, of marrying monsieur the dauphin, when a young child clad in white damask, and holding in her hand a daisy (a transparent personification of Mademoiselle Marguerite of Flanders) came to contest it with Venus.

Theatrical effect and change.

After a dispute, Venus, Marguerite, and the assistants agreed to submit to the good judgment of time holy Virgin. There was another good part, that of the king of Mesopotamia; but through so many interruptions, it was difficult to make out what end he served. All these persons had ascended by the ladder to the stage.

But all was over; none of these beauties had been felt nor understood. On the entrance of the cardinal, one would have said that an invisible magic thread had suddenly drawn all glances from the marble table to the gallery, from the southern to the western extremity of the hall. Nothing could disenchant the audience; all eyes remained fixed there, and the new-comers and their accursed names, and their faces, and their costumes, afforded a continual diversion. This was very distressing. With the exception of Gisquette and Liénarde, who turned round from time to time when Gringoire plucked them by the sleeve; with the exception of the big, patient neighbor, no one listened, no one looked at the poor, deserted morality full face. Gringoire saw only profiles.

With what bitterness did he behold his whole erection of glory and of poetry crumble away bit by bit! And to think that these people had been upon the point of instituting a revolt against the bailiff through impatience to hear his work! now that they had it they did not care for it. This same representation which had been begun amid so unanimous an acclamation! Eternal flood and ebb of popular favor! To think that they had been on the point of hanging the bailiff's sergeant! What would he not have given to be still at that hour of honey!

But the usher's brutal monologue came to an end; every one had arrived, and Gringoire breathed freely once more; the actors continued bravely. But Master Coppenole, the hosier, must needs rise of a sudden, and Gringoire was forced to listen to him deliver, amid universal attention, the following abominable harangue.

"Messieurs the **bourgeois** and squires of Paris, I don't know, cross of God! what we are doing here. I certainly do see yonder in the corner on that stage, some people who appear to be fighting. I don't know whether that is what you call a "mystery," but it is not amusing; they quarrel with their tongues and nothing more. I have been waiting for the first blow this quarter of an hour; nothing comes; they are cowards who only scratch each other with insults. You ought to send for the fighters of London or Rotterdam; and, I can tell you! you would have had blows of the fist that could be heard in the Place; but these men excite our pity. They ought at least, to give us a moorish dance, or some other mummer! That is not what was told me; I was promised a feast of fools, with the election of a pope. We have our pope of fools at Ghent also; we're not behindhand in that, cross of God! But this is the way we manage it; we collect a crowd like this one here, then each person in turn passes his head through a hole, and makes a grimace at the rest; time one who makes the ugliest, is elected pope by general acclamation; that's the way it is. It is very diverting. Would you like to make your pope after the fashion of my country? At all events, it will be less wearisome than to listen to chatterers. If they wish to come and make their grimaces through the hole, they can join the game. What say you, Messieurs les **bourgeois**? You have here enough grotesque specimens of both sexes, to allow of laughing in Flemish fashion, and there are enough of us ugly in countenance to hope for a fine grinning match."

Gringoire would have liked to retort; stupefaction, rage, indignation, deprived him of words. Moreover, the suggestion of the popular hosier was received with such enthusiasm by these **bourgeois** who were flattered at being called “squires,” that all resistance was useless. There was nothing to be done but to allow one’s self to drift with the torrent. Gringoire hid his face between his two hands, not being so fortunate as to have a mantle with which to veil his head, like Agamemnon of Timantis.

CHAPTER FIVE

Quasimodo

IN THE TWINKLING OF an eye, all was ready to execute Coppenole's idea. **Bourgeois**, scholars and law clerks all set to work. The little chapel situated opposite the marble table was selected for the scene of the grinning match. A pane broken in the pretty rose window above the door, left free a circle of stone through which it was agreed that the competitors should thrust their heads. In order to reach it, it was only necessary to mount upon a couple of hogsheads, which had been produced from I know not where, and perched one upon the other, after a fashion. It was settled that each candidate, man or woman (for it was possible to choose a female pope), should, for the sake of leaving the impression of his grimace fresh and complete, cover his face and remain concealed in the chapel until the moment of his appearance. In less than an instant, the chapel was crowded with competitors, upon whom the door was then closed.

Coppenole, from his post, ordered all, directed all, arranged all. During the uproar, the cardinal, no less abashed than Gringoire, had retired with all his suite, under the pretext of business and vespers, without the crowd which his arrival had so deeply stirred being in the least moved by his departure. Guillaume Rym was the only one who noticed his eminence's discomfiture. The attention of the populace, like the sun, pursued its revolution; having set out from one end of the hall, and halted for a space in the middle, it had now reached the other end. The marble table, the brocaded gallery had each had their day; it was now the turn of the chapel of Louis XI. Henceforth, the field was open to all folly. There was no one there now, but the Flemings and the rabble.

The grimaces began. The first face which appeared at the aperture, with eyelids turned up to the reds, a mouth open like a maw, and a brow wrinkled like our hussar boots of the Empire, evoked such an inextinguishable peal of laughter that Homer would have taken all these louts for gods. Nevertheless, the grand hall was anything but Olympus, and Gringoire's poor Jupiter knew it better than any one else. A second and third grimace followed, then another and another; and the laughter and transports of delight went on increasing. There was in this spectacle, a peculiar power of intoxication and fascination, of which it would be difficult to convey to the reader of our day and our salons any idea.

Let the reader picture to himself a series of visages presenting successively all geometrical forms, from the triangle to the trapezium, from the cone to the polyhedron; all human expressions, from wrath to lewdness; all ages, from the wrinkles of the new-born babe to the wrinkles of the aged and dying; all religious phantasmagories, from Faun to Beelzebub; all animal profiles, from the maw to the beak, from the jowl to the muzzle. Let the reader imagine all these grotesque figures of the Pont Neuf, those nightmares petrified beneath the hand of Germain Pilon, assuming life and breath, and coming in turn to stare you in the face with burning eyes; all the masks of the Carnival of Venice passing in succession before your glass,–in a word, a human kaleidoscope.

The orgy grew more and more Flemish. Teniers could have given but a very imperfect idea of it. Let the reader picture to himself in bacchanal form, Salvator Rosa's battle. There were no longer either scholars or ambassadors or **bourgeois** or men or women; there was no longer any Clopin Trouillefou, nor Gilles Lecornu, nor Marie Quatrelivres, nor Robin Poussepain. All was universal license. The grand hall was no longer anything but a vast furnace of effrontry and joviality, where every mouth was a cry, every individual a posture; everything shouted and howled. The strange visages which came, in turn, to gnash their teeth in the rose window, were like so many brands cast into the brazier; and from the whole of this effervescing crowd, there escaped, as from a furnace, a sharp, piercing, stinging noise, hissing like the wings of a gnat.

"Ho hé! curse it!"

"Just look at that face!"

"It's not good for anything."

"Guillemette Maugerepuis, just look at that bull's muzzle; it only lacks the horns. It can't be your husband."

"Another!"

"Belly of the pope! what sort of a grimace is that?"

"Holà hé! that's cheating. One must show only one's face."

"That damned Perrette Callebotte! she's capable of that!"

"Good! Good!"

"I'm stifling!"

"There's a fellow whose ears won't go through!" Etc., etc.

But we must do justice to our friend Jehan. In the midst of this witches' sabbath, he was still to be seen on the top of his pillar, like the cabin-boy on the topmast. He floundered about with incredible fury. His mouth was wide open, and from it there escaped a cry which no one heard, not that it was covered by the general clamor, great as that was but because it attained, no doubt, the limit of perceptible sharp sounds, the thousand vibrations of Sauveur, or the eight thousand of Biot.

As for Gringoire, the first moment of depression having passed, he had regained his composure. He had hardened himself against adversity.–"Continue!" he had said for the third time, to his comedians, speaking machines; then as he was marching with great strides in front of the marble table, a fancy seized him to go and appear in his turn at the aperture of the chapel, were it only for the pleasure of making a grimace at that ungrateful populace.–"But no, that would not be worthy of us; no, vengeance! let us combat until the end," he repeated to himself; "the power of poetry over people is great; I will bring them back. We shall see which will carry the day, grimaces or polite literature."

Alas! he had been left the sole spectator of his piece. It was far worse than it had been a little while before. He no longer beheld anything but backs.

I am mistaken. The big, patient man, whom he had already consulted in a critical moment, had remained with his face turned towards the stage. As for Gisquette and Liénarde, they had deserted him long ago.

Gringoire was touched to the heart by the fidelity of his only spectator. He approached him and addressed him, shaking his arm slightly; for the good man was leaning on the balustrade and dozing a little.

“Monsieur,” said Gringoire, “I thank you!”

“Monsieur,” replied the big man with a yawn, “for what?”

“I see what wearies you,” resumed the poet; “’tis all this noise which prevents your hearing comfortably. But be at ease! your name shall descend to posterity! Your name, if you please?”

“Renauld Chateau, guardian of the seals of the Châtelet of Paris, at your service.”

“Monsieur, you are the only representative of the muses here,” said Gringoire.

“You are too kind, sir,” said the guardian of

the seals at the Châtelet.

"You are the only one," resumed Gringoire, "who has listened to the piece decorously. What do you think of it?"

"He! he!" replied the fat magistrate, half aroused, "it's tolerably jolly, that's a fact."

Gringoire was forced to content himself with this eulogy; for a thunder of applause, mingled with a prodigious acclamation, cut their conversation short. The Pope of the Fools had been elected.

"Noël! Noël! Noël!"[6] shouted the people on all sides. That was, in fact, a marvellous grimace which was beaming at that moment through the aperture in the rose window. After all the pentagonal, hexagonal, and whimsical faces, which had succeeded each other at that hole without realizing the ideal of the grotesque which their imaginations, excited by the orgy, had constructed, nothing less was

6 The ancient French hurrah.

needed to win their suffrages than the sublime grimace which had just dazzled the assembly. Master Coppenole himself applauded, and Clopin Trouillefou, who had been among the competitors (and God knows what intensity of ugliness his visage could attain), confessed himself conquered: We will do the same. We shall not try to give the reader an idea of that tetrahedral nose, that horseshoe mouth; that little left eye obstructed with a red, bushy, bristling eyebrow, while the right eye disappeared entirely beneath an enormous wart; of those teeth in disarray, broken here and there, like the embattled parapet of a fortress; of that callous lip, upon which one of these teeth encroached, like the tusk of an elephant; of that forked chin; and above all, of the expression spread over the whole; of that mixture of malice, amazement, and sadness. Let the reader dream of this whole, if he can.

The acclamation was unanimous; people

rushed towards the chapel. They made the lucky Pope of the Fools come forth in triumph. But it was then that surprise and admiration attained their highest pitch; the grimace was his face.

Or rather, his whole person was a grimace. A huge head, bristling with red hair; between his shoulders an enormous hump, a counterpart perceptible in front; a system of thighs and legs so strangely astray that they could touch each other only at the knees, and, viewed from the front, resembled the crescents of two scythes joined by the handles; large feet, monstrous hands; and, with all this deformity, an indescribable and redoubtable air of vigor, agility, and courage,–strange exception to the eternal rule which wills that force as well as beauty shall be the result of harmony. Such was the pope whom the fools had just chosen for themselves.

One would have pronounced him a giant who had been broken and badly put together again.

When this species of cyclops appeared on the threshold of the chapel, motionless, squat, and almost as broad as he was tall; **squared** on the **base**, as a great man says; with his doublet half red, half violet, sown with silver bells, and, above all, in the perfection of his ugliness, the populace recognized him on the instant, and shouted with one voice,–

"'Tis Quasimodo, the bellringer! 'tis Quasimodo, the hunchback of Notre-Dame! Quasimodo, the one-eyed! Quasimodo, the bandy-legged! Noël! Noël!"

It will be seen that the poor fellow had a choice of surnames.

"Let the women with child beware!" shouted the scholars.

"Or those who wish to be," resumed Joannes.

The women did, in fact, hide their faces.

"Oh! the horrible monkey!" said one of them.

"As wicked as he is ugly," retorted another.

"He's the devil," added a third.

"I have the misfortune to live near Notre-Dame; I hear him prowling round the eaves by night."

"With the cats."

"He's always on our roofs."

"He throws spells down our chimneys."

"The other evening, he came and made a grimace at me through my attic window. I thought that it was a man. Such a fright as I had!"

"I'm sure that he goes to the witches' sabbath. Once he left a broom on my leads."

"Oh! what a displeasing hunchback's face!"

"Oh! what an ill-favored soul!"

"Whew!"

The men, on the contrary, were delighted and applauded. Quasimodo, the object of the tumult, still stood on the threshold of the chapel, sombre and grave, and allowed them to admire him.

One scholar (Robin Poussepain, I think), came and laughed in his face, and too close. Quasimodo contented himself with taking him by the girdle, and hurling him ten paces off amid the crowd; all without uttering a word.

Master Coppenole, in amazement, approached him.

"Cross of God! Holy Father! you possess the handsomest ugliness that I have ever beheld in my life. You would deserve to be pope at Rome, as well as at Paris."

So saying, he placed his hand gayly on his shoulder. Quasimodo did not stir. Coppenole went on,–

"You are a rogue with whom I have a fancy for carousing, were it to cost me a new dozen of twelve livres of Tours. How does it strike you?"

Quasimodo made no reply.

"Cross of God!" said the hosier, "are you deaf?"

He was, in truth, deaf.

Nevertheless, he began to grow impatient with Coppenole's behavior, and suddenly turned towards him with so formidable a gnashing of teeth, that the Flemish giant recoiled, like a bull-dog before a cat.

Then there was created around that strange personage, a circle of terror and respect, whose radius was at least fifteen geometrical feet. An old woman explained to Coppenole that Quasimodo was deaf.

"Deaf!" said the hosier, with his great Flemish laugh. "Cross of God! He's a perfect pope!"

"Hé! I recognize him," exclaimed Jehan, who had, at last, descended from his capital, in order to see Quasimodo at closer quarters, "he's the bellringer of my brother, the archdeacon. Good-day, Quasimodo!"

"What a devil of a man!" said Robin Poussepain still all bruised with his fall. "He shows himself; he's a hunchback. He walks; he's bandy-legged. He looks at you;

he's one-eyed. You speak to him; he's deaf. And what does this Polyphemus do with his tongue?"

"He speaks when he chooses," said the old woman; "he became deaf through ringing the bells. He is not dumb."

"That he lacks," remarks Jehan.

"And he has one eye too many," added Robin Poussepain.

"Not at all," said Jehan wisely. "A one-eyed man is far less complete than a blind man. He knows what he lacks."

In the meantime, all the beggars, all the lackeys, all the cutpurses, joined with the scholars, had gone in procession to seek, in the cupboard of the law clerks' company, the cardboard tiara, and the derisive robe of the Pope of the Fools. Quasimodo allowed them to array him in them without wincing, and with a sort of proud docility. Then they made him seat himself on a motley litter. Twelve officers of the fraternity of fools raised him on their shoulders; and a sort of bitter and disdainful joy lighted up the morose face of the cyclops, when he beheld beneath his deformed feet all those heads of handsome, straight, well-made men. Then the ragged and howling procession set out on its march, according to custom, around the inner galleries of the Courts, before making the circuit of the streets and squares.

CHAPTER SIX

Esmeralda

WE ARE DELIGHTED TO be able to inform the reader, that during the whole of this scene, Gringoire and his piece had stood firm. His actors, spurred on by him, had not ceased to spout his comedy, and he had not ceased to listen to it. He had made up his mind about the tumult, and was determined to proceed to the end, not giving up the hope of a return of attention on the part of the public. This gleam of hope acquired fresh life, when he saw Quasimodo, Coppenole, and the deafening escort of the pope of the procession of fools quit the hall amid great uproar. The throng rushed eagerly after them. "Good," he said to himself, "there go all the mischief-makers." Unfortunately, all the mischief-makers constituted the entire audience. In the twinkling of an eye, the grand hall was empty.

To tell the truth, a few spectators still remained, some scattered, others in groups around the pillars, women, old men, or children, who had had enough of the uproar and tumult. Some scholars were still perched astride of the window-sills, engaged in gazing into the Place.

"Well," thought Gringoire, "here are still as many as are required to hear the end of my mystery. They are few in number, but it is a choice audience, a lettered audience."

An instant later, a symphony which had been intended to produce the greatest effect on the arrival of the Virgin, was lacking. Gringoire perceived that his music had been carried off by the procession of the Pope of the Fools. "Skip it," said he, stoically.

He approached a group of **bourgeois**, who seemed to him to be discussing his piece. This is the fragment of conversation which he caught,–

"You know, Master Cheneteau, the Hôtel de Navarre, which belonged to Monsieur de Nemours?"

"Yes, opposite the Chapelle de Braque."

"Well, the treasury has just let it to Guillaume Alixandre, historian, for six livres, eight sols, parisian, a year."

"How rents are going up!"

"Come," said Gringoire to himself, with a sigh, "the others are listening."

"Comrades," suddenly shouted one of the young scamps from the window, "La Esmeralda! La Esmeralda in the Place!"

This word produced a magical effect. Every one who was left in the hall flew to the windows, climbing the walls in order to see, and repeating, “La Esmeralda! La Esmeralda?” At the same time, a great sound of applause was heard from without.

“What’s the meaning of this, of the Esmeralda?” said Gringoire, wringing his hands in despair. “Ah, good heavens! it seems to be the turn of the windows now.”

He returned towards the marble table, and saw that the representation had been interrupted. It was precisely at the instant when Jupiter should have appeared with his thunder. But Jupiter was standing motionless at the foot of the stage.

“Michel Giborne!” cried the irritated poet, “what are you doing there? Is that your part? Come up!”

“Alas!” said Jupiter, “a scholar has just seized the ladder.”

Gringoire looked. It was but too true. All communication between his plot and its solution was intercepted.

“The rascal,” he murmured. “And why did

he take that ladder?"

"In order to go and see the Esmeralda," replied Jupiter piteously. "He said, 'Come, here's a ladder that's of no use!' and he took it."

This was the last blow. Gringoire received it with resignation.

"May the devil fly away with you!" he said to the comedian, "and if I get my pay, you shall receive yours."

Then he beat a retreat, with drooping head, but the last in the field, like a general who has fought well.

And as he descended the winding stairs of the courts: "A fine rabble of asses and dolts these Parisians!" he muttered between his teeth; "they come to hear a mystery and don't listen to it at all! They are engrossed by every one, by Clopin Trouillefou, by the cardinal, by Coppenole, by Quasimodo, by the devil! but by Madame the Virgin Mary, not at all. If I had known, I'd have given you Virgin Mary; you ninnies! And I! to come to see faces and behold only backs! to be a poet, and to reap the success of an apothecary! It is true that Homerus begged through the Greek towns, and that Naso died in exile among the Muscovites. But may the devil flay me if I understand what they mean with their Esmeralda! What is that word, in the first place?–'tis Egyptian!"

VOLUME ONE

BOOK SECOND

CHAPTER ONE

From Charybdis to Scylla

NIGHT COMES ON EARLY in January. The streets were already dark when Gringoire issued forth from the Courts. This gloom pleased him; he was in haste to reach some obscure and deserted alley, in order there to meditate at his ease, and in order that the philosopher might place the first dressing upon the wound of the poet. Philosophy, moreover, was his sole refuge, for he did not know where he was to lodge for the night. After the brilliant failure of his first theatrical venture, he dared not return to the lodging which he occupied in the Rue Grenier-sur-l'Eau, opposite to the Port-au-Foin, having depended upon receiving from monsieur the provost for his epithalamium, the wherewithal to pay Master Guillaume Doulx-Sire, farmer of the taxes on cloven-footed animals in Paris, the rent which he owed him, that is to say, twelve sols parisian; twelve times the value of all that he possessed in the world, including his trunk-hose, his shirt, and his cap. After reflecting a moment, temporarily sheltered beneath the little wicket of the prison of the treasurer of the Sainte-Chappelle, as to the shelter which he would select for the night, having all the pavements of Paris to choose from, he remembered to have noticed the week previously in the Rue de la Savaterie, at the door of a councillor of the parliament, a stepping stone for mounting a mule, and to have said to himself that that stone would furnish, on occasion, a very excellent pillow for a mendicant or a poet. He thanked Providence for having sent this happy idea to him; but, as he was preparing to cross the Place, in order to reach the tortuous labyrinth of the city, where meander all those old sister streets, the Rues de la Barillerie, de la Vieille-Draperie, de la Savaterie, de la Juiverie, etc., still extant to-day, with their nine-story houses, he saw the procession of the Pope of the Fools, which was also emerging from the court house, and rushing across the courtyard, with great cries, a great flashing of torches, and the music which belonged to him, Gringoire. This sight revived the pain of his self-love; he fled. In the bitterness of his dramatic misadventure, everything which reminded him of the festival of that day irritated his wound and made it bleed.

He was on the point of turning to the Pont Saint-Michel; children were running about here and there with fire lances and rockets.

"Pest on firework candles!" said Gringoire; and he fell back on the Pont au Change. To the house at the head of the bridge there had been affixed three small banners, representing the king, the dauphin, and Marguerite of Flanders, and six little pennons on which were portrayed the Duke of Austria, the Cardinal de Bourbon, M. de Beaujeu, and Madame Jeanne de France, and Monsieur the Bastard of Bourbon, and I know not whom else; all being illuminated with torches. The rabble were admiring.

"Happy painter, Jehan Fourbault!" said Gringoire with a deep sigh; and he turned his back upon the bannerets and pennons. A street opened before him; he thought it so dark and deserted that he hoped to there escape from all the rumors as well as from all the gleams of the festival. At the end of a few moments his foot came in contact with an obstacle; he stumbled and fell. It was the May truss, which the clerks of the clerks' law court had deposited that morning at the door of a president of the parliament, in honor of the solemnity of the day. Gringoire bore this new disaster heroically; he picked himself up, and reached the water's edge. After leaving behind him the civic Tournelle[7] and the criminal tower, and skirted the great walls of the king's garden, on that unpaved strand where the mud reached to his ankles, he reached the western point of the city, and considered for some time the islet of the Passeur-aux-Vaches, which has disappeared beneath the bronze horse of the Pont Neuf. The islet appeared to him in the shadow like a black mass, beyond the narrow strip of whitish water which separated him from it. One could divine by the ray of a tiny light the sort of hut in the form of a beehive where the ferryman of cows took refuge at night.

7 A chamber of the ancient parliament of Paris.

"Happy ferryman!" thought Gringoire; "you do not dream of glory, and you do not make marriage songs! What matters it to you, if kings and Duchesses of Burgundy marry? You know no other daisies (**marguerites**) than those which your April greensward gives your cows to browse upon; while I, a poet, am hooted, and shiver, and owe twelve sous, and the soles of my shoes are so transparent, that they might serve as glasses for your lantern! Thanks, ferryman, your cabin rests my eyes, and makes me forget Paris!"

He was roused from his almost lyric ecstacy, by a big double Saint-Jean cracker, which suddenly went off from the happy cabin. It was the cow ferryman, who was taking his part in the rejoicings of the day, and letting off fireworks.

This cracker made Gringoire's skin bristle up all over.

"Accursed festival!" he exclaimed, "wilt thou pursue me everywhere? Oh! good

God! even to the ferryman's!"

Then he looked at the Seine at his feet, and a horrible temptation took possession of him:

"Oh!" said he, "I would gladly drown myself, were the water not so cold!"

Then a desperate resolution occurred to him. It was, since he could not escape from the Pope of the Fools, from Jehan Fourbault's bannerets, from May trusses, from squibs and crackers, to go to the Place de Grève.

"At least," he said to himself, "I shall there have a firebrand of joy wherewith to warm myself, and I can sup on some crumbs of the three great armorial bearings of royal sugar which have been erected on the public refreshment-stall of the city."

CHAPTER TWO

The Place de Grève

THERE REMAINS TO-DAY but a very imperceptible vestige of the Place de Grève, such as it existed then; it consists in the charming little turret, which occupies the angle north of the Place, and which, already enshrouded in the ignoble plaster which fills with paste the delicate lines of its sculpture, would soon have disappeared, perhaps submerged by that flood of new houses which so rapidly devours all the ancient façades of Paris.

The persons who, like ourselves, never cross the Place de Grève without casting a glance of pity and sympathy on that poor turret strangled between two hovels of the time of Louis XV., can easily reconstruct in their minds the aggregate of edifices to which it belonged, and find again entire in it the ancient Gothic place of the fifteenth century.

It was then, as it is to-day, an irregular trapezoid, bordered on one side by the quay, and on the other three by a series of lofty, narrow, and gloomy houses. By day, one could admire the variety of its edifices, all sculptured in stone or wood, and already presenting complete specimens of the different domestic architectures of the Middle Ages, running back from the fifteenth to the eleventh century, from the casement which had begun to dethrone the arch, to the Roman semicircle, which had been supplanted by the ogive, and which still occupies, below it, the first story of that ancient house de la Tour Roland, at the corner of the Place upon the Seine, on the side of the street with the Tannerie. At night, one could distinguish nothing of all that mass of buildings, except the black indentation of the roofs, unrolling their chain of acute angles round the place; for one of the radical differences between the cities of that time, and the cities of the present day, lay in the façades which looked upon the places and streets, and which were then gables. For the last two centuries the houses have been turned round.

In the centre of the eastern side of the Place, rose a heavy and hybrid construction, formed of three buildings placed in juxtaposition. It was called by three names which explain its history, its destination, and its architecture: "The House of the Dauphin," because Charles V., when Dauphin, had inhabited it; "The

Marchandise," because it had served as town hall; and "The Pillared House" (**domus ad piloria**), because of a series of large pillars which sustained the three stories. The city found there all that is required for a city like Paris; a chapel in which to pray to God; a **plaidoyer**, or pleading room, in which to hold hearings, and to repel, at need, the King's people; and under the roof, an **arsenac** full of artillery. For the **bourgeois** of Paris were aware that it is not sufficient to pray in every conjuncture, and to plead for the franchises of the city, and they had always in reserve, in the garret of the town hall, a few good rusty arquebuses. The Grève had then that sinister aspect which it preserves to-day from the execrable ideas which it awakens, and from the sombre town hall of Dominique Bocador, which has replaced the Pillared House. It must be admitted that a permanent gibbet and a pillory, "a justice and a ladder," as they were called in that day, erected side by side in the centre of the pavement, contributed not a little to cause eyes to be turned away from that fatal place, where so many beings full of life and health have agonized; where, fifty years later, that fever of Saint Vallier was destined to have its birth, that terror of the scaffold, the most monstrous of all maladies because it comes not from God, but from man.

It is a consoling idea (let us remark in passing), to think that the death penalty, which three hundred years ago still encumbered with its iron wheels, its stone gibbets, and all its paraphernalia of torture, permanent and riveted to the pavement, the Grève, the Halles, the Place Dauphine, the Cross du Trahoir, the Marché aux Pourceaux, that hideous Montfaucon, the barrier des Sergents, the Place aux Chats, the Porte Saint-Denis, Champeaux, the Porte Baudets, the Porte Saint Jacques, without reckoning the innumerable ladders of the provosts, the bishop of the chapters, of the abbots, of the priors, who had the decree of life and death,–without reckoning the judicial drownings in the river Seine; it is consoling to-day, after having lost successively all the pieces of its armor, its luxury of torment, its penalty of imagination and fancy, its torture for which it reconstructed every five years a leather bed at the Grand Châtelet, that ancient suzerain of feudal society almost expunged from our laws and our cities, hunted from code to code, chased from place to place, has no longer, in our immense Paris, any more than a dishonored corner of the Grève,–than a miserable guillotine, furtive, uneasy, shameful, which seems always afraid of being caught in the act, so quickly does it disappear after having dealt its blow.

CHAPTER THREE

Kisses for Blows

WHEN PIERRE GRINGOIRE ARRIVED on the Place de Grève, he was paralyzed. He had directed his course across the Pont aux Meuniers, in order to avoid the rabble on the Pont au Change, and the pennons of Jehan Fourbault; but the wheels of all the bishop's mills had splashed him as he passed, and his doublet was drenched; it seemed to him besides, that the failure of his piece had rendered him still more sensible to cold than usual. Hence he made haste to draw near the bonfire, which was burning magnificently in the middle of the Place. But a considerable crowd formed a circle around it.

"Accursed Parisians!" he said to himself (for Gringoire, like a true dramatic poet, was subject to monologues) "there they are obstructing my fire! Nevertheless, I am greatly in need of a chimney corner; my shoes drink in the water, and all those cursed mills wept upon me! That devil of a Bishop of Paris, with his mills! I'd just like to know what use a bishop can make of a mill! Does he expect to become a miller instead of a bishop? If only my malediction is needed for that, I bestow it upon him! and his cathedral, and his mills! Just see if those boobies will put themselves out! Move aside! I'd like to know what they are doing there! They are warming themselves, much pleasure may it give them! They are watching a hundred fagots burn; a fine spectacle!"

On looking more closely, he perceived that the circle was much larger than was required simply for the purpose of getting warm at the king's fire, and that this concourse of people had not been attracted solely by the beauty of the hundred fagots which were burning.

In a vast space left free between the crowd and the fire, a young girl was dancing.

Whether this young girl was a human being, a fairy, or an angel, is what Gringoire, sceptical philosopher and ironical poet that he was, could not decide at the first moment, so fascinated was he by this dazzling vision.

She was not tall, though she seemed so, so boldly did her slender form dart about. She was swarthy of complexion, but one divined that, by day, her skin must possess that beautiful golden tone of the Andalusians and the Roman women. Her little foot, too, was Andalusian, for it was both pinched and at ease in its graceful shoe. She danced, she turned, she whirled rapidly about on an old Persian rug, spread negligently under her feet; and each time that her radiant face passed before you, as she whirled, her great black eyes darted a flash of lightning at you.

All around her, all glances were riveted, all mouths open; and, in fact, when she danced thus, to the humming of the Basque tambourine, which her two pure, rounded arms raised above her head, slender, frail and vivacious as a wasp, with her corsage of gold without a fold, her variegated gown puffing out, her bare shoulders, her delicate limbs, which her petticoat revealed at times, her black hair, her eyes of flame, she was a supernatural creature.

"In truth," said Gringoire to himself, "she is a salamander, she is a nymph, she is a goddess, she is a bacchante of the Menelean Mount!"

At that moment, one of the salamander's braids of hair became unfastened, and a piece of yellow copper which was attached to it, rolled to the ground.

"Hé, no!" said he, "she is a gypsy!"

All illusions had disappeared.

She began her dance once more; she took from the ground two swords, whose points she rested against her brow, and which she made to turn in one direction, while she turned in the other; it was a purely gypsy effect. But, disenchanted though Gringoire was, the whole effect of this picture was not without its charm and its magic; the bonfire illuminated, with a red flaring light, which trembled, all alive, over the circle of faces in the crowd, on the brow of the young girl, and at the background of the Place cast a pallid reflection, on one side upon the ancient, black, and wrinkled façade of the House of Pillars, on the other, upon the old stone gibbet.

Among the thousands of visages which

that light tinged with scarlet, there was one which seemed, even more than all the others, absorbed in contemplation of the dancer. It was the face of a man, austere, calm, and sombre. This man, whose costume was concealed by the crowd which surrounded him, did not appear to be more than five and thirty years of age; nevertheless, he was bald; he had merely a few tufts of thin, gray hair on his temples; his broad, high forehead had begun to be furrowed with wrinkles, but his deep-set eyes sparkled with extraordinary youthfulness, an ardent life, a profound passion. He kept them fixed incessantly on the gypsy, and, while the giddy young girl of sixteen danced and whirled, for the pleasure of all, his revery seemed to become more and more sombre. From time to time, a smile and a sigh met upon his lips, but the smile was more melancholy than the sigh.

The young girl, stopped at length, breathless, and the people applauded her lovingly.

"Djali!" said the gypsy.

Then Gringoire saw come up to her, a pretty little white goat, alert, wide-awake, glossy, with gilded horns, gilded hoofs, and gilded collar, which he had not hitherto perceived, and which had remained lying curled up on one corner of the carpet watching his mistress dance.

"Djali!" said the dancer, "it is your turn."

And, seating herself, she gracefully presented her tambourine to the goat.

"Djali," she continued, "what month is this?"

The goat lifted its fore foot, and struck one blow upon the tambourine. It was the first month in the year, in fact.

"Djali," pursued the young girl, turning her tambourine round, "what day of the month is this?"

Djali raised his little gilt hoof, and struck six blows on the tambourine.

"Djali," pursued the Egyptian, with still

another movement of the tambourine, "what hour of the day is it?"

Djali struck seven blows. At that moment, the clock of the Pillar House rang out seven.

The people were amazed.

"There's sorcery at the bottom of it," said a sinister voice in the crowd. It was that of the bald man, who never removed his eyes from the gypsy.

She shuddered and turned round; but applause broke forth and drowned the morose exclamation.

It even effaced it so completely from her mind, that she continued to question her goat.

"Djali, what does Master Guichard Grand-Remy, captain of the pistoliers of the town do, at the procession of Candlemas?"

Djali reared himself on his hind legs, and began to bleat, marching along with so much dainty gravity, that the entire circle of spectators burst into a laugh at this parody of the interested devoutness of the captain of pistoliers.

"Djali," resumed the young girl, emboldened by her growing success, "how preaches Master Jacques Charmolue, procurator to the king in the ecclesiastical court?"

The goat seated himself on his hind quarters, and began to bleat, waving his fore feet in so strange a manner, that, with the exception of the bad French, and worse Latin, Jacques Charmolue was there complete,–gesture, accent, and attitude.

And the crowd applauded louder than ever.

"Sacrilege! profanation!" resumed the voice of the bald man.

The gypsy turned round once more.

"Ah!" said she, "'tis that villanous man!" Then, thrusting her under lip out beyond the upper, she made a little pout, which appeared to be familiar to her, executed a pirouette on her heel, and set about collecting in her tambourine the gifts of the multitude.

Big blanks, little blanks, targes[8] and eagle liards showered into it.

All at once, she passed in front of Gringoire. Gringoire put his hand so recklessly into his pocket that she halted. "The devil!" said the poet, finding at the bottom of his pocket the reality, that is, to say, a void. In the meantime, the pretty girl stood there, gazing at him with her big eyes, and holding out her tambourine to him and waiting. Gringoire broke into a violent perspiration.

If he had all Peru in his pocket, he would certainly have given it to the dancer; but Gringoire had not Peru, and, moreover, America had not yet been discovered.

Happily, an unexpected incident came to his rescue.

"Will you take yourself off, you Egyptian grasshopper?" cried a sharp voice, which proceeded from the darkest corner of the

---

8 A blank: an old French coin; six blanks were worth two sous and a half; targe, an ancient coin of Burgundy, a farthing.

Place.

The young girl turned round in affright. It was no longer the voice of the bald man; it was the voice of a woman, bigoted and malicious.

However, this cry, which alarmed the gypsy, delighted a troop of children who were prowling about there.

"It is the recluse of the Tour-Roland," they exclaimed, with wild laughter, "it is the sacked nun who is scolding! Hasn't she supped? Let's carry her the remains of the city refreshments!"

All rushed towards the Pillar House.

In the meanwhile, Gringoire had taken advantage of the dancer's embarrassment, to disappear. The children's shouts had reminded him that he, also, had not supped, so he ran to the public buffet. But the little rascals had better legs than he; when he arrived, they had stripped the table. There remained not so much as a miserable **camichon** at five sous the pound. Nothing remained upon the wall but slender fleurs-de-lis, mingled with rose bushes, painted in 1434 by Mathieu Biterne. It was a meagre supper.

It is an unpleasant thing to go to bed without supper, it is a still less pleasant thing not to sup and not to know where one is to sleep. That was Gringoire's condition. No supper, no shelter; he saw himself pressed on all sides by necessity, and he found necessity very crabbed. He had long ago discovered the truth, that Jupiter created men during a fit of misanthropy, and that during a wise man's whole life, his destiny holds his philosophy in a state of siege. As for himself, he had never seen the blockade so complete; he heard his stomach sounding a parley, and he considered it very much out of place that evil destiny should capture his philosophy by famine.

This melancholy revery was absorbing him more and more, when a song, quaint but full of sweetness, suddenly tore him from it. It was the young gypsy who was singing.

Her voice was like her dancing, like her beauty. It was indefinable and charming; something pure and sonorous, aerial, winged, so to speak. There were continual outbursts, melodies, unexpected cadences, then simple phrases strewn with aerial and hissing notes; then floods of scales which would have put a nightingale to rout, but in which harmony was always present; then soft modulations of octaves which rose and fell, like the bosom of the young singer. Her beautiful face followed, with singular mobility, all the caprices of her song, from the wildest inspiration to the chastest dignity. One would have pronounced her now a mad creature, now a queen.

The words which she sang were in a tongue unknown to Gringoire, and which seemed to him to be unknown to herself, so little relation did the expression which she imparted to her song bear to the sense of the words. Thus, these four lines, in her mouth, were madly gay,–

Un cofre de gran riqueza
  Hallaron dentro un pilar,
Dentro del, nuevas banderas
  Con figuras de espantar.[9]

And an instant afterwards, at the accents which she imparted to this stanza,–

Alarabes de cavallo
  Sin poderse menear,
Con espadas, y los cuellos,
  Ballestas de buen echar,

Gringoire felt the tears start to his eyes. Nevertheless, her song breathed joy, most

---

9 A coffer of great richness
  In a pillar's heart they found,
Within it lay new banners,
  With figures to astound.

of all, and she seemed to sing like a bird, from serenity and heedlessness.

The gypsy's song had disturbed Gringoire's revery as the swan disturbs the water. He listened in a sort of rapture, and forgetfulness of everything. It was the first moment in the course of many hours when he did not feel that he suffered.

The moment was brief.

The same woman's voice, which had interrupted the gypsy's dance, interrupted her song.

"Will you hold your tongue, you cricket of hell?" it cried, still from the same obscure corner of the place.

The poor "cricket" stopped short. Gringoire covered up his ears.

"Oh!" he exclaimed, "accursed saw with missing teeth, which comes to break the lyre!"

Meanwhile, the other spectators murmured like himself; "To the devil with the sacked nun!" said some of them. And the old invisible kill-joy might have had occasion to repent of her aggressions against the gypsy had their attention not been diverted at this moment by the procession of the Pope of the Fools, which, after having traversed many streets and squares, debouched on the Place de Grève, with all its torches and all its uproar.

This procession, which our readers have seen set out from the Palais de Justice, had organized on the way, and had been recruited by all the knaves, idle thieves, and unemployed vagabonds in Paris; so that it presented a very respectable aspect when it arrived at the Grève.

First came Egypt. The Duke of Egypt headed it, on horseback, with his counts on foot holding his bridle and stirrups for him; behind them, the male and female Egyptians, pell-mell, with their little children crying on their shoulders; all–duke, counts, and populace–in rags and tatters. Then came the Kingdom of Argot; that is to say, all the thieves of France, arranged according to the order of their dignity; the minor people walking first. Thus defiled by fours, with the divers insignia of their grades, in that strange faculty, most of them lame, some cripples, others one-armed, shop clerks, pilgrims, **hubins**, bootblacks, thimble-riggers, street arabs, beggars, the blear-eyed beggars, thieves, the weakly, vagabonds, merchants, sham soldiers, goldsmiths, passed masters of pickpockets, isolated thieves. A catalogue that would weary Homer. In the centre of the conclave of the passed masters of pickpockets, one had some difficulty in distinguishing the King of Argot, the grand coësre, so called, crouching in a little cart drawn by two big dogs. After the kingdom of the Argotiers, came the Empire of Galilee. Guillaume Rousseau, Emperor of the Empire of Galilee, marched majestically in his robe of purple, spotted with wine, preceded by buffoons wrestling and executing military dances; surrounded by his macebearers, his pickpockets and clerks of the chamber of accounts. Last of all came the corporation of law clerks, with its maypoles crowned with flowers, its black robes, its music worthy of the orgy, and its large candles of yellow wax. In the centre of this crowd, the grand officers of the Brotherhood of Fools bore on their shoulders a litter more loaded down with candles than the reliquary of Sainte-Geneviève in time of pest; and on this litter shone resplendent, with crosier, cope, and mitre, the new Pope of the Fools, the bellringer of Notre-Dame, Quasimodo the hunchback.

Each section of this grotesque procession had its own music. The Egyptians made their drums and African tambourines resound. The slang men, not a very musical race, still clung to the goat's horn trumpet and the Gothic rubebbe of the twelfth century. The Empire of Galilee was not much more advanced; among its music one could hardly distinguish some miserable rebec, from the infancy of the art, still imprisoned in the **ré-la-mi**. But it was around the Pope of the Fools that all the musical riches of the epoch were displayed in a magnificent discord. It was nothing but soprano rebecs, counter-tenor rebecs, and tenor rebecs, not to reckon the flutes and brass instruments. Alas! our readers will remember that this was Gringoire's orchestra.

It is difficult to convey an idea of the degree of proud and blissful expansion to which the sad and hideous visage of Quasimodo had attained during the transit from the Palais de Justice, to the Place de Grève. It was the first enjoyment of self-love that he had ever experienced. Down to that day, he had known only humiliation, disdain for his condition, disgust for his person. Hence, deaf though he was, he enjoyed, like a veritable pope, the acclamations of that throng, which he hated because he felt that he was hated by it. What mattered it that his people consisted of a pack of fools, cripples, thieves, and beggars? it was still a people and he was its sovereign. And he accepted seriously all this ironical applause, all this derisive respect, with which the crowd mingled, it must be admitted, a good deal of very real fear. For the hunchback was robust; for the bandy-legged fellow was agile; for the deaf man was malicious: three qualities which temper ridicule.

We are far from believing, however, that the new Pope of the Fools understood both the sentiments which he felt and the sentiments which he inspired. The spirit which was lodged in this failure of a body had, necessarily, something incomplete and deaf about it. Thus, what he felt at the moment was to him, absolutely vague, indistinct, and confused. Only joy made itself felt, only pride dominated. Around that sombre and unhappy face, there hung a radiance.

It was, then, not without surprise and alarm, that at the very moment when

Quasimodo was passing the Pillar House, in that semi-intoxicated state, a man was seen to dart from the crowd, and to tear from his hands, with a gesture of anger, his crosier of gilded wood, the emblem of his mock popeship.

This man, this rash individual, was the man with the bald brow, who, a moment earlier, standing with the gypsy's group had chilled the poor girl with his words of menace and of hatred. He was dressed in an ecclesiastical costume. At the moment when he stood forth from the crowd, Gringoire, who had not noticed him up to that time, recognized him: "Hold!" he said, with an exclamation of astonishment. "Eh! 'tis my master in Hermes, Dom Claude Frollo, the archdeacon! What the devil does he want of that old one-eyed fellow? He'll get himself devoured!"

A cry of terror arose, in fact. The formidable Quasimodo had hurled himself from the litter, and the women turned aside their eyes in order not to see him tear the archdeacon asunder.

He made one bound as far as the priest, looked at him, and fell upon his knees.

The priest tore off his tiara, broke his crozier, and rent his tinsel cope.

Quasimodo remained on his knees, with head bent and hands clasped. Then there was established between them a strange dialogue of signs and gestures, for neither of them spoke. The priest, erect on his feet, irritated, threatening, imperious; Quasimodo, prostrate, humble, suppliant. And, nevertheless, it is certain that Quasimodo could have crushed the priest with his thumb.

At length the archdeacon, giving Quasimodo's powerful shoulder a rough shake, made him a sign to rise and follow him.

Quasimodo rose.

Then the Brotherhood of Fools, their first stupor having passed off, wished to defend their pope, so abruptly dethroned. The

Egyptians, the men of slang, and all the fraternity of law clerks, gathered howling round the priest.

Quasimodo placed himself in front of the priest, set in play the muscles of his athletic fists, and glared upon the assailants with the snarl of an angry tiger.

The priest resumed his sombre gravity, made a sign to Quasimodo, and retired in silence.

Quasimodo walked in front of him, scattering the crowd as he passed.

When they had traversed the populace and the Place, the cloud of curious and idle were minded to follow them. Quasimodo then constituted himself the rearguard, and followed the archdeacon, walking backwards, squat, surly, monstrous, bristling, gathering up his limbs, licking his boar's tusks, growling like a wild beast, and imparting to the crowd immense vibrations, with a look or a gesture.

Both were allowed to plunge into a dark and narrow street, where no one dared to venture after them; so thoroughly did the mere chimera of Quasimodo gnashing his teeth bar the entrance.

"Here's a marvellous thing," said Gringoire; "but where the deuce shall I find some supper?"

CHAPTER FOUR

The Inconveniences of Following a Pretty Woman through the Streets in the Evening

GRINGOIRE SET OUT TO follow the gypsy at all hazards. He had seen her, accompanied by her goat, take to the Rue de la Coutellerie; he took the Rue de la Coutellerie.

"Why not?" he said to himself.

Gringoire, a practical philosopher of the streets of Paris, had noticed that nothing is more propitious to revery than following a pretty woman without knowing whither she is going. There was in this voluntary abdication of his freewill, in this fancy submitting itself to another fancy, which suspects it not, a mixture of fantastic independence and blind obedience, something indescribable, intermediate between slavery and liberty, which pleased Gringoire,–a spirit essentially compound, undecided, and complex, holding the extremities of all extremes, incessantly suspended between all human propensities, and neutralizing one by the other. He was fond of comparing himself to Mahomet's coffin, attracted in two different directions by two loadstones, and hesitating eternally between the heights and the depths, between the vault and the pavement, between fall and ascent, between zenith and nadir.

If Gringoire had lived in our day, what a

fine middle course he would hold between classicism and romanticism!

But he was not sufficiently primitive to live three hundred years, and 'tis a pity. His absence is a void which is but too sensibly felt to-day.

Moreover, for the purpose of thus following passers-by (and especially female passers-by) in the streets, which Gringoire was fond of doing, there is no better disposition than ignorance of where one is going to sleep.

So he walked along, very thoughtfully, behind the young girl, who hastened her pace and made her goat trot as she saw the **bourgeois** returning home and the taverns–the only shops which had been open that day–closing.

"After all," he half thought to himself, "she must lodge somewhere; gypsies have kindly hearts. Who knows?–"

And in the points of suspense which he placed after this reticence in his mind, there lay I know not what flattering ideas.

Meanwhile, from time to time, as he passed the last groups of **bourgeois** closing their doors, he caught some scraps of their conversation, which broke the thread of his pleasant hypotheses.

Now it was two old men accosting each other.

“Do you know that it is cold, Master Thibaut Fernicle?” (Gringoire had been aware of this since the beginning of the winter.)

“Yes, indeed, Master Boniface Disome! Are we going to have a winter such as we had three years ago, in ’80, when wood cost eight sous the measure?”

“Bah! that’s nothing, Master Thibaut, compared with the winter of 1407, when it froze from St. Martin’s Day until Candlemas! and so cold that the pen of the registrar of the parliament froze every three words, in the Grand Chamber! which interrupted the registration of justice.”

Further on there were two female neighbors

at their windows, holding candles, which the fog caused to sputter.

"Has your husband told you about the mishap, Mademoiselle la Boudraque?"

"No. What is it, Mademoiselle Turquant?"

"The horse of M. Gilles Godin, the notary at the Châtelet, took fright at the Flemings and their procession, and overturned Master Philippe Avrillot, lay monk of the Célestins."

"Really?"

"Actually."

"A **bourgeois** horse! 'tis rather too much! If it had been a cavalry horse, well and good!"

And the windows were closed. But Gringoire had lost the thread of his ideas, nevertheless.

Fortunately, he speedily found it again, and he knotted it together without difficulty, thanks to the gypsy, thanks to Djali, who still walked in front of him; two fine, delicate, and charming creatures, whose tiny feet, beautiful forms, and graceful manners he was engaged in admiring, almost confusing them in his contemplation; believing them to be both young girls, from their intelligence and good friendship; regarding them both as goats,–so far as the lightness, agility, and dexterity of their walk were concerned.

But the streets were becoming blacker and more deserted every moment. The curfew had sounded long ago, and it was only at rare intervals now that they encountered a passer-by in the street, or a light in the windows. Gringoire had become involved, in his pursuit of the gypsy, in that inextricable labyrinth of alleys, squares, and closed courts which surround the ancient sepulchre of the Saints-Innocents, and which resembles a ball of thread tangled by a cat. “Here are streets which possess but little logic!” said Gringoire, lost in the thousands of circuits which returned upon themselves incessantly, but where the young girl pursued a road which seemed familiar to her, without hesitation and with a step which became ever more rapid. As for him, he would have been utterly ignorant of his situation had he not espied, in passing, at the turn of a street, the octagonal mass of the pillory of the fish markets, the openwork summit of which threw its black, fretted outlines clearly upon a window which was still lighted in the Rue Verdelet.

The young girl's attention had been attracted to him for the last few moments; she had repeatedly turned her head towards him with uneasiness; she had even once come to a standstill, and taking advantage of a ray of light which escaped from a half-open bakery to survey him intently, from head to foot, then, having cast this glance, Gringoire had seen her make that little pout which he had already noticed, after which she passed on.

This little pout had furnished Gringoire with food for thought. There was certainly both disdain and mockery in that graceful grimace. So he dropped his head, began to count the paving-stones, and to follow the young girl at a little greater distance, when, at the turn of a street, which had caused him to lose sight of her, he heard her utter a piercing cry.

He hastened his steps.

The street was full of shadows. Nevertheless, a twist of tow soaked in oil, which burned in a cage at the feet of the Holy Virgin at the street corner, permitted Gringoire to make out the gypsy struggling in the arms of two men, who were endeavoring to stifle her cries. The poor little goat, in great alarm, lowered his horns and bleated.

"Help! gentlemen of the watch!" shouted Gringoire, and advanced bravely. One of the men who held the young girl turned towards him. It was the formidable visage of Quasimodo.

Gringoire did not take to flight, but neither did he advance another step.

Quasimodo came up to him, tossed him four paces away on the pavement with a backward turn of the hand, and plunged rapidly into the gloom, bearing the young girl folded across one arm like a silken scarf. His companion followed him, and the poor goat ran after them all, bleating plaintively.

"Murder! murder!" shrieked the unhappy gypsy.

"Halt, rascals, and yield me that wench!" suddenly shouted in a voice of thunder, a cavalier who appeared suddenly from a neighboring square.

It was a captain of the king's archers, armed from head to foot, with his sword in his hand.

He tore the gypsy from the arms of the dazed Quasimodo, threw her across his saddle, and at the moment when the terrible hunchback, recovering from his surprise, rushed upon him to regain his prey, fifteen or sixteen archers, who followed their captain closely, made their appearance, with their two-edged swords in their fists. It was a squad of the king's police, which was making the rounds, by order of Messire Robert d'Estouteville, guard of the provostship of Paris.

Quasimodo was surrounded, seized, garroted; he roared, he foamed at the mouth, he bit; and had it been broad daylight, there is no doubt that his face alone, rendered more hideous by wrath, would have put the entire squad to flight. But by night he was deprived of his most formidable weapon, his ugliness.

His companion had disappeared during the struggle.

The gypsy gracefully raised herself upright upon the officer's saddle, placed both hands upon the young man's shoulders, and gazed fixedly at him for several seconds, as though enchanted with his good looks and with the aid which he had just rendered her. Then breaking silence first, she said to him, making her sweet voice still sweeter than usual,–

"What is your name, monsieur le gendarme?"

"Captain Phœbus de Châteaupers, at your service, my beauty!" replied the officer, drawing himself up.

"Thanks," said she.

And while Captain Phœbus was turning

up his moustache in Burgundian fashion, she slipped from the horse, like an arrow falling to earth, and fled.

A flash of lightning would have vanished less quickly.

"Nombrill of the Pope!" said the captain, causing Quasimodo's straps to be drawn tighter, "I should have preferred to keep the wench."

"What would you have, captain?" said one gendarme. "The warbler has fled, and the bat remains."

CHAPTER FIVE

Result of the Dangers

GRINGOIRE, THOROUGHLY STUNNED by his fall, remained on the pavement in front of the Holy Virgin at the street corner. Little by little, he regained his senses; at first, for several minutes, he was floating in a sort of half-somnolent revery, which was not without its charm, in which æriel figures of the gypsy and her goat were coupled with Quasimodo's heavy fist. This state lasted but a short time.

A decidedly vivid sensation of cold in the part of his body which was in contact with the pavement, suddenly aroused him and caused his spirit to return to the surface.

"Whence comes this chill?" he said abruptly, to himself. He then perceived that he was lying half in the middle of the gutter.

"That devil of a hunchbacked cyclops!" he muttered between his teeth; and he tried to rise. But he was too much dazed and bruised; he was forced to remain where he was. Moreover, his hand was tolerably free; he stopped up his nose and resigned himself.

"The mud of Paris," he said to himself– for decidedly he thought that he was sure that the gutter would prove his refuge for the night; and what can one do in a refuge, except dream?–"the mud of Paris is particularly stinking; it must contain a great deal of volatile and nitric salts. That, moreover, is the opinion of Master Nicholas Flamel, and of the alchemists–"

The word **alchemists** suddenly suggested

to his mind the idea of Archdeacon Claude Frollo. He recalled the violent scene which he had just witnessed in part; that the gypsy was struggling with two men, that Quasimodo had a companion; and the morose and haughty face of the archdeacon passed confusedly through his memory. "That would be strange!" he said to himself. And on that fact and that basis he began to construct a fantastic edifice of hypothesis, that card-castle of philosophers; then, suddenly returning once more to reality, "Come! I'm freezing!" he ejaculated.

The place was, in fact, becoming less and less tenable. Each molecule of the gutter bore away a molecule of heat radiating from Gringoire's loins, and the equilibrium between the temperature of his body and the temperature of the brook, began to be established in rough fashion.

Quite a different annoyance suddenly assailed him. A group of children, those little bare-footed savages who have always roamed the pavements of Paris under the eternal name of **gamins**, and who, when we were also children ourselves, threw stones at all of us in the afternoon, when we came out of school, because our trousers were not torn–a swarm of these young scamps rushed towards the square where Gringoire lay, with shouts and laughter which seemed to pay but little heed to the sleep of the neighbors. They were dragging after them some sort of hideous sack; and the noise of their wooden shoes alone would have roused the dead. Gringoire who was not quite dead yet, half raised himself.

"Ohé, Hennequin Dandèche! Ohé, Jehan Pincebourde!" they shouted in deafening tones, "old Eustache Moubon, the merchant at the corner, has just died. We've got his straw pallet, we're going to have a bonfire out of it. It's the turn of the Flemish to-day!"

And behold, they flung the pallet directly upon Gringoire, beside whom they had arrived, without espying him. At the same time, one of them took a handful of straw and set off to light it at the wick of the good Virgin.

"S'death!" growled Gringoire, "am I going to be too warm now?"

It was a critical moment. He was caught between fire and water; he made a superhuman effort, the effort of a counterfeiter of money who is on the point of being boiled, and who seeks to escape. He rose to his feet, flung aside the straw pallet upon the street urchins, and fled.

"Holy Virgin!" shrieked the children; "'tis the merchant's ghost!"

And they fled in their turn.

The straw mattress remained master of the field. Belleforêt, Father Le Juge, and Corrozet affirm that it was picked up on the morrow, with great pomp, by the clergy of the quarter, and borne to the treasury of the church of Saint Opportune, where the sacristan, even as late as 1789, earned a tolerably handsome revenue out of the great miracle of the Statue of the Virgin at the corner of the Rue Mauconseil, which had, by its mere presence, on the memorable night between the sixth and seventh of January, 1482, exorcised the defunct Eustache Moubon, who, in order to play a trick on the devil, had at his death maliciously concealed his soul in his straw pallet.

CHAPTER SIX

The Broken Jug

AFTER HAVING RUN FOR some time at the top of his speed, without knowing whither, knocking his head against many a street corner, leaping many a gutter, traversing many an alley, many a court, many a square, seeking flight and passage through all the meanderings of the ancient passages of the Halles, exploring in his panic terror what the fine Latin of the maps calls **tota via, cheminum et viaria**, our poet suddenly halted for lack of breath in the first place, and in the second, because he had been collared, after a fashion, by a dilemma which had just occurred to his mind. “It strikes me, Master Pierre Gringoire,” he said to himself, placing his finger to his brow, “that you are running like a madman. The little scamps are no less afraid of you than you are of them. It strikes me, I say, that you heard the clatter of their wooden shoes fleeing southward, while you were fleeing northward. Now, one of two things, either they have taken flight, and the pallet, which they must have forgotten in their terror, is precisely that hospitable bed in search of which you have been running ever since morning, and which madame the Virgin miraculously sends you, in order to recompense you for having made a morality in her honor, accompanied by triumphs and mummeries; or the children have not taken flight, and in that case they have put the brand to the pallet, and that is precisely the good fire which you need to cheer, dry, and warm you. In either case, good fire or good bed, that straw pallet is a gift from heaven. The blessed Virgin Marie who stands at the corner of the Rue Mauconseil, could only have made Eustache Moubon die for that express purpose; and it is folly on your part to flee thus zigzag, like a Picard before a Frenchman, leaving behind you what you seek before you; and you are a fool!"

Then he retraced his steps, and feeling his way and searching, with his nose to the wind and his ears on the alert, he tried to find the blessed pallet again, but in vain. There was nothing to be found but intersections of houses, closed courts, and crossings of streets, in the midst of which he hesitated and doubted incessantly, being more perplexed and entangled in this medley of streets than he would have been even in the labyrinth of the Hôtel des Tournelles. At length he lost patience, and exclaimed solemnly: "Cursed be cross roads! 'tis the devil who has made them in the shape of his pitchfork!"

This exclamation afforded him a little solace, and a sort of reddish reflection which he caught sight of at that moment, at the extremity of a long and narrow lane, completed the elevation of his moral tone. "God be praised!" said he, "There it is yonder! There is my pallet burning." And comparing himself to the pilot who suffers shipwreck by night, "**Salve**," he added piously, "**salve, maris stella**!"

Did he address this fragment of litany to the Holy Virgin, or to the pallet? We are utterly unable to say.

He had taken but a few steps in the long street, which sloped downwards, was unpaved, and more and more muddy and steep, when he noticed a very singular thing. It was not deserted; here and there along its extent crawled certain vague and formless masses, all directing their course towards the light which flickered at the end of the street, like those heavy insects which drag along by night, from blade to blade of grass, towards the shepherd's fire.

Nothing renders one so adventurous as not being able to feel the place where one's pocket is situated. Gringoire continued to advance, and had soon joined that one of the forms which dragged along most indolently, behind the others. On drawing near, he perceived that it was nothing else than a wretched legless cripple in a bowl, who was hopping along on his two hands like a wounded field-spider which has but two legs left. At the moment when he passed close to this species of spider with a human countenance, it raised towards him a lamentable voice: "**La buona mancia, signor! la buona mancia**!"[10]

"Deuce take you," said Gringoire, "and

10 Alms.

me with you, if I know what you mean!"

And he passed on.

He overtook another of these itinerant masses, and examined it. It was an impotent man, both halt and crippled, and halt and crippled to such a degree that the complicated system of crutches and wooden legs which sustained him, gave him the air of a mason's scaffolding on the march. Gringoire, who liked noble and classical comparisons, compared him in thought to the living tripod of Vulcan.

This living tripod saluted him as he passed, but stopping his hat on a level with Gringoire's chin, like a shaving dish, while he shouted in the latter's ears: "**Secor cabellero, para comprar un pedaso de pan**!"[11]

"It appears," said Gringoire, "that this one can also talk; but 'tis a rude language, and he is more fortunate than I if he understands it." Then, smiting his brow, in a sudden transition of ideas: "By the way, what the deuce did they

11 Give me the means to buy a bit of bread, sir.

mean this morning with their **Esmeralda?**"

He was minded to augment his pace, but for the third time something barred his way. This something or, rather, some one was a blind man, a little blind fellow with a bearded, Jewish face, who, rowing away in the space about him with a stick, and towed by a large dog, droned through his nose with a Hungarian accent: "**Facitote caritatem**!"

"Well, now," said Gringoire, "here's one at last who speaks a Christian tongue. I must have a very charitable aspect, since they ask alms of me in the present lean condition of my purse. My friend," and he turned towards the blind man, "I sold my last shirt last week; that is to say, since you understand only the language of Cicero: **Vendidi hebdomade nuper transita meam ultimam chemisam**."

That said, he turned his back upon the blind man, and pursued his way. But the blind man began to increase his stride at the same time; and, behold! the cripple and the legless man, in his bowl, came up on their side in great haste, and with great clamor of bowl and crutches, upon the pavement. Then all three, jostling each other at poor Gringoire's heels, began to sing their song to him,–

"**Caritatem**!" chanted the blind man.

"**La buona mancia**!" chanted the cripple in the bowl.

And the lame man took up the musical phrase by repeating: "**Un pedaso de pan**!"

Gringoire stopped up his ears. "Oh, tower of Babel!" he exclaimed.

He set out to run. The blind man ran! The lame man ran! The cripple in the bowl ran!

And then, in proportion as he plunged deeper into the street, cripples in bowls, blind men and lame men, swarmed about him, and men with one arm, and with one eye, and the leprous with their sores, some emerging from little streets adjacent, some from the air-holes of cellars, howling, bellowing, yelping, all limping and halting, all flinging themselves towards the light, and humped up in the mire, like snails after a shower.

Gringoire, still followed by his three persecutors, and not knowing very well what was to become of him, marched along in terror among them, turning out for the lame, stepping over the cripples in bowls, with his feet imbedded in that ant-hill of lame men, like the English captain who got caught in the quicksand of a swarm of crabs.

The idea occurred to him of making an effort to retrace his steps. But it was too late. This whole legion had closed in behind him, and his three beggars held him fast. So he proceeded, impelled both by this irresistible flood, by fear, and by a vertigo which converted all this into a sort of horrible dream.

At last he reached the end of the street. It opened upon an immense place, where a thousand scattered lights flickered in the confused mists of night. Gringoire flew thither, hoping to escape, by the swiftness of his legs, from the three infirm spectres who had clutched him.

"**Onde vas, hombre**?" (Where are you going, my man?) cried the cripple, flinging away his crutches, and running after him with the best legs that ever traced a geometrical step upon the pavements of Paris.

In the meantime the legless man, erect upon his feet, crowned Gringoire with his heavy iron bowl, and the blind man glared in his face with flaming eyes!

"Where am I?" said the terrified poet.

"In the Court of Miracles," replied a fourth spectre, who had accosted them.

"Upon my soul," resumed Gringoire, "I certainly do behold the blind who see, and the lame who walk, but where is the Saviour?"

They replied by a burst of sinister laughter.

The poor poet cast his eyes about him. It was, in truth, that redoubtable Cour des Miracles, whither an honest man had never penetrated at such an hour; the magic circle where the officers of the Châtelet and the sergeants of the provostship, who ventured thither, disappeared in morsels; a city of thieves, a hideous wart on the face of Paris; a sewer, from which escaped every morning, and whither returned every night to crouch, that stream of vices, of mendicancy and vagabondage which always overflows in the streets of capitals; a monstrous hive, to which returned at nightfall, with their booty, all the drones of the social order; a lying hospital where the bohemian, the disfrocked monk, the ruined scholar, the ne'er-do-wells of all nations, Spaniards, Italians, Germans,–of all religions, Jews, Christians, Mahometans, idolaters, covered with painted sores, beggars by day, were transformed by night into brigands; an immense dressing-room, in a word, where, at that epoch, the actors of that eternal comedy, which theft, prostitution, and murder play upon the pavements of Paris, dressed and undressed.

It was a vast place, irregular and badly paved, like all the squares of Paris at that date. Fires, around which swarmed strange groups, blazed here and there. Every one was going, coming, and shouting. Shrill laughter was to be heard, the wailing of children, the voices of women. The hands and heads of this throng, black against the luminous background, outlined against it a thousand eccentric gestures. At times, upon the ground, where trembled the light of the fires, mingled with large, indefinite shadows, one could behold a dog passing, which resembled a man, a man who resembled a dog. The limits of races and species seemed effaced in this city, as in a pandemonium. Men, women, beasts, age, sex, health, maladies, all seemed to be in common among these people; all went together, they mingled, confounded, superposed; each one there participated in all.

The poor and flickering flames of the fire permitted Gringoire to distinguish, amid his trouble, all around the immense place, a hideous frame of ancient houses, whose wormeaten, shrivelled, stunted façades, each pierced with one or two lighted attic windows, seemed to him, in the darkness, like enormous heads of old women, ranged in a circle, monstrous and crabbed, winking as they looked on at the Witches' Sabbath.

It was like a new world, unknown, unheard of, misshapen, creeping, swarming, fantastic.

Gringoire, more and more terrified, clutched by the three beggars as by three pairs of tongs, dazed by a throng of other faces which frothed and yelped around him, unhappy Gringoire endeavored to summon his presence of mind, in order to recall whether it was a Saturday. But his efforts were vain; the thread of his memory and of his thought was broken; and, doubting everything, wavering between what he saw and what he felt, he put to himself this unanswerable question,–

"If I exist, does this exist? if this exists, do

I exist?"

At that moment, a distinct cry arose in the buzzing throng which surrounded him, "Let's take him to the king! let's take him to the king!"

"Holy Virgin!" murmured Gringoire, "the king here must be a ram."

"To the king! to the king!" repeated all voices.

They dragged him off. Each vied with the other in laying his claws upon him. But the three beggars did not loose their hold and tore him from the rest, howling, "He belongs to us!"

The poet's already sickly doublet yielded its last sigh in this struggle.

While traversing the horrible place, his vertigo vanished. After taking a few steps, the sentiment of reality returned to him. He began to become accustomed to the atmosphere of the place. At the first moment there had arisen from his poet's head, or, simply and prosaically, from his empty stomach, a mist, a vapor, so to speak, which, spreading between objects and himself, permitted him to catch a glimpse of them only in the incoherent fog of nightmare,–in those shadows of dreams which distort every outline, agglomerating objects into unwieldy groups, dilating things into chimeras, and men into phantoms. Little by little, this hallucination was succeeded by a less bewildered and exaggerating view. Reality made its way to the light around him, struck his eyes, struck his feet, and demolished, bit by bit, all that frightful poetry with which he had, at first, believed himself to be surrounded. He was forced to perceive that he was not walking in the Styx, but in mud, that he was elbowed not by demons, but by thieves; that it was not his soul which was in question, but his life (since he lacked that precious conciliator, which places itself so effectually between the bandit and the honest man–a purse). In short, on examining the orgy more closely, and with more coolness, he fell from the witches' sabbath to the dram-shop.

The Cour des Miracles was, in fact, merely a dram-shop; but a brigand's dram-shop, reddened quite as much with blood as with wine.

The spectacle which presented itself to his eyes, when his ragged escort finally deposited him at the end of his trip, was not fitted to bear him back to poetry, even to the poetry of hell. It was more than ever the prosaic and brutal reality of the tavern. Were we not in the fifteenth century, we would say that Gringoire had descended from Michael Angelo to Callot.

Around a great fire which burned on a large, circular flagstone, the flames of which had heated red-hot the legs of a tripod, which was empty for the moment, some wormeaten tables were placed, here and there, haphazard, no lackey of a geometrical turn having deigned to adjust their parallelism, or to see to it that they did not make too unusual angles. Upon these tables gleamed several dripping pots of wine and beer, and round these pots were grouped many bacchic visages, purple with the fire and the wine. There was a man with a huge belly and a jovial face, noisily kissing a woman of the town, thickset and brawny. There was a sort of sham soldier, a "naquois," as the slang expression runs, who was whistling as he undid the bandages from his fictitious wound, and removing the numbness from his sound and vigorous knee, which had been swathed since morning in a thousand ligatures. On the other hand, there was a wretched fellow, preparing with celandine and beef's blood, his "leg of God," for the next day. Two tables further on, a palmer, with his pilgrim's costume complete, was practising the lament of the Holy Queen, not forgetting the drone and the nasal drawl. Further on, a young scamp was taking a lesson in epilepsy from an old pretender, who was instructing him in the art of foaming at the mouth, by chewing a morsel of soap. Beside him, a man with the dropsy was getting rid of his swelling, and making four or five female thieves, who were disputing at the same table, over a child who had been stolen that evening, hold their noses. All circumstances which, two centuries later, "seemed so ridiculous to the court," as Sauval says, "that they served as a pastime to the king, and as an introduction to the royal ballet of Night, divided into four parts and danced on the theatre of the Petit-Bourbon." "Never," adds an eye witness of 1653, "have the sudden metamorphoses of the Court of Miracles been more happily presented. Benserade prepared us for it by some very gallant verses."

Loud laughter everywhere, and obscene songs. Each one held his own course, carping and swearing, without listening to his neighbor. Pots clinked, and quarrels sprang up at the shock of the pots, and the broken pots made rents in the rags.

A big dog, seated on his tail, gazed at the fire. Some children were mingled in this orgy. The stolen child wept and cried. Another, a big boy four years of age, seated with legs dangling, upon a bench that was too high for him, before a table that reached to his chin, and uttering not a word. A third, gravely spreading out upon the table with his finger, the melted tallow which dripped from a candle. Last of all, a little fellow crouching in the mud, almost lost in a cauldron, which he was scraping with a tile, and from which he was evoking a sound that would have made Stradivarius swoon.

Near the fire was a hogshead, and on the hogshead a beggar. This was the king on his throne.

The three who had Gringoire in their clutches led him in front of this hogshead, and the entire bacchanal rout fell silent for a moment, with the exception of the cauldron inhabited by the child.

Gringoire dared neither breathe nor raise his eyes.

"**Hombre, quita tu sombrero**!" said one of the three knaves, in whose grasp he was, and, before he had comprehended the meaning, the other had snatched his hat–a wretched headgear, it is true, but still good on a sunny day or when there was but little rain. Gringoire sighed.

Meanwhile the king addressed him, from the summit of his cask,–

"Who is this rogue?"

Gringoire shuddered. That voice, although accentuated by menace, recalled to him another voice, which, that very morning, had dealt the deathblow to his mystery, by drawling, nasally, in the midst of the audience, "Charity, please!" He raised his head. It was indeed Clopin Trouillefou.

Clopin Trouillefou, arrayed in his royal insignia, wore neither one rag more nor one rag less. The sore upon his arm had already disappeared. He held in his hand one of those whips made of thongs of white leather, which police sergeants then used to repress the crowd, and which were called **boullayes**. On his head he wore a sort of headgear, bound round and closed at the top. But it was difficult to make out whether it was a child's cap or a king's crown, the two things bore so strong a resemblance to each other.

Meanwhile Gringoire, without knowing why, had regained some hope, on recognizing in the King of the Cour des Miracles his accursed mendicant of the Grand Hall.

"Master," stammered he; "monseigneur–sire–how ought I to address you?" he said at length, having reached the culminating point of his crescendo, and knowing neither how to mount higher, nor to descend again.

"Monseigneur, his majesty, or comrade, call me what you please. But make haste. What have you to say in your own defence?"

"**In your own defence?**" thought Gringoire,

"that displeases me." He resumed, stuttering, "I am he, who this morning–"

"By the devil's claws!" interrupted Clopin, "your name, knave, and nothing more. Listen. You are in the presence of three powerful sovereigns: myself, Clopin Trouillefou, King of Thunes, successor to the Grand Coësre, supreme suzerain of the Realm of Argot; Mathias Hunyadi Spicali, Duke of Egypt and of Bohemia, the old yellow fellow whom you see yonder, with a dish clout round his head; Guillaume Rousseau, Emperor of Galilee, that fat fellow who is not listening to us but caressing a wench. We are your judges. You have entered the Kingdom of Argot, without being an **argotier**; you have violated the privileges of our city. You must be punished unless you are a **capon**, a **franc-mitou** or a **rifodé**; that is to say, in the slang of honest folks,–a thief, a beggar, or a vagabond. Are you anything of that sort? Justify yourself; announce your titles."

"Alas!" said Gringoire, "I have not that

honor. I am the author–"

"That is sufficient," resumed Trouillefou, without permitting him to finish. "You are going to be hanged. 'Tis a very simple matter, gentlemen and honest **bourgeois**! as you treat our people in your abode, so we treat you in ours! The law which you apply to vagabonds, vagabonds apply to you. 'Tis your fault if it is harsh. One really must behold the grimace of an honest man above the hempen collar now and then; that renders the thing honorable. Come, friend, divide your rags gayly among these damsels. I am going to have you hanged to amuse the vagabonds, and you are to give them your purse to drink your health. If you have any mummery to go through with, there's a very good God the Father in that mortar yonder, in stone, which we stole from Saint-Pierre aux Bœufs. You have four minutes in which to fling your soul at his head."

The harangue was formidable.

"Well said, upon my soul! Clopin Trouillefou preaches like the Holy Father the Pope!" exclaimed the Emperor of Galilee, smashing his pot in order to prop up his table.

"Messeigneurs, emperors, and kings," said Gringoire coolly (for I know not how, firmness had returned to him, and he spoke with resolution), "don't think of such a thing; my name is Pierre Gringoire. I am the poet whose morality was presented this morning in the grand hall of the Courts."

"Ah! so it was you, master!" said Clopin. "I was there, **par la tête Dieu**! Well! comrade, is that any reason, because you bored us to death this morning, that you should not be hung this evening?"

"I shall find difficulty in getting out of it," said Gringoire to himself. Nevertheless, he made one more effort: "I don't see why poets are not classed with vagabonds," said he. "Vagabond, Æsopus certainly was; Homerus was a beggar; Mercurius was a thief–"

Clopin interrupted him: "I believe that you

are trying to blarney us with your jargon. Zounds! let yourself be hung, and don't kick up such a row over it!"

"Pardon me, monseigneur, the King of Thunes," replied Gringoire, disputing the ground foot by foot. "It is worth trouble–One moment!–Listen to me–You are not going to condemn me without having heard me"–

His unlucky voice was, in fact, drowned in the uproar which rose around him. The little boy scraped away at his cauldron with more spirit than ever; and, to crown all, an old woman had just placed on the tripod a frying-pan of grease, which hissed away on the fire with a noise similar to the cry of a troop of children in pursuit of a masker.

In the meantime, Clopin Trouillefou appeared to hold a momentary conference with the Duke of Egypt, and the Emperor of Galilee, who was completely drunk. Then he shouted shrilly: "Silence!" and, as the cauldron and the frying-pan did not heed him, and continued their duet, he jumped down from his hogshead, gave a kick to the boiler, which rolled ten paces away bearing the child with it, a kick to the frying-pan, which upset in the fire with all its grease, and gravely remounted his throne, without troubling himself about the stifled tears of the child, or the grumbling of the old woman, whose supper was wasting away in a fine white flame.

Trouillefou made a sign, and the duke, the emperor, and the passed masters of pickpockets, and the isolated robbers, came and ranged themselves around him in a horseshoe, of which Gringoire, still roughly held by the body, formed the centre. It was a semicircle of rags, tatters, tinsel, pitchforks, axes, legs staggering with intoxication, huge, bare arms, faces sordid, dull, and stupid. In the midst of this Round Table of beggary, Clopin Trouillefou,–as the doge of this senate, as the king of this peerage, as the pope of this conclave,–dominated; first by virtue of the height of his hogshead, and next by virtue of an indescribable, haughty, fierce, and formidable air, which caused his eyes to flash, and corrected in his savage profile the bestial type of the race of vagabonds. One would have pronounced him a boar amid a herd of swine.

"Listen," said he to Gringoire, fondling his misshapen chin with his horny hand; "I don't see why you should not be hung. It is true that it appears to be repugnant to you; and it is very natural, for you **bourgeois** are not accustomed to it. You form for yourselves a great idea of the thing. After all, we don't wish you any harm. Here is a means of extricating yourself from your predicament for the moment. Will you become one of us?"

The reader can judge of the effect which this proposition produced upon Gringoire, who beheld life slipping away from him, and who was beginning to lose his hold upon it. He clutched at it again with energy.

"Certainly I will, and right heartily," said he.

"Do you consent," resumed Clopin, "to enroll yourself among the people of the knife?"

"Of the knife, precisely," responded Gringoire.

"You recognize yourself as a member of the free **bourgeoisie?**"[12] added the King of Thunes.

"Of the free **bourgeoisie**."

"Subject of the Kingdom of Argot?"

"Of the Kingdom of Argot[13]."

"A vagabond?"

"A vagabond."

"In your soul?"

"In my soul."

"I must call your attention to the fact," continued the king, "that you will be hung all the same."

"The devil!" said the poet.

"Only," continued Clopin imperturbably, "you will be hung later on, with more ceremony, at

---

12 A high-toned sharper.

13 Thieves.

the expense of the good city of Paris, on a handsome stone gibbet, and by honest men. That is a consolation."

"Just so," responded Gringoire.

"There are other advantages. In your quality of a high-toned sharper, you will not have to pay the taxes on mud, or the poor, or lanterns, to which the **bourgeois** of Paris are subject."

"So be it," said the poet. "I agree. I am a vagabond, a thief, a sharper, a man of the knife, anything you please; and I am all that already, monsieur, King of Thunes, for I am a philosopher; **et omnia in philosophia, omnes in philosopho continentur**,–all things are contained in philosophy, all men in the philosopher, as you know."

The King of Thunes scowled.

"What do you take me for, my friend? What Hungarian Jew patter are you jabbering at us? I don't know Hebrew. One isn't a Jew because one is a bandit. I don't even steal any longer. I'm above that; I kill. Cut-throat, yes; cutpurse, no."

Gringoire tried to slip in some excuse between these curt words, which wrath rendered more and more jerky.

"I ask your pardon, monseigneur. It is not Hebrew; 'tis Latin."

"I tell you," resumed Clopin angrily, "that I'm not a Jew, and that I'll have you hung, belly of the synagogue, like that little shopkeeper of Judea, who is by your side, and whom I entertain strong hopes of seeing nailed to a counter one of these days, like the counterfeit coin that he is!"

So saying, he pointed his finger at the little, bearded Hungarian Jew who had accosted Gringoire with his **facitote caritatem**, and who, understanding no other language beheld with surprise the King of Thunes's ill-humor overflow upon him.

At length Monsieur Clopin calmed down.

"So you will be a vagabond, you knave?" he said to our poet.

"Of course," replied the poet.

"Willing is not all," said the surly Clopin; "good will doesn't put one onion the more into the soup, and 'tis good for nothing except to go to Paradise with; now, Paradise and the thieves' band are two different things. In order to be received among the thieves,[14] you must prove that you are good for something, and for that purpose, you must search the manikin."

"I'll search anything you like," said Gringoire.

Clopinmadeasign.Severalthievesdetached themselves from the circle, and returned a moment later. They brought two thick posts, terminated at their lower extremities in spreading timber supports, which made them stand readily upon the ground; to the upper extremity of the two posts they fitted a cross-beam, and the whole constituted a very pretty portable gibbet, which Gringoire had the satisfaction of beholding rise before

14 L'argot.

him, in a twinkling. Nothing was lacking, not even the rope, which swung gracefully over the cross-beam.

"What are they going to do?" Gringoire asked himself with some uneasiness. A sound of bells, which he heard at that moment, put an end to his anxiety; it was a stuffed manikin, which the vagabonds were suspending by the neck from the rope, a sort of scarecrow dressed in red, and so hung with mule-bells and larger bells, that one might have tricked out thirty Castilian mules with them. These thousand tiny bells quivered for some time with the vibration of the rope, then gradually died away, and finally became silent when the manikin had been brought into a state of immobility by that law of the pendulum which has dethroned the water clock and the hour-glass. Then Clopin, pointing out to Gringoire a rickety old stool placed beneath the manikin,–"Climb up there."

"Death of the devil!" objected Gringoire; "I shall break my neck. Your stool limps like one of Martial's distiches; it has one hexameter leg and one pentameter leg."

"Climb!" repeated Clopin.

Gringoire mounted the stool, and succeeded, not without some oscillations of head and arms, in regaining his centre of gravity.

"Now," went on the King of Thunes, "twist your right foot round your left leg, and rise on the tip of your left foot."

"Monseigneur," said Gringoire, "so you absolutely insist on my breaking some one of my limbs?"

Clopin tossed his head.

"Hark ye, my friend, you talk too much. Here's the gist of the matter in two words: you are to rise on tiptoe, as I tell you; in that way you will be able to reach the pocket of the manikin, you will rummage it, you will pull out the purse that is there,–and if you do all this without our hearing the sound of a bell, all is well: you shall be a vagabond. All we shall then have to do, will be to thrash you soundly for the space of a week."

"**Ventre-Dieu**! I will be careful," said Gringoire. "And suppose I do make the bells sound?"

"Then you will be hanged. Do you understand?"

"I don't understand at all," replied Gringoire.

"Listen, once more. You are to search the manikin, and take away its purse; if a single bell stirs during the operation, you will be hung. Do you understand that?"

"Good," said Gringoire; "I understand that. And then?"

"If you succeed in removing the purse without our hearing the bells, you are a vagabond, and you will be thrashed for eight consecutive days. You understand now, no doubt?"

"No, monseigneur; I no longer understand. Where is the advantage to me? hanged in one case, cudgelled in the other?"

"And a vagabond," resumed Clopin, "and a vagabond; is that nothing? It is for your interest that we should beat you, in order to harden you to blows."

"Many thanks," replied the poet.

"Come, make haste," said the king, stamping upon his cask, which resounded like a huge drum! "Search the manikin, and let there be an end to this! I warn you for the last time, that if I hear a single bell, you will take the place of the manikin."

The band of thieves applauded Clopin's words, and arranged themselves in a circle round the gibbet, with a laugh so pitiless that Gringoire perceived that he amused them too much not to have everything to fear from them. No hope was left for him, accordingly, unless it were the slight chance of succeeding in the formidable operation which was imposed upon him; he decided to risk it, but it was not without first having addressed a fervent prayer to the manikin he was about to plunder, and who would have been easier to move to pity than the vagabonds. These myriad bells, with their little copper tongues, seemed to him like the mouths of so many asps, open and ready to sting and to hiss.

"Oh!" he said, in a very low voice, "is it possible that my life depends on the slightest vibration of the least of these bells? Oh!" he added, with clasped hands, "bells, do not ring, hand-bells do not clang, mule-bells do not quiver!"

He made one more attempt upon Trouillefou.

"And if there should come a gust of wind?"

"You will be hanged," replied the other, without hesitation.

Perceiving that no respite, nor reprieve, nor subterfuge was possible, he bravely decided upon his course of action; he wound his right foot round his left leg, raised himself on his left foot, and stretched out his arm: but at the moment when his hand touched the manikin, his body, which was now supported upon one leg only, wavered on the stool which had but three; he made an involuntary effort to support himself by the manikin, lost his balance, and fell heavily to the ground, deafened by the fatal vibration of the thousand bells of the manikin, which, yielding to the impulse imparted by his hand, described first a rotary motion, and then swayed majestically between the two posts.

"Malediction!" he cried as he fell, and remained as though dead, with his face to the earth.

Meanwhile, he heard the dreadful peal above his head, the diabolical laughter of the vagabonds, and the voice of Trouillefou saying,–

"Pick me up that knave, and hang him without ceremony." He rose. They had already detached the manikin to make room for him.

The thieves made him mount the stool, Clopin came to him, passed the rope about his neck, and, tapping him on the shoulder,–

"Adieu, my friend. You can't escape now, even if you digested with the pope's guts."

The word "Mercy!" died away upon

Gringoire's lips. He cast his eyes about him; but there was no hope: all were laughing.

"Bellevigne de l'Étoile," said the King of Thunes to an enormous vagabond, who stepped out from the ranks, "climb upon the cross beam."

Bellevigne de l'Étoile nimbly mounted the transverse beam, and in another minute, Gringoire, on raising his eyes, beheld him, with terror, seated upon the beam above his head.

"Now," resumed Clopin Trouillefou, "as soon as I clap my hands, you, Andry the Red, will fling the stool to the ground with a blow of your knee; you, François Chanteprune, will cling to the feet of the rascal; and you, Bellevigne, will fling yourself on his shoulders; and all three at once, do you hear?"

Gringoire shuddered.

"Are you ready?" said Clopin Trouillefou to the three thieves, who held themselves in readiness to fall upon Gringoire. A moment of horrible suspense ensued for the poor victim, during which Clopin tranquilly thrust into the fire with the tip of his foot, some bits of vine shoots which the flame had not caught. "Are you ready?" he repeated, and opened his hands to clap. One second more and all would have been over.

But he paused, as though struck by a sudden thought.

"One moment!" said he; "I forgot! It is our custom not to hang a man without inquiring whether there is any woman who wants him. Comrade, this is your last resource. You must wed either a female vagabond or the noose."

This law of the vagabonds, singular as it may strike the reader, remains to-day written out at length, in ancient English legislation. (See **Burington's Observations**.)

Gringoire breathed again. This was the second time that he had returned to life within an hour. So he did not dare to trust to it too implicitly.

"Holà!" cried Clopin, mounted once more upon his cask, "holà! women, females, is there among you, from the sorceress to her cat, a wench who wants this rascal? Holà, Colette la Charonne! Elisabeth Trouvain! Simone Jodouyne! Marie Piédebou! Thonne la Longue! Bérarde Fanouel! Michelle Genaille! Claude Ronge-oreille! Mathurine Girorou!–Holà! Isabeau-la-Thierrye! Come and see! A man for nothing! Who wants him?"

Gringoire, no doubt, was not very appetizing in this miserable condition. The female vagabonds did not seem to be much affected by the proposition. The unhappy wretch heard them answer: "No! no! hang him; there'll be the more fun for us all!"

Nevertheless, three emerged from the throng and came to smell of him. The first was a big wench, with a square face. She examined the philosopher's deplorable doublet attentively. His garment was worn, and more full of holes than a stove for roasting chestnuts. The girl made a wry face.

"Old rag!" she muttered, and addressing Gringoire, "Let's see your cloak!" "I have lost it," replied Gringoire. "Your hat?" "They took it away from me." "Your shoes?" "They have hardly any soles left." "Your purse?" "Alas!" stammered Gringoire, "I have not even a sou." "Let them hang you, then, and say 'Thank you!'" retorted the vagabond wench, turning her back on him.

The second,–old, black, wrinkled, hideous, with an ugliness conspicuous even in the Cour des Miracles, trotted round Gringoire. He almost trembled lest she should want him. But she mumbled between her teeth, "He's too thin," and went off.

The third was a young girl, quite fresh, and not too ugly. "Save me!" said the poor fellow to her, in a low tone. She gazed at him for a moment with an air of pity, then dropped her eyes, made a plait in her petticoat, and remained in indecision. He followed all these movements with his eyes; it was the last gleam of hope. "No," said the young girl, at length, "no! Guillaume Longuejoue would beat me." She retreated into the crowd.

"You are unlucky, comrade," said Clopin.

Then rising to his feet, upon his hogshead. "No one wants him," he exclaimed, imitating the accent of an auctioneer, to the great delight of all; "no one wants him? once, twice, three times!" and, turning towards the gibbet with a sign of his hand, "Gone!"

Bellevigne de l'Étoile, Andry the Red, François Chanteprune, stepped up to Gringoire.

At that moment a cry arose among the thieves: "**La Esmeralda! La Esmeralda!**"

Gringoire shuddered, and turned towards the side whence the clamor proceeded.

The crowd opened, and gave passage to a pure and dazzling form.

It was the gypsy.

"La Esmeralda!" said Gringoire, stupefied in the midst of his emotions, by the abrupt manner in which that magic word knotted together all his reminiscences of the day.

This rare creature seemed, even in the Cour des Miracles, to exercise her sway of charm and beauty. The vagabonds, male and female, ranged themselves gently along her path, and their brutal faces beamed beneath her glance.

She approached the victim with her light step. Her pretty Djali followed her. Gringoire was more dead than alive. She examined him for a moment in silence.

"You are going to hang this man?" she said gravely, to Clopin.

"Yes, sister," replied the King of Thunes, "unless you will take him for your husband."

She made her pretty little pout with her under lip. "I'll take him," said she.

Gringoire firmly believed that he had been in a dream ever since morning, and that this was the continuation of it.

The change was, in fact, violent, though a gratifying one. They undid the noose, and made the poet step down from the stool. His emotion was so lively that he was obliged to sit down.

The Duke of Egypt brought an earthenware crock, without uttering a word. The gypsy offered it to Gringoire: “Fling it on the ground,” said she.

The crock broke into four pieces.

“Brother,” then said the Duke of Egypt, laying his hands upon their foreheads, “she is your wife; sister, he is your husband for four years. Go.”

CHAPTER SEVEN

A Bridal Night

A FEW MOMENTS LATER our poet found himself in a tiny arched chamber, very cosy, very warm, seated at a table which appeared to ask nothing better than to make some loans from a larder hanging near by, having a good bed in prospect, and alone with a pretty girl. The adventure smacked of enchantment. He began seriously to take himself for a personage in a fairy tale; he cast his eyes about him from time to time to time, as though to see if the chariot of fire, harnessed to two-winged chimeras, which alone could have so rapidly transported him from Tartarus to Paradise, were still there. At times, also, he fixed his eyes obstinately upon the holes in his doublet, in order to cling to reality, and not lose the ground from under his feet completely. His reason, tossed about in imaginary space, now hung only by this thread.

The young girl did not appear to pay any attention to him; she went and came, displaced a stool, talked to her goat, and indulged in a pout now and then. At last she came and seated herself near the table, and Gringoire was able to scrutinize her at his ease.

You have been a child, reader, and you would, perhaps, be very happy to be one still. It is quite certain that you have not, more than once (and for my part, I have passed whole days, the best employed of my life, at it) followed from thicket to thicket, by the side of running water, on a sunny day, a beautiful green or blue dragon-fly, breaking its flight in abrupt angles, and kissing the tips of all the branches. You recollect with what amorous curiosity your thought and your gaze were riveted upon this little whirlwind, hissing and humming with wings of purple and azure, in the midst of which floated an imperceptible body, veiled by the very rapidity of its movement. The aerial being which was dimly outlined amid this quivering of wings, appeared to you chimerical, imaginary, impossible to touch, impossible to see. But when, at length, the dragon-fly alighted on the tip of a reed, and, holding your breath the while, you were able to examine the long, gauze wings, the long enamel robe, the two globes of crystal, what astonishment you felt, and what fear lest you should again behold the form disappear into a shade, and the creature into a chimera! Recall these impressions, and you will readily appreciate what Gringoire felt on contemplating, beneath her visible and palpable form, that Esmeralda of whom, up to that time, he had only caught a glimpse, amidst a whirlwind of dance, song, and tumult.

Sinking deeper and deeper into his revery: "So this," he said to himself, following her vaguely with his eyes, "is **la Esmeralda!** a celestial creature! a street dancer! so much, and so little! 'Twas she who dealt the death-blow to my mystery this morning, 'tis she who saves my life this evening! My evil genius! My good angel! A pretty woman, on my word! and who must needs love me madly to have taken me in that fashion. By the way," said he, rising suddenly, with that sentiment of the true which formed the foundation of his character and his philosophy, "I don't know very well how it happens, but I am her husband!"

With this idea in his head and in his eyes, he stepped up to the young girl in a manner so military and so gallant that she drew back.

"What do you want of me?" said she.

"Can you ask me, adorable Esmeralda?" replied Gringoire, with so passionate an accent that he was himself astonished at it on hearing himself speak.

The gypsy opened her great eyes. "I don't know what you mean."

"What!" resumed Gringoire, growing warmer and warmer, and supposing that, after all, he had to deal merely with a virtue of the Cour des Miracles; "am I not thine, sweet friend, art thou not mine?"

And, quite ingenuously, he clasped her waist.

The gypsy's corsage slipped through his hands like the skin of an eel. She bounded from one end of the tiny room to the other, stooped down, and raised herself again, with a little poniard in her hand, before Gringoire had even had time to see whence the poniard came; proud and angry, with swelling lips and inflated nostrils, her cheeks as red as an api apple,[15] and her eyes darting lightnings. At the same time, the white goat placed itself in front of her, and presented to Gringoire a hostile front, bristling with two pretty horns, gilded and very sharp. All this took place in the twinkling of an eye.

The dragon-fly had turned into a wasp, and asked nothing better than to sting.

Our philosopher was speechless, and turned his astonished eyes from the goat to the young girl. "Holy Virgin!" he said at last, when surprise permitted him to speak, "here are two hearty dames!"

The gypsy broke the silence on her side.

"You must be a very bold knave!"

"Pardon, mademoiselle," said Gringoire, with a smile. "But why did you take me for

15 A small dessert apple, bright red on one side and greenish-white on the other.

your husband?"

"Should I have allowed you to be hanged?"

"So," said the poet, somewhat disappointed in his amorous hopes. "You had no other idea in marrying me than to save me from the gibbet?"

"And what other idea did you suppose that I had?"

Gringoire bit his lips. "Come," said he, "I am not yet so triumphant in Cupido, as I thought. But then, what was the good of breaking that poor jug?"

Meanwhile Esmeralda's dagger and the goat's horns were still upon the defensive.

"Mademoiselle Esmeralda," said the poet, "let us come to terms. I am not a clerk of the court, and I shall not go to law with you for thus carrying a dagger in Paris, in the teeth of the ordinances and prohibitions of M. the Provost. Nevertheless, you are not ignorant of the fact that Noël Lescrivain was condemned, a week ago, to pay ten Parisian sous, for having carried a cutlass.

But this is no affair of mine, and I will come to the point. I swear to you, upon my share of Paradise, not to approach you without your leave and permission, but do give me some supper."

The truth is, Gringoire was, like M. Despreaux, "not very voluptuous." He did not belong to that chevalier and musketeer species, who take young girls by assault. In the matter of love, as in all other affairs, he willingly assented to temporizing and adjusting terms; and a good supper, and an amiable tête-à-tête appeared to him, especially when he was hungry, an excellent interlude between the prologue and the catastrophe of a love adventure.

The gypsy did not reply. She made her disdainful little grimace, drew up her head like a bird, then burst out laughing, and the tiny poniard disappeared as it had come, without Gringoire being able to see where the wasp concealed its sting.

A moment later, there stood upon the

table a loaf of rye bread, a slice of bacon, some wrinkled apples and a jug of beer. Gringoire began to eat eagerly. One would have said, to hear the furious clashing of his iron fork and his earthenware plate, that all his love had turned to appetite.

The young girl seated opposite him, watched him in silence, visibly preoccupied with another thought, at which she smiled from time to time, while her soft hand caressed the intelligent head of the goat, gently pressed between her knees.

A candle of yellow wax illuminated this scene of voracity and revery.

Meanwhile, the first cravings of his stomach having been stilled, Gringoire felt some false shame at perceiving that nothing remained but one apple.

"You do not eat, Mademoiselle Esmeralda?"

She replied by a negative sign of the head, and her pensive glance fixed itself upon the vault of the ceiling.

"What the deuce is she thinking of?" thought

Gringoire, staring at what she was gazing at; "'tis impossible that it can be that stone dwarf carved in the keystone of that arch, which thus absorbs her attention. What the deuce! I can bear the comparison!"

He raised his voice, "Mademoiselle!"

She seemed not to hear him.

He repeated, still more loudly, "Mademoiselle Esmeralda!"

Trouble wasted. The young girl's mind was elsewhere, and Gringoire's voice had not the power to recall it. Fortunately, the goat interfered. She began to pull her mistress gently by the sleeve.

"What dost thou want, Djali?" said the gypsy, hastily, as though suddenly awakened.

"She is hungry," said Gringoire, charmed to enter into conversation. Esmeralda began to crumble some bread, which Djali ate gracefully from the hollow of her hand.

Moreover, Gringoire did not give her time to resume her revery. He hazarded a delicate question.

"So you don't want me for your husband?"

The young girl looked at him intently, and said, "No."

"For your lover?" went on Gringoire.

She pouted, and replied, "No."

"For your friend?" pursued Gringoire.

She gazed fixedly at him again, and said, after a momentary reflection, "Perhaps."

This "perhaps," so dear to philosophers, emboldened Gringoire.

"Do you know what friendship is?" he asked.

"Yes," replied the gypsy; "it is to be brother and sister; two souls which touch without mingling, two fingers on one hand."

"And love?" pursued Gringoire.

"Oh! love!" said she, and her voice trembled, and her eye beamed. "That is to be two and to be but one. A man and a woman mingled into one angel. It is heaven."

The street dancer had a beauty as she

spoke thus, that struck Gringoire singularly, and seemed to him in perfect keeping with the almost oriental exaltation of her words. Her pure, red lips half smiled; her serene and candid brow became troubled, at intervals, under her thoughts, like a mirror under the breath; and from beneath her long, drooping, black eyelashes, there escaped a sort of ineffable light, which gave to her profile that ideal serenity which Raphael found at the mystic point of intersection of virginity, maternity, and divinity.

Nevertheless, Gringoire continued,–

"What must one be then, in order to please you?"

"A man."

"And I–" said he, "what, then, am I?"

"A man has a helmet on his head, a sword in his hand, and golden spurs on his heels."

"Good," said Gringoire, "without a horse, no man. Do you love any one?"

"As a lover?–"

"Yes."

She remained thoughtful for a moment, then said with a peculiar expression: "That I shall know soon."

"Why not this evening?" resumed the poet tenderly. "Why not me?"

She cast a grave glance upon him and said,–

"I can never love a man who cannot protect me."

Gringoire colored, and took the hint. It was evident that the young girl was alluding to the slight assistance which he had rendered her in the critical situation in which she had found herself two hours previously. This memory, effaced by his own adventures of the evening, now recurred to him. He smote his brow.

"By the way, mademoiselle, I ought to have begun there. Pardon my foolish absence of mind. How did you contrive to escape from the claws of Quasimodo?"

This question made the gypsy shudder.

"Oh! the horrible hunchback," said she, hiding her face in her hands. And she shuddered as though with violent cold.

"Horrible, in truth," said Gringoire, who clung to his idea; "but how did you manage to escape him?"

La Esmeralda smiled, sighed, and remained silent.

"Do you know why he followed you?" began Gringoire again, seeking to return to his question by a circuitous route.

"I don't know," said the young girl, and she added hastily, "but you were following me also, why were you following me?"

"In good faith," responded Gringoire, "I don't know either."

Silence ensued. Gringoire slashed the table with his knife. The young girl smiled and seemed to be gazing through the wall at something. All at once she began to sing in a barely articulate voice,–

Quando las pintadas aves,

Mudas estan, y la tierra–[16]

She broke off abruptly, and began to caress Djali.

"That's a pretty animal of yours," said Gringoire.

"She is my sister," she answered.

"Why are you called **la Esmeralda?**" asked the poet.

"I do not know."

"But why?"

She drew from her bosom a sort of little oblong bag, suspended from her neck by a string of adrézarach beads. This bag exhaled a strong odor of camphor. It was covered with green silk, and bore in its centre a large piece of green glass, in imitation of an emerald.

"Perhaps it is because of this," said she.

Gringoire was on the point of taking the bag in his hand. She drew back.

"Don't touch it! It is an amulet. You would injure the charm or the charm would injure

16 When the gay-plumaged birds grow weary, and the earth—

you."

The poet's curiosity was more and more aroused.

"Who gave it to you?"

She laid one finger on her mouth and concealed the amulet in her bosom. He tried a few more questions, but she hardly replied.

"What is the meaning of the words, **la Esmeralda?**"

"I don't know," said she.

"To what language do they belong?"

"They are Egyptian, I think."

"I suspected as much," said Gringoire, "you are not a native of France?"

"I don't know."

"Are your parents alive?"

She began to sing, to an ancient air,–

Mon père est oiseau,
Ma mère est oiselle.
Je passe l'eau sans nacelle,
Je passe l'eau sans bateau,
Ma mère est oiselle,

Mon père est oiseau.[17]

"Good," said Gringoire. "At what age did you come to France?"

"When I was very young."

"And when to Paris?"

"Last year. At the moment when we were entering the papal gate I saw a reed warbler flit through the air, that was at the end of August; I said, it will be a hard winter."

"So it was," said Gringoire, delighted at this beginning of a conversation. "I passed it in blowing my fingers. So you have the gift of prophecy?"

She retired into her laconics again.

"Is that man whom you call the Duke of Egypt, the chief of your tribe?"

"Yes."

---

17 My father is a bird,
my mother is a bird.
I cross the water without a barque,
I cross the water without a boat.
My mother is a bird,
my father is a bird.

"But it was he who married us," remarked the poet timidly.

She made her customary pretty grimace.

"I don't even know your name."

"My name? If you want it, here it is,–Pierre Gringoire."

"I know a prettier one," said she.

"Naughty girl!" retorted the poet. "Never mind, you shall not provoke me. Wait, perhaps you will love me more when you know me better; and then, you have told me your story with so much confidence, that I owe you a little of mine. You must know, then, that my name is Pierre Gringoire, and that I am a son of the farmer of the notary's office of Gonesse. My father was hung by the Burgundians, and my mother disembowelled by the Picards, at the siege of Paris, twenty years ago. At six years of age, therefore, I was an orphan, without a sole to my foot except the pavements of Paris. I do not know how I passed the interval from six to sixteen. A fruit dealer gave me a plum here, a baker flung me a crust there;

in the evening I got myself taken up by the watch, who threw me into prison, and there I found a bundle of straw. All this did not prevent my growing up and growing thin, as you see. In the winter I warmed myself in the sun, under the porch of the Hôtel de Sens, and I thought it very ridiculous that the fire on Saint John's Day was reserved for the dog days. At sixteen, I wished to choose a calling. I tried all in succession. I became a soldier; but I was not brave enough. I became a monk; but I was not sufficiently devout; and then I'm a bad hand at drinking. In despair, I became an apprentice of the woodcutters, but I was not strong enough; I had more of an inclination to become a schoolmaster; 'tis true that I did not know how to read, but that's no reason. I perceived at the end of a certain time, that I lacked something in every direction; and seeing that I was good for nothing, of my own free will I became a poet and rhymester. That is a trade which one can always adopt when one is a vagabond, and it's better than stealing, as some young brigands of my acquaintance advised me to do. One day I met by luck, Dom Claude Frollo, the reverend archdeacon of Notre-Dame. He took an interest in me, and it is to him that I to-day owe it that I am a veritable man of letters, who knows Latin from the **de Officiis** of Cicero to the mortuology of the Celestine Fathers, and a barbarian neither in scholastics, nor in politics, nor in rhythmics, that sophism of sophisms. I am the author of the Mystery which was presented to-day with great triumph and a great concourse of populace, in the grand hall of the Palais de Justice. I have also made a book which will contain six hundred pages, on the wonderful comet of 1465, which sent one man mad. I have enjoyed still other successes. Being somewhat of an artillery carpenter, I lent a hand to Jean Mangue's great bombard, which burst, as you know, on the day when it was tested, on the Pont de Charenton, and killed four and twenty curious spectators. You see that I am not a bad match in marriage. I know a great many sorts of very engaging tricks, which I will teach your goat; for example, to mimic the Bishop of Paris, that cursed Pharisee whose mill wheels splash passers-by the whole length of the Pont aux Meuniers. And then my mystery will bring me in a great deal of coined money, if they will only pay me. And finally, I am at your orders, I and my wits, and my science and my letters, ready to live with you, damsel, as it shall please you, chastely or joyously; husband and wife, if you see fit; brother and sister, if you think that better."

Gringoire ceased, awaiting the effect of his harangue on the young girl. Her eyes were fixed on the ground.

"**Phœbus,**" she said in a low voice. Then, turning towards the poet, "**Phœbus**,–what does that mean?"

Gringoire, without exactly understanding what the connection could be between his address and this question, was not sorry to display his erudition. Assuming an air of importance, he replied,–

"It is a Latin word which means **sun.**"

"Sun!" she repeated.

"It is the name of a handsome archer, who was a god," added Gringoire.

"A god!" repeated the gypsy, and there was something pensive and passionate in her tone.

At that moment, one of her bracelets became unfastened and fell. Gringoire stooped quickly to pick it up; when he straightened up, the young girl and the goat had disappeared. He heard the sound of a bolt. It was a little door, communicating, no doubt, with a neighboring cell, which was being fastened on the outside.

"Has she left me a bed, at least?" said our philosopher.

He made the tour of his cell. There was no piece of furniture adapted to sleeping purposes, except a tolerably long wooden coffer; and its cover was carved, to boot;

which afforded Gringoire, when he stretched himself out upon it, a sensation somewhat similar to that which Micromégas would feel if he were to lie down on the Alps.

"Come!" said he, adjusting himself as well as possible, "I must resign myself. But here's a strange nuptial night. 'Tis a pity. There was something innocent and antediluvian about that broken crock, which quite pleased me."

VOLUME ONE

BOOK THIRD

CHAPTER ONE

Notre-Dame

THE CHURCH OF NOTRE-Dame de Paris is still no doubt, a majestic and sublime edifice. But, beautiful as it has been preserved in growing old, it is difficult not to sigh, not to wax indignant, before the numberless degradations and mutilations which time and men have both caused the venerable monument to suffer, without respect for Charlemagne, who laid its first stone, or for Philip Augustus, who laid the last.

On the face of this aged queen of our cathedrals, by the side of a wrinkle, one always finds a scar. **Tempus edax, homo edacior**[18]; which I should be glad to translate thus: time is blind, man is stupid.

If we had leisure to examine with the reader, one by one, the diverse traces of destruction imprinted upon the old church, time's share would be the least, the share of men the most, especially **the men of art**, since there have been individuals who assumed the title of architects during the last two centuries.

And, in the first place, to cite only a few leading examples, there certainly are few finer architectural pages than this façade, where, successively and at once, the

---

18 Time is a devourer; man, more so.

three portals hollowed out in an arch; the broidered and dentated cordon of the eight and twenty royal niches; the immense central rose window, flanked by its two lateral windows, like a priest by his deacon and subdeacon; the frail and lofty gallery of trefoil arcades, which supports a heavy platform above its fine, slender columns; and lastly, the two black and massive towers with their slate penthouses, harmonious parts of a magnificent whole, superposed in five gigantic stories;–develop themselves before the eye, in a mass and without confusion, with their innumerable details of statuary, carving, and sculpture, joined powerfully to the tranquil grandeur of the whole; a vast symphony in stone, so to speak; the colossal work of one man and one people, all together one and complex, like the Iliads and the Romanceros, whose sister it is; prodigious product of the grouping together of all the forces of an epoch, where, upon each stone, one sees the fancy of the workman disciplined by the genius of the artist start forth in a hundred fashions; a sort of human creation, in a word, powerful and fecund as the divine creation of which it seems to have stolen the double character,–variety, eternity.

And what we here say of the façade must be said of the entire church; and what we say of the cathedral church of Paris, must be said of all the churches of Christendom in the Middle Ages. All things are in place in that art, self-created, logical, and well proportioned. To measure the great toe of the foot is to measure the giant.

Let us return to the façade of Notre-Dame, as it still appears to us, when we go piously to admire the grave and puissant cathedral, which inspires terror, so its chronicles assert: **quæ mole sua terrorem incutit spectantibus**.

Three important things are to-day lacking in that façade: in the first place, the staircase of eleven steps which formerly raised it above the soil; next, the lower series of statues which occupied the niches of the three portals; and lastly the upper series, of the twenty-eight most ancient kings of France, which garnished the gallery of the first story, beginning with Childebert, and ending with Phillip Augustus, holding in his hand “the imperial apple.”

Time has caused the staircase to disappear, by raising the soil of the city with a slow and irresistible progress; but, while thus causing the eleven steps which added to the majestic height of the edifice, to be devoured, one by one, by the rising tide of the pavements of Paris,–time has bestowed upon the church perhaps more than it has taken away, for it is time which has spread over the façade that sombre hue of the centuries which makes the old age of monuments the period of their beauty.

But who has thrown down the two rows of statues? who has left the niches empty?

who has cut, in the very middle of the central portal, that new and bastard arch? who has dared to frame therein that commonplace and heavy door of carved wood, à la Louis XV., beside the arabesques of Biscornette? The men, the architects, the artists of our day.

And if we enter the interior of the edifice, who has overthrown that colossus of Saint Christopher, proverbial for magnitude among statues, as the grand hall of the Palais de Justice was among halls, as the spire of Strasbourg among spires? And those myriads of statues, which peopled all the spaces between the columns of the nave and the choir, kneeling, standing, equestrian, men, women, children, kings, bishops, gendarmes, in stone, in marble, in gold, in silver, in copper, in wax even,–who has brutally swept them away? It is not time.

And who substituted for the ancient gothic altar, splendidly encumbered with shrines and reliquaries, that heavy marble sarcophagus, with angels' heads and clouds, which seems a specimen pillaged from the Val-de-Grâce or the Invalides? Who stupidly sealed that heavy anachronism of stone in the Carlovingian pavement of Hercandus? Was it not Louis XIV., fulfilling the request of Louis XIII.?

And who put the cold, white panes in the place of those windows, "high in color," which caused the astonished eyes of our fathers to hesitate between the rose of the grand portal and the arches of the apse? And what would a sub-chanter of the sixteenth century say, on beholding the beautiful yellow wash, with which our archiepiscopal vandals have desmeared their cathedral? He would remember that it was the color with which the hangman smeared "accursed" edifices; he would recall the Hôtel du Petit-Bourbon, all smeared thus, on account of the constable's treason. "Yellow, after all, of so good a quality," said Sauval, "and so well recommended, that more than a century has not yet caused it to lose its color." He would think that the sacred place had become infamous, and would flee.

And if we ascend the cathedral, without mentioning a thousand barbarisms of every sort,–what has become of that charming little bell tower, which rested upon the point of intersection of the cross-roofs, and which, no less frail and no less bold than its neighbor (also destroyed), the spire of the Sainte-Chapelle, buried itself in the sky, farther forward than the towers, slender, pointed, sonorous, carved in open work. An architect of good taste amputated it (1787), and considered it sufficient to mask the wound with that large, leaden plaster, which resembles a pot cover.

'Tis thus that the marvellous art of the Middle Ages has been treated in nearly every country, especially in France. One can distinguish on its ruins three sorts of lesions, all three of which cut into it at different depths; first, time, which has insensibly notched its surface here and there, and gnawed it everywhere; next, political and religious revolution, which, blind and wrathful by nature, have flung themselves tumultuously upon it, torn its rich garment of carving and sculpture, burst its rose windows, broken its necklace of arabesques and tiny figures, torn out its statues, sometimes because of their mitres, sometimes because of their crowns; lastly, fashions, even more grotesque and foolish, which, since the anarchical and splendid deviations of the Renaissance, have followed each other in the necessary decadence of architecture. Fashions have wrought more harm than revolutions. They have cut to the quick; they have attacked the very bone and framework of art; they have cut, slashed, disorganized, killed the edifice, in form as in the symbol, in its consistency as well as in its beauty. And then they have made it over; a presumption of which neither time nor revolutions at least have been guilty. They have audaciously adjusted, in the name of "good taste," upon the wounds of gothic architecture, their miserable gewgaws of a day, their ribbons of marble, their pompons of metal, a veritable leprosy of egg-shaped ornaments, volutes, whorls, draperies, garlands, fringes, stone flames, bronze clouds, pudgy cupids, chubby-cheeked cherubim, which begin to devour the face of art in the oratory of Catherine de Medicis, and cause it to expire, two centuries later, tortured and grimacing, in the boudoir of the Dubarry.

Thus, to sum up the points which we have just indicated, three sorts of ravages to-day disfigure Gothic architecture. Wrinkles and warts on the epidermis; this is the work of time. Deeds of violence, brutalities, contusions, fractures; this is the work of the revolutions from Luther to Mirabeau. Mutilations, amputations, dislocation of the joints, **restorations**; this is the Greek,

Roman, and barbarian work of professors according to Vitruvius and Vignole. This magnificent art produced by the Vandals has been slain by the academies. The centuries, the revolutions, which at least devastate with impartiality and grandeur, have been joined by a cloud of school architects, licensed, sworn, and bound by oath; defacing with the discernment and choice of bad taste, substituting the **chicorées** of Louis XV. for the Gothic lace, for the greater glory of the Parthenon. It is the kick of the ass at the dying lion. It is the old oak crowning itself, and which, to heap the measure full, is stung, bitten, and gnawed by caterpillars.

How far it is from the epoch when Robert Cenalis, comparing Notre-Dame de Paris to the famous temple of Diana at Ephesus, **so much lauded by the ancient pagans**, which Erostatus **has** immortalized, found the Gallic temple "more excellent in length, breadth, height, and structure."[19]

Notre-Dame is not, moreover, what can be called a complete, definite, classified monument. It is no longer a Romanesque church; nor is it a Gothic church. This edifice is not a type. Notre-Dame de Paris has not, like the Abbey of Tournus, the grave and massive frame, the large and round vault, the glacial bareness, the majestic simplicity of the edifices which have the rounded arch for their progenitor. It is not, like the Cathedral of Bourges, the magnificent, light, multiform, tufted, bristling efflorescent product of the pointed arch. Impossible to class it in that ancient family of sombre, mysterious churches, low and crushed as it were by the round arch, almost Egyptian, with the exception of the ceiling; all hieroglyphics, all sacerdotal, all symbolical, more loaded in their ornaments, with lozenges and

19 Histoire Gallicane, liv. II. Periode III. fo. 130, p. 1.

zigzags, than with flowers, with flowers than with animals, with animals than with men; the work of the architect less than of the bishop; first transformation of art, all impressed with theocratic and military discipline, taking root in the Lower Empire, and stopping with the time of William the Conqueror. Impossible to place our Cathedral in that other family of lofty, aerial churches, rich in painted windows and sculpture; pointed in form, bold in attitude; communal and **bourgeois** as political symbols; free, capricious, lawless, as a work of art; second transformation of architecture, no longer hieroglyphic, immovable and sacerdotal, but artistic, progressive, and popular, which begins at the return from the crusades, and ends with Louis IX. Notre-Dame de Paris is not of pure Romanesque, like the first; nor of pure Arabian race, like the second.

It is an edifice of the transition period. The Saxon architect completed the erection of the first pillars of the nave, when the pointed arch, which dates from the Crusade, arrived and placed itself as a conqueror upon the large Romanesque capitals which should support only round arches. The pointed arch, mistress since that time, constructed the rest of the church. Nevertheless, timid and inexperienced at the start, it sweeps out, grows larger, restrains itself, and dares no longer dart upwards in spires and lancet windows, as it did later on, in so many marvellous cathedrals. One would say that it were conscious of the vicinity of the heavy Romanesque pillars.

However, these edifices of the transition from the Romanesque to the Gothic, are no less precious for study than the pure types. They express a shade of the art which would be lost without them. It is the graft of the pointed upon the round arch.

Notre-Dame de Paris is, in particular, a curious specimen of this variety. Each face, each stone of the venerable monument, is a page not only of the history of the country, but of the history of science and art as well. Thus, in order to indicate here only the principal details, while the little Red Door almost attains to the limits of the Gothic delicacy of the fifteenth century, the pillars of the nave, by their size and weight, go back to the Carlovingian Abbey of Saint-Germain-des-Prés. One would suppose that six centuries separated these pillars from that door. There is no one, not even the hermetics, who does not find in the symbols of the grand portal a satisfactory compendium of their science, of which the Church of Saint-Jacques de la Boucherie was so complete a hieroglyph. Thus, the Roman abbey, the philosophers' church, the Gothic art, Saxon art, the heavy, round pillar, which recalls Gregory VII., the hermetic symbolism, with which Nicolas Flamel played the prelude to Luther, papal unity, schism, Saint-Germain des Prés, Saint-Jacques de la Boucherie,– all are mingled, combined, amalgamated in Notre-Dame. This central mother church is, among the ancient churches of Paris, a sort of chimera; it has the head of one, the limbs of another, the haunches of another, something of all.

We repeat it, these hybrid constructions are not the least interesting for the artist, for the antiquarian, for the historian. They make one feel to what a degree architecture is a primitive thing, by demonstrating (what is also demonstrated by the cyclopean vestiges, the pyramids of Egypt, the gigantic Hindoo pagodas) that the greatest products of architecture are less the works of individuals than of society; rather the offspring of a nation's effort, than the inspired flash of a man of genius; the deposit left by a whole people; the heaps accumulated by centuries; the residue of successive evaporations of human society,–in a word, species of formations. Each wave of time contributes its alluvium, each race deposits its layer on the monument, each individual brings his stone. Thus do the beavers, thus do the bees, thus do men. The great symbol of architecture, Babel, is a hive.

Great edifices, like great mountains, are the work of centuries. Art often undergoes a transformation while they are pending, **pendent opera interrupta**; they proceed quietly in accordance with the transformed art. The new art takes the monument where it finds it, incrusts itself there, assimilates it to itself, develops it according to its fancy, and finishes it if it can. The thing is accomplished without trouble, without effort, without reaction,–following a natural and tranquil law. It is a graft which shoots up, a sap which circulates, a vegetation which starts forth anew. Certainly there is matter here for many large volumes, and often the universal history of humanity in the successive engrafting of many arts at many levels, upon the same monument. The man, the artist, the individual, is effaced in these great masses, which lack the name of their author; human intelligence is there summed up and totalized. Time is the architect, the nation is the builder.

Not to consider here anything except the Christian architecture of Europe, that younger sister of the great masonries of the Orient, it appears to the eyes as an immense formation divided into three well-defined zones, which are superposed, the one upon the other: the Romanesque zone[20], the Gothic zone, the zone of the Renaissance, which we would gladly call the Greco-Roman zone. The Roman layer, which is the most

---

20 This is the same which is called, according to locality, climate, and races, Lombard, Saxon, or Byzantine. There are four sister and parallel architectures, each having its special character, but derived from the same origin, the round arch.

Facies non omnibus una, Non diversa tamen, qualem, etc.

Their faces not all alike, nor yet different, but such as the faces of sisters ought to be.

ancient and deepest, is occupied by the round arch, which reappears, supported by the Greek column, in the modern and upper layer of the Renaissance. The pointed arch is found between the two. The edifices which belong exclusively to any one of these three layers are perfectly distinct, uniform, and complete. There is the Abbey of Jumiéges, there is the Cathedral of Reims, there is the Sainte-Croix of Orléans. But the three zones mingle and amalgamate along the edges, like the colors in the solar spectrum. Hence, complex monuments, edifices of gradation and transition. One is Roman at the base, Gothic in the middle, Greco-Roman at the top. It is because it was six hundred years in building. This variety is rare. The donjon keep of d'Étampes is a specimen of it. But monuments of two formations are more frequent. There is Notre-Dame de Paris, a pointed-arch edifice, which is imbedded by its pillars in that Roman zone, in which are plunged the portal of Saint-Denis, and the nave of Saint-Germain des Prés. There is the charming, half-Gothic chapter-house of Bocherville, where the Roman layer extends half way up. There is the cathedral of Rouen, which would be entirely Gothic if it did not bathe the tip of its central spire in the zone of the Renaissance.[21]

However, all these shades, all these differences, do not affect the surfaces of edifices only. It is art which has changed its skin. The very constitution of the Christian church is not attacked by it. There is always the same internal woodwork, the same logical arrangement of parts. Whatever may be the carved and embroidered envelope of a cathedral, one always finds beneath it–in the state of a germ, and of a rudiment at the least–the Roman basilica. It is eternally developed upon the soil according to the same law. There are, invariably, two naves,

21 This portion of the spire, which was of woodwork, is precisely that which was consumed by lightning, in 1823.

which intersect in a cross, and whose upper portion, rounded into an apse, forms the choir; there are always the side aisles, for interior processions, for chapels,–a sort of lateral walks or promenades where the principal nave discharges itself through the spaces between the pillars. That settled, the number of chapels, doors, bell towers, and pinnacles are modified to infinity, according to the fancy of the century, the people, and art. The service of religion once assured and provided for, architecture does what she pleases. Statues, stained glass, rose windows, arabesques, denticulations, capitals, bas-reliefs,–she combines all these imaginings according to the arrangement which best suits her. Hence, the prodigious exterior variety of these edifices, at whose foundation dwells so much order and unity. The trunk of a tree is immovable; the foliage is capricious.

CHAPTER TWO

A Bird's-Eye View of Paris

WE HAVE JUST ATTEMPTED to restore, for the reader's benefit, that admirable church of Notre-Dame de Paris. We have briefly pointed out the greater part of the beauties which it possessed in the fifteenth century, and which it lacks to-day; but we have omitted the principal thing,–the view of Paris which was then to be obtained from the summits of its towers.

That was, in fact,–when, after having long groped one's way up the dark spiral which perpendicularly pierces the thick wall of the belfries, one emerged, at last abruptly, upon one of the lofty platforms inundated with light and air,–that was, in fact, a fine picture which spread out, on all sides at once, before the eye; a spectacle **sui generis**, of which those of our readers who have had the good fortune to see a Gothic city entire, complete, homogeneous,–a few of which still remain, Nuremberg in Bavaria and Vittoria in Spain,–can readily form an idea; or even smaller specimens, provided that they are well preserved,–Vitré in Brittany, Nordhausen in Prussia.

The Paris of three hundred and fifty years ago–the Paris of the fifteenth century–was already a gigantic city. We Parisians generally make a mistake as to the ground which we think that we have gained, since Paris has not increased much over one-third since the time of Louis XI. It has certainly lost more in beauty than it has gained in size.

Paris had its birth, as the reader knows, in that old island of the City which has the form of a cradle. The strand of that island was its first boundary wall, the Seine its first moat. Paris remained for many centuries in its island state, with two bridges, one on the north, the other on the south; and two bridge heads, which were at the same time its gates and its fortresses,–the Grand-Châtelet on the right bank, the Petit-Châtelet on the left. Then, from the date of the kings of the first race, Paris, being too cribbed and confined in its island, and unable to return thither, crossed the water. Then, beyond the Grand, beyond the Petit-Châtelet, a first circle of walls and towers began to infringe upon the country on the two sides of the Seine. Some vestiges of this ancient enclosure still remained in the last century; to-day, only the memory of it is left, and here and there a tradition, the Baudets or Baudoyer gate, **Porta Bagauda**.

Little by little, the tide of houses, always thrust from the heart of the city outwards, overflows, devours, wears away, and effaces this wall. Philip Augustus makes a new dike for it. He imprisons Paris in a circular chain of great towers, both lofty and solid. For the period of more than a century, the houses press upon each other, accumulate, and raise their level in this basin, like water in a reservoir. They begin to deepen; they pile story upon story; they mount upon each other; they gush forth at the top, like all laterally compressed growth, and there is a rivalry as to which shall thrust its head above its neighbors, for the sake of getting a little air. The street glows narrower and deeper, every space is overwhelmed and disappears. The houses finally leap the wall of Philip Augustus, and scatter joyfully over the plain, without order, and all askew, like runaways. There they plant themselves squarely, cut themselves gardens from the fields, and take their ease. Beginning with 1367, the city spreads to such an extent into the suburbs, that a new wall becomes necessary, particularly on the right bank; Charles V. builds it. But a city like Paris is perpetually growing. It is only such cities that become capitals. They are funnels, into which all the geographical, political, moral, and intellectual water-sheds of a country, all the natural slopes of a people, pour; wells of civilization, so to speak, and also sewers, where commerce, industry, intelligence, population,–all that is sap, all that is life, all that is the soul of a nation, filters and amasses unceasingly, drop by drop, century by century.

So Charles V.'s wall suffered the fate of that of Philip Augustus. At the end of the fifteenth century, the Faubourg strides across it, passes beyond it, and runs farther. In the sixteenth, it seems to retreat visibly, and to bury itself deeper and deeper in the old city, so thick had the new city already become outside of it. Thus, beginning with the fifteenth century, where our story finds us, Paris had already outgrown the three concentric circles of walls which, from the time of Julian the Apostate, existed, so to speak, in germ in the Grand-Châtelet and the Petit-Châtelet. The mighty city had cracked, in succession, its four enclosures of walls, like a child grown too large for his garments of last year. Under Louis XI., this sea of houses was seen to be pierced at intervals by several groups of ruined towers, from the ancient wall, like the summits of hills in an inundation,–like archipelagos of the old Paris submerged beneath the new. Since that time Paris has undergone yet another transformation, unfortunately for our eyes; but it has passed only one more wall, that of Louis XV., that miserable wall of mud and spittle, worthy of the king who built it, worthy of the poet who sung it,–

Le mur murant Paris rend Paris

murmurant.[22]

In the fifteenth century, Paris was still divided into three wholly distinct and separate towns, each having its own physiognomy, its own specialty, its manners, customs, privileges, and history: the City, the University, the Town. The City, which occupied the island, was the most ancient, the smallest, and the mother of the other two, crowded in between them like (may we be pardoned the comparison) a little old woman between two large and handsome maidens. The University covered the left bank of the Seine, from the Tournelle to the Tour de Nesle, points which correspond in the Paris of to-day, the one to the wine market, the other to the mint. Its wall included a large part of that plain where Julian had built his hot baths. The hill of Sainte-Geneviève was enclosed in it. The culminating point of this sweep

---

22 The wall walling Paris makes Paris murmur.

of walls was the Papal gate, that is to say, near the present site of the Pantheon. The Town, which was the largest of the three fragments of Paris, held the right bank. Its quay, broken or interrupted in many places, ran along the Seine, from the Tour de Billy to the Tour du Bois; that is to say, from the place where the granary stands to-day, to the present site of the Tuileries. These four points, where the Seine intersected the wall of the capital, the Tournelle and the Tour de Nesle on the right, the Tour de Billy and the Tour du Bois on the left, were called pre-eminently, **the four towers of Paris**. The Town encroached still more extensively upon the fields than the University. The culminating point of the Town wall (that of Charles V.) was at the gates of Saint-Denis and Saint-Martin, whose situation has not been changed.

As we have just said, each of these three great divisions of Paris was a town, but too special a town to be complete, a city which could not get along without the other two. Hence three entirely distinct aspects: churches abounded in the City; palaces, in the Town; and colleges, in the University. Neglecting here the originalities, of secondary importance in old Paris, and the capricious regulations regarding the public highways, we will say, from a general point of view, taking only masses and the whole group, in this chaos of communal jurisdictions, that the island belonged to the bishop, the right bank to the provost of the merchants, the left bank to the Rector; over all ruled the provost of Paris, a royal not a municipal official. The City had Notre-Dame; the Town, the Louvre and the Hôtel de Ville; the University, the Sorbonne. The Town had the markets (Halles); the city, the Hospital; the University, the Pré-aux-Clercs. Offences committed by the scholars on the left bank were tried in the law courts on the island, and were punished on the right bank at Montfaucon; unless the rector, feeling the university to be strong and the king weak, intervened; for it was the students' privilege to be hanged on their own grounds.

The greater part of these privileges, it may be noted in passing, and there were some even better than the above, had been extorted from the kings by revolts and mutinies. It is the course of things from time immemorial; the king only lets go when the people tear away. There is an old charter which puts the matter naively: **àpropos** of fidelity: **Civibus fidelitas in reges, quæ tamen aliquoties seditionibus interrupta, multa peperit privilegia**.

In the fifteenth century, the Seine bathed five islands within the walls of Paris: Louviers island, where there were then trees, and where there is no longer anything but wood; l'île aux Vaches, and l'île Notre-Dame, both deserted, with the exception of one house, both fiefs of the bishop–in the seventeenth century, a single island was formed out of these two, which was built upon and named l'île Saint-Louis–, lastly the City, and at its point, the little islet of the cow tender, which was afterwards engulfed beneath the platform of the Pont-Neuf. The City then had five bridges: three on the right, the Pont Notre-Dame, and the Pont au Change, of stone, the Pont aux Meuniers, of wood; two on the left, the Petit Pont, of stone, the Pont Saint-Michel, of wood; all loaded with houses.

The University had six gates, built by Philip Augustus; there were, beginning with la Tournelle, the Porte Saint-Victor, the Porte Bordelle, the Porte Papale, the Porte Saint-Jacques, the Porte Saint-Michel, the Porte Saint-Germain. The Town had six gates, built by Charles V.; beginning with the Tour de Billy they were: the Porte Saint-Antoine, the Porte du Temple, the Porte Saint-Martin, the Porte Saint-Denis, the Porte Montmartre, the Porte Saint-Honoré. All these gates were strong, and also handsome, which does not detract from strength. A large, deep moat, with a brisk current during the high water of winter, bathed the base of the wall round Paris; the Seine furnished the water. At night, the gates were shut, the river was barred at both ends of the city with huge iron chains, and Paris slept tranquilly.

From a bird's-eye view, these three burgs, the City, the Town, and the University, each presented to the eye an inextricable skein of eccentrically tangled streets. Nevertheless, at first sight, one recognized the fact that these three fragments formed but one body. One immediately perceived three long parallel streets, unbroken, undisturbed, traversing, almost in a straight line, all three cities, from one end to the other; from North to South, perpendicularly, to the Seine, which bound them together, mingled them, infused them in each other, poured and transfused the people incessantly, from one to the other, and made one out of the three. The first of these streets ran from the Porte Saint-Martin: it was called the Rue

Saint-Jacques in the University, Rue de la Juiverie in the City, Rue Saint-Martin in the Town; it crossed the water twice, under the name of the Petit Pont and the Pont Notre-Dame. The second, which was called the Rue de la Harpe on the left bank, Rue de la Barillerié in the island, Rue Saint-Denis on the right bank, Pont Saint-Michel on one arm of the Seine, Pont au Change on the other, ran from the Porte Saint-Michel in the University, to the Porte Saint-Denis in the Town. However, under all these names, there were but two streets, parent streets, generating streets,–the two arteries of Paris. All the other veins of the triple city either derived their supply from them or emptied into them.

Independently of these two principal streets, piercing Paris diametrically in its whole breadth, from side to side, common to the entire capital, the City and the University had also each its own great special street, which ran lengthwise by them, parallel to the

Seine, cutting, as it passed, at right angles, the two arterial thoroughfares. Thus, in the Town, one descended in a straight line from the Porte Saint-Antoine to the Porte Saint-Honoré; in the University from the Porte Saint-Victor to the Porte Saint-Germain. These two great thoroughfares intersected by the two first, formed the canvas upon which reposed, knotted and crowded together on every hand, the labyrinthine network of the streets of Paris. In the incomprehensible plan of these streets, one distinguished likewise, on looking attentively, two clusters of great streets, like magnified sheaves of grain, one in the University, the other in the Town, which spread out gradually from the bridges to the gates.

Some traces of this geometrical plan still exist to-day.

Now, what aspect did this whole present, when, as viewed from the summit of the towers of Notre-Dame, in 1482? That we shall try to describe.

For the spectator who arrived, panting, upon that pinnacle, it was first a dazzling confusing view of roofs, chimneys, streets, bridges, places, spires, bell towers. Everything struck your eye at once: the carved gable, the pointed roof, the turrets suspended at the angles of the walls; the stone pyramids of the eleventh century, the slate obelisks of the fifteenth; the round, bare tower of the donjon keep; the square and fretted tower of the church; the great and the little, the massive and the aerial. The eye was, for a long time, wholly lost in this labyrinth, where there was nothing which did not possess its originality, its reason, its genius, its beauty,–nothing which did not proceed from art; beginning with the smallest house, with its painted and carved front, with external beams, elliptical door, with projecting stories, to the royal Louvre, which then had a colonnade of towers. But these are the principal masses which were then to be distinguished when the eye began to accustom itself to this tumult of edifices.

In the first place, the City.–"The island of the City," as Sauval says, who, in spite of his confused medley, sometimes has such happy turns of expression,–"the island of the city is made like a great ship, stuck in the mud and run aground in the current, near the centre of the Seine."

We have just explained that, in the fifteenth century, this ship was anchored to the two banks of the river by five bridges. This form of a ship had also struck the heraldic scribes; for it is from that, and not from the siege by the Normans, that the ship which blazons the old shield of Paris, comes, according to Favyn and Pasquier. For him who understands how to decipher them, armorial bearings are algebra, armorial bearings have a tongue. The whole history of the second half of the Middle Ages is written in armorial bearings,–the first half is in the symbolism of the Roman churches.

They are the hieroglyphics of feudalism, succeeding those of theocracy.

Thus the City first presented itself to the eye, with its stern to the east, and its prow to the west. Turning towards the prow, one had before one an innumerable flock of ancient roofs, over which arched broadly the lead-covered apse of the Sainte-Chapelle, like an elephant's haunches loaded with its tower. Only here, this tower was the most audacious, the most open, the most ornamented spire of cabinet-maker's work that ever let the sky peep through its cone of lace. In front of Notre-Dame, and very near at hand, three streets opened into the cathedral square,–a fine square, lined with ancient houses. Over the south side of this place bent the wrinkled and sullen façade of the Hôtel Dieu, and its roof, which seemed covered with warts and pustules. Then, on the right and the left, to east and west, within that wall of the City, which was yet so contracted, rose the bell towers of its one and twenty churches, of every date, of every form, of every size, from the low and wormeaten belfry of Saint-Denis du Pas (**Carcer Glaucini**) to the slender needles of Saint-Pierre aux Bœufs and Saint-Landry.

Behind Notre-Dame, the cloister and its Gothic galleries spread out towards the north; on the south, the half-Roman palace of the bishop; on the east, the desert point of the Terrain. In this throng of houses the eye also distinguished, by the lofty open-work mitres of stone which then crowned the roof itself, even the most elevated windows of the palace, the hotel given by the city, under Charles VI., to Juvénal des Ursins; a little farther on, the pitch-covered sheds of the Palus Market; in still another quarter the new apse of Saint-Germain le Vieux, lengthened in 1458, with a bit of the Rue aux Febves; and then, in places, a square crowded with people; a pillory, erected at the corner of a street; a fine fragment of the pavement of Philip Augustus, a magnificent flagging, grooved for the horses' feet, in the middle of the road, and so badly replaced in the sixteenth century by the miserable cobblestones, called the **pavement of the League;** a deserted back courtyard, with one of those diaphanous staircase turrets, such as were erected in the fifteenth century, one of which is still to be seen in the Rue des Bourdonnais. Lastly, at the right of the Sainte-Chapelle, towards the west, the Palais de Justice rested its group of towers at the edge of the water. The thickets of the king's gardens, which covered the western point of the City, masked the Island du Passeur. As for the water, from the summit of the towers of Notre-Dame one hardly saw it, on either side of the City; the Seine was hidden by bridges, the bridges by houses.

And when the glance passed these bridges, whose roofs were visibly green, rendered mouldy before their time by the vapors from the water, if it was directed to the left, towards the University, the first edifice which struck it was a large, low sheaf of towers, the Petit-Châtelet, whose yawning gate devoured the end of the Petit-Pont. Then, if your view ran along the bank, from east to west, from the Tournelle to the Tour de Nesle, there was a long cordon of houses, with carved beams, stained-glass windows, each story projecting over that beneath it, an interminable zigzag of **bourgeois** gables, frequently interrupted by the mouth of a street, and from time to time also by the front or angle of a huge stone mansion, planted at its ease, with courts and gardens, wings and detached buildings, amid this populace of crowded and narrow houses, like a grand gentleman among a throng of rustics. There were five or six of these mansions on the quay, from the house of Lorraine, which shared with the Bernardins the grand enclosure adjoining the Tournelle, to the Hôtel de Nesle, whose principal tower ended Paris, and whose pointed roofs were in a position, during three months of the year, to encroach, with their black triangles, upon the scarlet disk of the setting sun.

This side of the Seine was, however, the least mercantile of the two. Students furnished more of a crowd and more noise there than artisans, and there was not, properly speaking, any quay, except from the Pont Saint-Michel to the Tour de Nesle. The rest of the bank of the Seine was now a naked strand, the same as beyond the Bernardins; again, a throng of houses, standing with their feet in the water, as between the two bridges.

There was a great uproar of laundresses; they screamed, and talked, and sang from morning till night along the beach, and beat a great deal of linen there, just as in our day. This is not the least of the gayeties of Paris.

The University presented a dense mass to the eye. From one end to the other, it was homogeneous and compact. The thousand roofs, dense, angular, clinging to each other, composed, nearly all, of the same geometrical element, offered, when viewed from above, the aspect of a crystallization of the same substance.

The capricious ravine of streets did not cut this block of houses into too disproportionate slices. The forty-two colleges were scattered about in a fairly equal manner, and there were some everywhere. The amusingly varied crests of these beautiful edifices were the product of the same art as the simple roofs which they overshot, and were, actually, only a multiplication of the square or the cube of the same geometrical figure. Hence they complicated the whole effect, without disturbing it; completed, without overloading it. Geometry is harmony. Some fine mansions here and there made magnificent outlines against the picturesque attics of the left bank. The house of Nevers, the house of Rome, the house of Reims, which have disappeared; the Hôtel de Cluny, which still exists, for the consolation of the artist, and whose tower was so stupidly deprived of its crown a few years ago. Close to Cluny, that Roman palace, with fine round arches, were once the hot baths of Julian. There were a great many abbeys, of a beauty more devout, of a grandeur more solemn than the mansions, but not less beautiful, not less grand. Those which first caught the eye were the Bernardins, with their three bell towers; Sainte-Geneviève, whose square tower, which still exists, makes us regret the rest; the Sorbonne, half college, half monastery, of which so admirable a nave survives; the fine quadrilateral cloister of the Mathurins; its neighbor, the cloister of Saint-Benoît, within whose walls they have had time to cobble up a theatre, between the seventh and eighth editions of this book; the Cordeliers, with their three enormous adjacent gables; the Augustins, whose graceful spire formed, after the Tour de Nesle, the second denticulation on this side of Paris, starting from the west. The colleges, which are, in fact, the intermediate ring between the cloister and the world, hold the middle position in the monumental series between the hotels and the abbeys, with a severity full of elegance, sculpture less giddy than the palaces, an architecture less severe than the convents. Unfortunately, hardly anything remains of these monuments, where Gothic art combined with so just a balance, richness and economy. The churches (and they were numerous and splendid in the University, and they were graded there also in all the ages of architecture, from the round arches of Saint-Julian to the pointed arches of Saint-Séverin), the churches dominated the whole; and, like one harmony more in this mass of harmonies, they pierced in quick succession the multiple open work of the gables with slashed spires, with open-work bell towers, with slender pinnacles, whose line was also only a magnificent exaggeration of the acute angle of the roofs.

The ground of the University was hilly; Mount Sainte-Geneviève formed an enormous mound to the south; and it was a sight to see from the summit of Notre-Dame how that throng of narrow and tortuous streets (to-day the Latin Quarter), those bunches of houses which, spread out in every direction from the top of this eminence, precipitated themselves in disorder, and almost perpendicularly down its flanks, nearly to the water's edge, having the air, some of falling, others of clambering up again, and all of holding to one another. A continual flux of a thousand black points which passed each other on the pavements made everything move before the eyes; it was the populace seen thus from aloft and afar.

Lastly, in the intervals of these roofs, of these spires, of these accidents of numberless edifices, which bent and writhed, and jagged in so eccentric a manner the extreme line of the University, one caught a glimpse, here and there, of a great expanse of moss-grown wall, a thick, round tower, a crenellated city gate, shadowing forth the fortress; it was the wall of Philip Augustus. Beyond, the fields gleamed green; beyond, fled the roads, along which were scattered a few more suburban houses, which became more infrequent as they became more distant. Some of these faubourgs were important: there were, first, starting from la Tournelle, the Bourg Saint-Victor, with its one arch bridge over the Bièvre, its abbey where one could read the epitaph of Louis le Gros, **epitaphium Ludovici Grossi**, and its church with an octagonal spire, flanked with four little bell towers of the eleventh century (a similar one can be seen at Étampes; it is not yet destroyed); next, the Bourg Saint-Marceau, which already had three churches and one convent; then, leaving the mill of the Gobelins and its four white walls on the left, there was the Faubourg Saint-Jacques with the beautiful carved cross in its square; the church of Saint-Jacques du Haut-Pas, which was then Gothic, pointed, charming; Saint-Magloire, a fine nave of the fourteenth century, which Napoleon turned into a hayloft; Notre-Dame des Champs, where there were Byzantine mosaics; lastly, after having left behind, full in the country, the Monastery des Chartreux, a rich edifice contemporary with the Palais de Justice, with its little garden divided into compartments, and the haunted ruins of Vauvert, the eye fell, to the west, upon the three Roman spires of Saint-Germain des Prés. The Bourg Saint-Germain, already a large community, formed fifteen or twenty streets in the rear; the pointed bell tower of Saint-Sulpice marked one corner of the town. Close beside it one descried the quadrilateral enclosure of the fair of Saint-Germain, where the market is situated to-day; then the abbot's pillory, a pretty little round tower, well capped with a leaden cone; the brickyard was further on, and the Rue du Four, which led to the common bakehouse, and the mill on its hillock, and the lazar house, a tiny house, isolated and half seen.

But that which attracted the eye most of all, and fixed it for a long time on that point, was the abbey itself. It is certain that this monastery, which had a grand air, both as a church and as a seignory; that abbatial palace, where the bishops of Paris counted themselves happy if they could pass the night; that refectory, upon which the architect had bestowed the air, the beauty, and the rose window of a cathedral; that elegant chapel of the Virgin; that monumental dormitory; those vast gardens; that portcullis; that drawbridge; that envelope of battlements which notched to the eye the verdure of the surrounding meadows; those courtyards, where gleamed men at arms, intermingled with golden copes;–the whole grouped and clustered about three lofty spires, with round arches, well planted upon a Gothic apse, made a magnificent figure against the horizon.

When, at length, after having contemplated the University for a long time, you turned towards the right bank, towards the Town, the character of the spectacle was abruptly altered. The Town, in fact much larger than the University, was also less of a unit. At the first glance, one saw that it was divided into many masses, singularly distinct. First, to the eastward, in that part of the town which still takes its name from the marsh where Camulogènes entangled Cæsar, was a pile of palaces. The block extended to the very water's edge. Four almost contiguous hotels, Jouy, Sens, Barbeau, the house of the Queen, mirrored their slate peaks, broken with slender turrets, in the Seine.

These four edifices filled the space from the Rue des Nonaindières, to the abbey of the

Celestins, whose spire gracefully relieved their line of gables and battlements. A few miserable, greenish hovels, hanging over the water in front of these sumptuous hotels, did not prevent one from seeing the fine angles of their façades, their large, square windows with stone mullions, their pointed porches overloaded with statues, the vivid outlines of their walls, always clear cut, and all those charming accidents of architecture, which cause Gothic art to have the air of beginning its combinations afresh with every monument.

Behind these palaces, extended in all directions, now broken, fenced in, battlemented like a citadel, now veiled by great trees like a Carthusian convent, the immense and multiform enclosure of that miraculous Hôtel de Saint-Pol, where the King of France possessed the means of lodging superbly two and twenty princes of the rank of the dauphin and the Duke of Burgundy, with their domestics and their suites, without counting the great lords, and the emperor when he came to view Paris, and the lions, who had their separate hotel at the royal hotel. Let us say here that a prince's apartment was then composed of never less than eleven large rooms, from the chamber of state to the oratory, not to mention the galleries, baths, vapor-baths, and other "superfluous places," with which each apartment was provided; not to mention the private gardens for each of the king's guests; not to mention the kitchens, the cellars, the domestic offices, the general refectories of the house, the poultry-yards, where there were twenty-two general laboratories, from the bakehouses to the wine-cellars; games of a thousand sorts, malls, tennis, and riding at the ring; aviaries, fishponds, menageries, stables, barns, libraries, arsenals and foundries. This was what a king's palace, a Louvre, a Hôtel de Saint-Pol was then. A city within a city.

From the tower where we are placed, the

Hôtel Saint-Pol, almost half hidden by the four great houses of which we have just spoken, was still very considerable and very marvellous to see. One could there distinguish, very well, though cleverly united with the principal building by long galleries, decked with painted glass and slender columns, the three hotels which Charles V. had amalgamated with his palace: the Hôtel du Petit-Muce, with the airy balustrade, which formed a graceful border to its roof; the Hôtel of the Abbé de Saint-Maur, having the vanity of a stronghold, a great tower, machicolations, loopholes, iron gratings, and over the large Saxon door, the armorial bearings of the abbé, between the two mortises of the drawbridge; the Hôtel of the Comte d'Étampes, whose donjon keep, ruined at its summit, was rounded and notched like a cock's comb; here and there, three or four ancient oaks, forming a tuft together like enormous cauliflowers; gambols of swans, in the clear water of the fishponds, all in folds of light and shade; many courtyards of which one beheld picturesque bits; the Hôtel of the Lions, with its low, pointed arches on short, Saxon pillars, its iron gratings and its perpetual roar; shooting up above the whole, the scale-ornamented spire of the Ave-Maria; on the left, the house of the Provost of Paris, flanked by four small towers, delicately grooved, in the middle; at the extremity, the Hôtel Saint-Pol, properly speaking, with its multiplied façades, its successive enrichments from the time of Charles V., the hybrid excrescences, with which the fancy of the architects had loaded it during the last two centuries, with all the apses of its chapels, all the gables of its galleries, a thousand weathercocks for the four winds, and its two lofty contiguous towers, whose conical roof, surrounded by battlements at its base, looked like those pointed caps which have their edges turned up.

Continuing to mount the stories of this

amphitheatre of palaces spread out afar upon the ground, after crossing a deep ravine hollowed out of the roofs in the Town, which marked the passage of the Rue Saint-Antoine, the eye reached the house of Angoulême, a vast construction of many epochs, where there were perfectly new and very white parts, which melted no better into the whole than a red patch on a blue doublet. Nevertheless, the remarkably pointed and lofty roof of the modern palace, bristling with carved eaves, covered with sheets of lead, where coiled a thousand fantastic arabesques of sparkling incrustations of gilded bronze, that roof, so curiously damascened, darted upwards gracefully from the midst of the brown ruins of the ancient edifice; whose huge and ancient towers, rounded by age like casks, sinking together with old age, and rending themselves from top to bottom, resembled great bellies unbuttoned. Behind rose the forest of spires of the Palais des Tournelles.

Not a view in the world, either at Chambord or at the Alhambra, is more magic, more aerial, more enchanting, than that thicket of spires, tiny bell towers, chimneys, weather-vanes, winding staircases, lanterns through which the daylight makes its way, which seem cut out at a blow, pavilions, spindle-shaped turrets, or, as they were then called, **tournelles**, all differing in form, in height, and attitude. One would have pronounced it a gigantic stone chess-board.

To the right of the Tournelles, that truss of enormous towers, black as ink, running into each other and tied, as it were, by a circular moat; that donjon keep, much more pierced with loopholes than with windows; that drawbridge, always raised; that portcullis, always lowered,–is the Bastille. Those sorts of black beaks which project from between the battlements, and which you take from a distance to be cave spouts, are cannons.

Beneath them, at the foot of the formidable

edifice, behold the Porte Sainte-Antoine, buried between its two towers.

Beyond the Tournelles, as far as the wall of Charles V., spread out, with rich compartments of verdure and of flowers, a velvet carpet of cultivated land and royal parks, in the midst of which one recognized, by its labyrinth of trees and alleys, the famous Dædalus garden which Louis XI. had given to Coictier. The doctor's observatory rose above the labyrinth like a great isolated column, with a tiny house for a capital. Terrible astrologies took place in that laboratory.

There to-day is the Place Royale.

As we have just said, the quarter of the palace, of which we have just endeavored to give the reader some idea by indicating only the chief points, filled the angle which Charles V.'s wall made with the Seine on the east. The centre of the Town was occupied by a pile of houses for the populace. It was there, in fact, that the three bridges disgorged upon the right bank, and bridges lead to the building of houses rather than palaces. That congregation of **bourgeois** habitations, pressed together like the cells in a hive, had a beauty of its own. It is with the roofs of a capital as with the waves of the sea,– they are grand. First the streets, crossed and entangled, forming a hundred amusing figures in the block; around the market-place, it was like a star with a thousand rays.

The Rues Saint-Denis and Saint-Martin, with their innumerable ramifications, rose one after the other, like trees intertwining their branches; and then the tortuous lines, the Rues de la Plâtrerie, de la Verrerie, de la Tixeranderie, etc., meandered over all. There were also fine edifices which pierced the petrified undulations of that sea of gables. At the head of the Pont aux Changeurs, behind which one beheld the Seine foaming beneath the wheels of the Pont aux Meuniers, there was the Châlelet, no longer a Roman tower, as under Julian the Apostate, but a feudal tower of the thirteenth century, and of a stone so hard that the pickaxe could not break away so much as the thickness of the fist in a space of three hours; there was the rich square bell tower of Saint-Jacques de la Boucherie, with its angles all frothing with carvings, already admirable, although it was not finished in the fifteenth century. (It lacked, in particular, the four monsters, which, still perched to-day on the corners of its roof, have the air of so many sphinxes who are propounding to new Paris the riddle of the ancient Paris. Rault, the sculptor, only placed them in position in 1526, and received twenty francs for his pains.) There was the Maison-aux-Piliers, the Pillar House, opening upon that Place de Grève of which we have given the reader some idea; there was Saint-Gervais, which a front "in good taste" has since spoiled; Saint-Méry, whose ancient pointed arches were still almost round arches; Saint-Jean, whose magnificent spire was proverbial;

there were twenty other monuments, which did not disdain to bury their wonders in that chaos of black, deep, narrow streets. Add the crosses of carved stone, more lavishly scattered through the squares than even the gibbets; the cemetery of the Innocents, whose architectural wall could be seen in the distance above the roofs; the pillory of the Markets, whose top was visible between two chimneys of the Rue de la Cossonnerie; the ladder of the Croix-du-Trahoir, in its square always black with people; the circular buildings of the wheat mart; the fragments of Philip Augustus's ancient wall, which could be made out here and there, drowned among the houses, its towers gnawed by ivy, its gates in ruins, with crumbling and deformed stretches of wall; the quay with its thousand shops, and its bloody knacker's yards; the Seine encumbered with boats, from the Port au Foin to For-l'Évêque, and you will have a confused picture of what the central trapezium of the Town was like in 1482.

With these two quarters, one of hotels, the other of houses, the third feature of aspect presented by the city was a long zone of abbeys, which bordered it in nearly the whole of its circumference, from the rising to the setting sun, and, behind the circle of fortifications which hemmed in Paris, formed a second interior enclosure of convents and chapels. Thus, immediately adjoining the park des Tournelles, between the Rue Saint-Antoine and the Vieille Rue du Temple, there stood Sainte-Catherine, with its immense cultivated lands, which were terminated only by the wall of Paris. Between the old and the new Rue du Temple, there was the Temple, a sinister group of towers, lofty, erect, and isolated in the middle of a vast, battlemented enclosure. Between the Rue Neuve-du-Temple and the Rue Saint-Martin, there was the Abbey of Saint-Martin, in the midst of its gardens, a superb fortified church, whose girdle of towers, whose diadem of bell towers, yielded in force and splendor only to Saint-Germain des Prés. Between the Rue Saint-Martin and the Rue Saint-Denis, spread the enclosure of the Trinité.

Lastly, between the Rue Saint-Denis, and the Rue Montorgueil, stood the Filles-Dieu. On one side, the rotting roofs and unpaved enclosure of the Cour des Miracles could be descried. It was the sole profane ring which was linked to that devout chain of convents.

Finally, the fourth compartment, which stretched itself out in the agglomeration of the roofs on the right bank, and which occupied the western angle of the enclosure, and the banks of the river down stream, was a fresh cluster of palaces and hôtels pressed close about the base of the Louvre. The old Louvre of Philip Augustus, that immense edifice whose great tower rallied about it three and twenty chief towers, not to reckon the lesser towers, seemed from a distance to be enshrined in the Gothic roofs of the

Hôtel d'Alençon, and the Petit-Bourbon. This hydra of towers, giant guardian of Paris, with its four and twenty heads, always erect, with its monstrous haunches, loaded or scaled with slates, and all streaming with metallic reflections, terminated with wonderful effect the configuration of the Town towards the west.

Thus an immense block, which the Romans called **insula**, or island, of **bourgeois** houses, flanked on the right and the left by two blocks of palaces, crowned, the one by the Louvre, the other by the Tournelles, bordered on the north by a long girdle of abbeys and cultivated enclosures, all amalgamated and melted together in one view; upon these thousands of edifices, whose tiled and slated roofs outlined upon each other so many fantastic chains, the bell towers, tattooed, fluted, and ornamented with twisted bands, of the four and forty churches on the right bank; myriads of cross streets; for boundary on one side, an enclosure of lofty walls with square towers (that of the University had round towers); on the other, the Seine, cut by bridges, and bearing on its bosom a multitude of boats; behold the Town of Paris in the fifteenth century.

Beyond the walls, several suburban villages pressed close about the gates, but less numerous and more scattered than those of the University. Behind the Bastille there were twenty hovels clustered round the curious sculptures of the Croix-Faubin and the flying buttresses of the Abbey of Saint-Antoine des Champs; then Popincourt, lost amid wheat fields; then la Courtille, a merry village of wine-shops; the hamlet of Saint-Laurent with its church whose bell tower, from afar, seemed to add itself to the pointed towers of the Porte Saint-Martin; the Faubourg Saint-Denis, with the vast enclosure of Saint-Ladre; beyond the Montmartre Gate, the Grange-Batelière, encircled with white walls; behind it, with its chalky slopes, Montmartre, which had then almost as many churches as windmills, and which has kept only the windmills, for society no longer demands anything but bread for the body. Lastly, beyond the Louvre, the Faubourg Saint-Honoré, already considerable at that time, could be seen stretching away into the fields, and Petit-Bretagne gleaming green, and the Marché aux Pourceaux spreading abroad, in whose centre swelled the horrible apparatus used for boiling counterfeiters. Between la Courtille and Saint-Laurent, your eye had already noticed, on the summit of an eminence crouching amid desert plains, a sort of edifice which resembled from a distance a ruined colonnade, mounted upon a basement with its foundation laid bare. This was neither a Parthenon, nor a temple of the Olympian Jupiter. It was Montfaucon.

Now, if the enumeration of so many edifices, summary as we have endeavored to make it, has not shattered in the reader's mind the general image of old Paris, as we have constructed it, we will recapitulate it in a few words. In the centre, the island of the City, resembling as to form an enormous tortoise, and throwing out its bridges with tiles for scales; like legs from beneath its gray shell of roofs. On the left, the monolithic trapezium, firm, dense, bristling, of the University; on the right, the vast semicircle of the Town, much more intermixed with gardens and monuments. The three blocks, city, university, and town, marbled with innumerable streets. Across all, the Seine, "foster-mother Seine," as says Father Du Breul, blocked with islands, bridges, and boats. All about an immense plain, patched with a thousand sorts of cultivated plots, sown with fine villages. On the left, Issy, Vanvres, Vaugirarde, Montrouge, Gentilly, with its round tower and its square tower, etc.; on the right, twenty others, from Conflans to Ville-l'Évêque. On the horizon, a border of hills arranged in a circle like the rim of the basin. Finally, far away to the east, Vincennes, and its seven quadrangular towers to the south, Bicêtre and its pointed turrets; to the north, Saint-Denis and its spire; to the west, Saint Cloud and its donjon keep. Such was the Paris which the ravens, who lived in 1482, beheld from the summits of the towers of Notre-Dame.

Nevertheless, Voltaire said of this city, that "before Louis XIV., it possessed but four fine monuments": the dome of the Sorbonne, the Val-de-Grâce, the modern Louvre, and I know not what the fourth was– the Luxembourg, perhaps. Fortunately, Voltaire was the author of "Candide" in spite of this, and in spite of this, he is, among all the men who have followed each other in the long series of humanity, the one who has best possessed the diabolical laugh. Moreover, this proves that one can be a fine genius, and yet understand nothing of an art to which one does not belong. Did not Molière imagine that he was doing

Raphael and Michael-Angelo a very great honor, by calling them "those Mignards of their age?"

Let us return to Paris and to the fifteenth century.

It was not then merely a handsome city; it was a homogeneous city, an architectural and historical product of the Middle Ages, a chronicle in stone. It was a city formed of two layers only; the Romanesque layer and the Gothic layer; for the Roman layer had disappeared long before, with the exception of the Hot Baths of Julian, where it still pierced through the thick crust of the Middle Ages. As for the Celtic layer, no specimens were any longer to be found, even when sinking wells.

Fifty years later, when the Renaissance began to mingle with this unity which was so severe and yet so varied, the dazzling luxury of its fantasies and systems, its debasements of Roman round arches, Greek columns, and Gothic bases, its sculpture which was so tender and so ideal, its peculiar taste for arabesques and acanthus leaves, its architectural paganism, contemporary with Luther, Paris, was perhaps, still more beautiful, although less harmonious to the eye, and to the thought.

But this splendid moment lasted only for a short time; the Renaissance was not impartial; it did not content itself with building, it wished to destroy; it is true that it required the room. Thus Gothic Paris was complete only for a moment. Saint-Jacques de la Boucherie had barely been completed when the demolition of the old Louvre was begun.

After that, the great city became more disfigured every day. Gothic Paris, beneath which Roman Paris was effaced, was effaced in its turn; but can any one say what Paris has replaced it?

There is the Paris of Catherine de Medicis at the Tuileries;[23]–the Paris of Henri II., at

23 We have seen with sorrow mingled with indignation, that it is the intention to increase, to recast, to make over, that is to say, to destroy

the Hôtel de Ville, two edifices still in fine taste;–the Paris of Henri IV., at the Place Royale: façades of brick with stone corners, and slated roofs, tri-colored houses;–the Paris of Louis XIII., at the Val-de-Grâce: a crushed and squat architecture, with vaults like basket-handles, and something

---

this admirable palace. The architects of our day have too heavy a hand to touch these delicate works of the Renaissance. We still cherish a hope that they will not dare. Moreover, this demolition of the Tuileries now, would be not only a brutal deed of violence, which would make a drunken vandal blush—it would be an act of treason. The Tuileries is not simply a masterpiece of the art of the sixteenth century, it is a page of the history of the nineteenth. This palace no longer belongs to the king, but to the people. Let us leave it as it is. Our revolution has twice set its seal upon its front. On one of its two façades, there are the cannon-balls of the 10th of August; on the other, the balls of the 29th of July. It is sacred. Paris, April 7, 1831. (Note to the fifth edition.)

indescribably pot-bellied in the column, and thickset in the dome;–the Paris of Louis XIV., in the Invalides: grand, rich, gilded, cold;–the Paris of Louis XV., in Saint-Sulpice: volutes, knots of ribbon, clouds, vermicelli and chiccory leaves, all in stone;–the Paris of Louis XVI., in the Pantheon: Saint Peter of Rome, badly copied (the edifice is awkwardly heaped together, which has not amended its lines);–the Paris of the Republic, in the School of Medicine: a poor Greek and Roman taste, which resembles the Coliseum or the Parthenon as the constitution of the year III., resembles the laws of Minos,–it is called in architecture, "the Messidor"[24] taste;–the Paris of Napoleon in the Place Vendôme: this one is sublime, a column of bronze made of cannons;–the Paris of the Restoration, at the Bourse: a very white colonnade supporting a very smooth frieze; the whole is square and

24 The tenth month of the French republican calendar, from the 19th of June to the 18th of July.

cost twenty millions.

To each of these characteristic monuments there is attached by a similarity of taste, fashion, and attitude, a certain number of houses scattered about in different quarters and which the eyes of the connoisseur easily distinguishes and furnishes with a date. When one knows how to look, one finds the spirit of a century, and the physiognomy of a king, even in the knocker on a door.

The Paris of the present day has then, no general physiognomy. It is a collection of specimens of many centuries, and the finest have disappeared. The capital grows only in houses, and what houses! At the rate at which Paris is now proceeding, it will renew itself every fifty years.

Thus the historical significance of its architecture is being effaced every day. Monuments are becoming rarer and rarer, and one seems to see them gradually engulfed, by the flood of houses. Our fathers had a Paris of stone; our sons will have one of plaster.

So far as the modern monuments of new Paris are concerned, we would gladly be excused from mentioning them. It is not that we do not admire them as they deserve. The Sainte-Geneviève of M. Soufflot is certainly the finest Savoy cake that has ever been made in stone. The Palace of the Legion of Honor is also a very distinguished bit of pastry. The dome of the wheat market is an English jockey cap, on a grand scale. The towers of Saint-Sulpice are two huge clarinets, and the form is as good as any other; the telegraph, contorted and grimacing, forms an admirable accident upon their roofs. Saint-Roch has a door which, for magnificence, is comparable only to that of Saint-Thomas d'Aquin. It has, also, a crucifixion in high relief, in a cellar, with a sun of gilded wood. These things are fairly marvellous. The lantern of the labyrinth of the Jardin des Plantes is also very ingenious.

As for the Palace of the Bourse, which is Greek as to its colonnade, Roman in the round arches of its doors and windows, of the Renaissance by virtue of its flattened vault, it is indubitably a very correct and very pure monument; the proof is that it is crowned with an attic, such as was never seen in Athens, a beautiful, straight line, gracefully broken here and there by stovepipes. Let us add that if it is according to rule that the architecture of a building should be adapted to its purpose in such a manner that this purpose shall be immediately apparent from the mere aspect of the building, one cannot be too much amazed at a structure which might be indifferently–the palace of a king, a chamber of communes, a town-hall, a college, a riding-school, an academy, a warehouse, a court-house, a museum, a barracks, a sepulchre, a temple, or a theatre. However, it is an Exchange. An edifice ought to be, moreover, suitable to the climate. This one is evidently constructed expressly for our cold and rainy skies. It has a roof almost as flat as roofs in the East, which involves sweeping the roof in winter, when it snows; and of course roofs are made to be swept. As for its purpose, of which we just spoke, it fulfils it to a marvel; it is a bourse in France as it would have been a temple in Greece. It is true that the architect was at a good deal of trouble to conceal the clock face, which would have destroyed the purity of the fine lines of the façade; but, on the other hand, we have that colonnade which circles round the edifice and under which, on days of high religious ceremony, the theories of the stock-brokers and the courtiers of commerce can be developed so majestically.

These are very superb structures. Let us add a quantity of fine, amusing, and varied streets, like the Rue de Rivoli, and I do not despair of Paris presenting to the eye, when viewed from a balloon, that richness of line, that opulence of detail, that diversity of aspect, that grandiose something in the simple, and unexpected in the beautiful, which characterizes a checker-board.

However, admirable as the Paris of to-day may seem to you, reconstruct the Paris of the fifteenth century, call it up before you in thought; look at the sky athwart that surprising forest of spires, towers, and belfries; spread out in the centre of the city, tear away at the point of the islands, fold at the arches of the bridges, the Seine, with its broad green and yellow expanses, more variable than the skin of a serpent; project clearly against an azure horizon the Gothic profile of this ancient Paris. Make its contour float in a winter's mist which clings to its numerous chimneys; drown it in profound night and watch the odd play of lights and shadows in that sombre labyrinth of edifices; cast upon it a ray of light which shall vaguely outline it and cause to emerge from the fog the great heads of the towers; or take that black silhouette again, enliven with shadow the thousand acute angles of the spires and gables, and make it start out more toothed than a shark's jaw against a copper-colored western sky,–and then compare.

And if you wish to receive of the ancient city an impression with which the modern one can no longer furnish you, climb–on the morning of some grand festival, beneath the rising sun of Easter or of Pentecost–climb upon some elevated point, whence you command the entire capital; and be present at the wakening of the chimes. Behold, at a signal given from heaven, for it is the sun which gives it, all those churches quiver simultaneously. First come scattered strokes, running from one church to another, as when musicians give warning that they are about to begin. Then, all at once, behold!–for it seems at times, as though the ear also possessed a sight of its own,–behold, rising from each bell tower, something like a column of sound, a cloud of harmony. First, the vibration of each bell mounts straight upwards, pure and, so to speak, isolated from the others, into the splendid morning sky; then, little by little, as they swell they melt together, mingle, are lost in each other, and amalgamate in a magnificent concert. It is no longer anything but a mass of sonorous vibrations incessantly sent forth from the numerous belfries; floats, undulates, bounds, whirls over the city, and prolongs far beyond the horizon the deafening circle of its oscillations.

Nevertheless, this sea of harmony is not a chaos; great and profound as it is, it has not lost its transparency; you behold the windings of each group of notes which escapes from the belfries. You can follow the dialogue, by turns grave and shrill, of the treble and the bass; you can see the octaves leap from one tower to another; you watch them spring forth, winged, light, and whistling, from the silver bell, to fall, broken and limping from the bell of wood; you admire in their midst the rich gamut which incessantly ascends and re-ascends the seven bells of Saint-Eustache; you see light and rapid notes running across it, executing three or four luminous zigzags, and vanishing like flashes of lightning. Yonder is the Abbey of Saint-Martin, a shrill, cracked singer; here the gruff and gloomy voice of the Bastille; at the other end, the great tower of the Louvre, with its bass. The royal chime of the palace scatters on all sides, and without relaxation, resplendent trills, upon which fall, at regular intervals, the heavy strokes from the belfry of Notre-Dame, which makes them sparkle like the anvil under the hammer. At intervals you behold the passage of sounds of all forms which come from the triple peal of Saint-Germain-des-Prés. Then, again, from time to time, this mass of sublime noises opens and gives passage to the beats of the Ave Maria, which bursts forth and sparkles like an aigrette of stars. Below, in the very depths of the concert, you confusedly distinguish the interior chanting of the churches, which exhales through the vibrating pores of their vaulted roofs.

Assuredly, this is an opera which it is worth the trouble of listening to. Ordinarily, the noise which escapes from Paris by day is the city speaking; by night, it is the city breathing; in this case, it is the city singing. Lend an ear, then, to this concert of bell towers; spread over all the murmur of half a million men, the eternal plaint of the river, the infinite breathings of the wind, the grave and distant quartette of the four forests arranged upon the hills, on the horizon, like immense stacks of organ pipes; extinguish, as in a half shade, all that is too hoarse and too shrill about the central chime, and say whether you know anything in the world more rich and joyful, more golden, more dazzling, than this tumult of bells and chimes;–than this furnace of music,–than these ten thousand brazen voices chanting simultaneously in the flutes of stone, three hundred feet high,–than this city which is no longer anything but an orchestra,–than this symphony which produces the noise of a tempest.

VOLUME ONE

BOOK FOURTH

CHAPTER ONE

Good Souls

SIXTEEN YEARS PREVIOUS TO the epoch when this story takes place, one fine morning, on Quasimodo Sunday, a living creature had been deposited, after mass, in the church of Notre-Dame, on the wooden bed securely fixed in the vestibule on the left, opposite that great image of Saint Christopher, which the figure of Messire Antoine des Essarts, chevalier, carved in stone, had been gazing at on his knees since 1413, when they took it into their heads to overthrow the saint and the faithful follower. Upon this bed of wood it was customary to expose foundlings for public charity. Whoever cared to take them did so. In front of the wooden bed was a copper basin for alms.

The sort of living being which lay upon that plank on the morning of Quasimodo, in the year of the Lord, 1467, appeared to excite to a high degree, the curiosity of the numerous group which had congregated about the wooden bed. The group was formed for the most part of the fair sex. Hardly any one was there except old women.

In the first row, and among those who were most bent over the bed, four were noticeable, who, from their gray **cagoule**, a sort of cassock, were recognizable as attached to some devout sisterhood. I do not see why history has not transmitted to posterity the names of these four discreet and venerable damsels. They were Agnès la Herme, Jehanne de la Tarme, Henriette la Gaultière, Gauchère la Violette, all four widows, all four dames of the Chapel Étienne Haudry, who had quitted their house with the permission of their mistress, and in conformity with the statutes of Pierre d'Ailly, in order to come and hear the sermon.

However, if these good Haudriettes were, for the moment, complying with the statutes of Pierre d'Ailly, they certainly violated with joy those of Michel de Brache, and the Cardinal of Pisa, which so inhumanly enjoined silence upon them.

"What is this, sister?" said Agnès to Gauchère, gazing at the little creature exposed, which was screaming and writhing on the wooden bed, terrified by so many glances.

"What is to become of us," said Jehanne, "if that is the way children are made now?"

"I'm not learned in the matter of children,"

resumed Agnès, "but it must be a sin to look at this one."

"'Tis not a child, Agnès."

"'Tis an abortion of a monkey," remarked Gauchère.

"'Tis a miracle," interposed Henriette la Gaultière.

"Then," remarked Agnès, "it is the third since the Sunday of the **Lætare**: for, in less than a week, we had the miracle of the mocker of pilgrims divinely punished by Notre-Dame d'Aubervilliers, and that was the second miracle within a month."

"This pretended foundling is a real monster of abomination," resumed Jehanne.

"He yells loud enough to deafen a chanter," continued Gauchère. "Hold your tongue, you little howler!"

"To think that Monsieur of Reims sent this enormity to Monsieur of Paris," added la Gaultière, clasping her hands.

"I imagine," said Agnès la Herme, "that it is a beast, an animal,–the fruit of a Jew and a sow; something not Christian, in short, which ought to be thrown into the fire or into the water."

"I really hope," resumed la Gaultière, "that nobody will apply for it."

"Ah, good heavens!" exclaimed Agnès; "those poor nurses yonder in the foundling asylum, which forms the lower end of the lane as you go to the river, just beside Monseigneur the bishop! what if this little monster were to be carried to them to suckle? I'd rather give suck to a vampire."

"How innocent that poor la Herme is!" resumed Jehanne; "don't you see, sister, that this little monster is at least four years old, and that he would have less appetite for your breast than for a turnspit."

The "little monster" we should find it difficult ourselves to describe him otherwise, was, in fact, not a new-born child. It was a very angular and very lively little mass, imprisoned in its linen sack, stamped with the cipher of Messire Guillaume Chartier, then bishop of

Paris, with a head projecting. That head was deformed enough; one beheld only a forest of red hair, one eye, a mouth, and teeth. The eye wept, the mouth cried, and the teeth seemed to ask only to be allowed to bite. The whole struggled in the sack, to the great consternation of the crowd, which increased and was renewed incessantly around it.

Dame Aloïse de Gondelaurier, a rich and noble woman, who held by the hand a pretty girl about five or six years of age, and dragged a long veil about, suspended to the golden horn of her headdress, halted as she passed the wooden bed, and gazed for a moment at the wretched creature, while her charming little daughter, Fleur-de-Lys de Gondelaurier, spelled out with her tiny, pretty finger, the permanent inscription attached to the wooden bed: "Foundlings."

"Really," said the dame, turning away in disgust, "I thought that they only exposed children here."

She turned her back, throwing into the

basin a silver florin, which rang among the liards, and made the poor goodwives of the chapel of Étienne Haudry open their eyes.

A moment later, the grave and learned Robert Mistricolle, the king's protonotary, passed, with an enormous missal under one arm and his wife on the other (Damoiselle Guillemette la Mairesse), having thus by his side his two regulators,–spiritual and temporal.

"Foundling!" he said, after examining the object; "found, apparently, on the banks of the river Phlegethon."

"One can only see one eye," observed Damoiselle Guillemette; "there is a wart on the other."

"It's not a wart," returned Master Robert Mistricolle, "it is an egg which contains another demon exactly similar, who bears another little egg which contains another devil, and so on."

"How do you know that?" asked Guillemette la Mairesse.

"I know it pertinently," replied the protonotary.

"Monsieur le protonotare," asked Gauchère, "what do you prognosticate of this pretended foundling?"

"The greatest misfortunes," replied Mistricolle.

"Ah! good heavens!" said an old woman among the spectators, "and that besides our having had a considerable pestilence last year, and that they say that the English are going to disembark in a company at Harfleur."

"Perhaps that will prevent the queen from coming to Paris in the month of September," interposed another; "trade is so bad already."

"My opinion is," exclaimed Jehanne de la Tarme, "that it would be better for the louts of Paris, if this little magician were put to bed on a fagot than on a plank."

"A fine, flaming fagot," added the old woman.

"It would be more prudent," said Mistricolle.

For several minutes, a young priest had been listening to the reasoning of the Haudriettes and the sentences of the notary. He had a severe face, with a large brow, a profound glance. He thrust the crowd silently aside, scrutinized the "little magician," and stretched out his hand upon him. It was high time, for all the devotees were already licking their chops over the "fine, flaming fagot."

"I adopt this child," said the priest.

He took it in his cassock and carried it off. The spectators followed him with frightened glances. A moment later, he had disappeared through the "Red Door," which then led from the church to the cloister.

When the first surprise was over, Jehanne de la Tarme bent down to the ear of la Gaultière,–

"I told you so, sister,–that young clerk, Monsieur Claude Frollo, is a sorcerer."

CHAPTER TWO

Claude Frollo

IN FACT, CLAUDE FROLLO was no common person.

He belonged to one of those middle-class families which were called indifferently, in the impertinent language of the last century, the high **bourgeoise** or the petty nobility. This family had inherited from the brothers Paclet the fief of Tirechappe, which was dependent upon the Bishop of Paris, and whose twenty-one houses had been in the thirteenth century the object of so many suits before the official. As possessor of this fief, Claude Frollo was one of the twenty-seven seigneurs keeping claim to a manor in fee in Paris and its suburbs; and for a long time, his name was to be seen inscribed in this quality, between the Hôtel de Tancarville, belonging to Master François Le Rez, and the college of Tours, in the records deposited at Saint Martin des Champs.

Claude Frollo had been destined from infancy, by his parents, to the ecclesiastical profession. He had been taught to read in Latin; he had been trained to keep his eyes on the ground and to speak low. While still a child, his father had cloistered him in the college of Torchi in the University. There it was that he had grown up, on the missal and the lexicon.

Moreover, he was a sad, grave, serious child, who studied ardently, and learned quickly; he never uttered a loud cry in recreation hour, mixed but little in the bacchanals of the Rue du Fouarre, did not know what it was to **dare alapas et capillos laniare**, and had cut no figure in that revolt of 1463, which the annalists register gravely, under the title of "The sixth trouble of the University." He seldom rallied the poor students of Montaigu on the **cappettes** from which they derived their name, or the bursars of the college of Dormans on their shaved tonsure, and their surtout parti-colored of bluish-green, blue, and violet cloth, **azurini coloris et bruni**, as says the charter of the Cardinal des Quatre-Couronnes.

On the other hand, he was assiduous at the great and the small schools of the Rue Saint Jean de Beauvais. The first pupil whom the Abbé de Saint Pierre de Val, at the moment of beginning his reading on canon law, always perceived, glued to a pillar of the school Saint-Vendregesile, opposite his rostrum, was Claude Frollo, armed with his horn ink-bottle, biting his pen, scribbling on his threadbare knee, and, in winter, blowing on his fingers. The first auditor whom Messire Miles d'Isliers, doctor in decretals, saw arrive every Monday morning, all breathless, at the opening of the gates of the school of the Chef-Saint-Denis, was Claude Frollo. Thus, at sixteen years of age, the young clerk might have held his own, in mystical theology, against a father of the church; in canonical theology, against a father of the councils; in scholastic theology, against a doctor of Sorbonne.

Theology conquered, he had plunged into decretals. From the "Master of Sentences," he had passed to the "Capitularies of Charlemagne;" and he had devoured in succession, in his appetite for science, decretals upon decretals, those of Theodore, Bishop of Hispalus; those of Bouchard, Bishop of Worms; those of Yves, Bishop of Chartres; next the decretal of Gratian, which succeeded the capitularies of Charlemagne; then the collection of Gregory IX.; then the Epistle of **Superspecula**, of Honorius III. He rendered clear and familiar to himself that vast and tumultuous period of civil law and canon law in conflict and at strife with each other, in the chaos of the Middle Ages,–a period which Bishop Theodore opens in 618, and which Pope Gregory closes in 1227.

Decretals digested, he flung himself upon medicine, on the liberal arts. He studied the science of herbs, the science of unguents; he became an expert in fevers and in contusions, in sprains and abcesses. Jacques d' Espars would have received him as a physician; Richard Hellain, as a surgeon. He also passed through all the degrees of licentiate, master, and doctor of arts. He studied the languages, Latin, Greek, Hebrew, a triple sanctuary then very little frequented. His was a veritable fever for acquiring and hoarding, in the matter of science. At the age of eighteen, he had made his way through the four faculties; it seemed to the young man that life had but one sole object: learning.

It was towards this epoch, that the excessive heat of the summer of 1466 caused that grand outburst of the plague which carried off more than forty thousand souls in the vicomty of Paris, and among others, as Jean de Troyes states, "Master Arnoul, astrologer to the king, who was a very fine man, both wise and pleasant." The rumor spread in the University that the Rue Tirechappe was especially devastated by the malady. It was there that Claude's parents resided, in the midst of their fief. The young scholar rushed in great alarm to the paternal mansion. When he entered it, he found that both father and mother had died on the preceding day. A very young brother of his, who was in swaddling clothes, was still alive and crying abandoned in his cradle. This was all that remained to Claude of his family; the young man took the child under his arm and went off in a pensive mood. Up to that moment, he had lived only in science; he now began to live in life.

This catastrophe was a crisis in Claude's existence. Orphaned, the eldest, head of the family at the age of nineteen, he felt himself rudely recalled from the reveries of school to the realities of this world. Then, moved with pity, he was seized with passion and devotion towards that child, his brother; a sweet and strange thing was a human affection to him, who had hitherto loved his books alone.

This affection developed to a singular point; in a soul so new, it was like a first love. Separated since infancy from his parents, whom he had hardly known; cloistered and immured, as it were, in his books; eager above all things to study and to learn; exclusively attentive up to that time, to his intelligence which broadened in science, to his imagination, which expanded in letters,–the poor scholar had not yet had time to feel the place of his heart.

This young brother, without mother or father, this little child which had fallen abruptly from heaven into his arms, made a new man of him. He perceived that there was something else in the world besides the speculations of the Sorbonne, and the verses of Homer; that man needed affections; that life without tenderness and without love was only a set of dry, shrieking, and rending wheels. Only, he imagined, for he was at the age when illusions are as yet replaced only by illusions, that the affections of blood and family were the sole ones necessary, and that a little brother to love sufficed to fill an entire existence.

He threw himself, therefore, into the love for his little Jehan with the passion of a character already profound, ardent, concentrated; that poor frail creature, pretty, fair-haired, rosy, and curly,–that orphan with another orphan for his only support, touched him to the bottom of his heart; and grave thinker as he was, he set to meditating upon Jehan with an infinite compassion. He kept watch and ward over him as over something very fragile, and very worthy of care. He was more than a brother to the child; he became a mother to him.

Little Jehan had lost his mother while he was still at the breast; Claude gave him to a nurse. Besides the fief of Tirechappe, he had inherited from his father the fief of Moulin, which was a dependency of the square tower of Gentilly; it was a mill on a hill, near the château of Winchestre (Bicêtre). There was a miller's wife there who was nursing a fine child; it was not far from the university, and Claude carried the little Jehan to her in his own arms.

From that time forth, feeling that he had a burden to bear, he took life very seriously. The thought of his little brother became not only his recreation, but the object of his studies. He resolved to consecrate himself entirely to a future for which he was responsible in the sight of God, and never to have any other wife, any other child than the happiness and fortune of his brother.

Therefore, he attached himself more closely than ever to the clerical profession. His merits, his learning, his quality of immediate vassal of the Bishop of Paris, threw the doors of the church wide open to him. At the age of twenty, by special dispensation of the Holy See, he was a priest, and served as the youngest of the chaplains of Notre-Dame the altar which is called, because of the late mass which is said there, **altare pigrorum**.

There, plunged more deeply than ever in his dear books, which he quitted only to run for an hour to the fief of Moulin, this mixture of learning and austerity, so rare at his age, had promptly acquired for him the respect and admiration of the monastery. From the cloister, his reputation as a learned man had passed to the people, among whom it had changed a little, a frequent occurrence at that time, into reputation as a sorcerer.

It was at the moment when he was returning, on Quasimodo day, from saying his mass at the Altar of the Lazy, which was by the side of the door leading to the nave on the right, near the image of the Virgin, that his attention had been attracted by the group of old women chattering around the bed for foundlings.

Then it was that he approached the unhappy little creature, which was so hated and so menaced. That distress, that deformity, that abandonment, the thought of his young brother, the idea which suddenly occurred to him, that if he were to die, his dear little Jehan might also be flung miserably on the plank for foundlings,–all this had gone to his heart simultaneously; a great pity had moved in him, and he had carried off the child.

When he removed the child from the sack, he found it greatly deformed, in very sooth. The poor little wretch had a wart on his left eye, his head placed directly on his shoulders, his spinal column was crooked, his breast bone prominent, and his legs bowed; but he appeared to be lively; and although it was impossible to say in what language he lisped, his cry indicated considerable force and health. Claude's compassion increased at the sight of this ugliness; and he made a vow in his heart to rear the child for the love of his brother, in order that, whatever might be the future faults of the little Jehan, he should have beside him that charity done for his sake. It was a sort of investment of good works, which he was effecting in the name of his young brother; it was a stock of good works which he wished to amass in advance for him, in case the little rogue should some day find himself short of that coin, the only sort which is received at the toll-bar of paradise.

He baptized his adopted child, and gave him the name of Quasimodo, either because he desired thereby to mark the day, when he had found him, or because he wished to designate by that name to what a degree the poor little creature was incomplete, and hardly sketched out. In fact, Quasimodo, blind, hunchbacked, knock-kneed, was only an "almost."

CHAPTER THREE

Immanis Pecoris Custos, Immanior Ipse

NOW, IN 1482, Quasimodo had grown up. He had become a few years previously the bellringer of Notre-Dame, thanks to his father by adoption, Claude Frollo,–who had become archdeacon of Josas, thanks to his suzerain, Messire Louis de Beaumont,–who had become Bishop of Paris, at the death of Guillaume Chartier in 1472, thanks to his patron, Olivier Le Daim, barber to Louis XI., king by the grace of God.

So Quasimodo was the ringer of the chimes of Notre-Dame.

In the course of time there had been formed a certain peculiarly intimate bond which united the ringer to the church. Separated forever from the world, by the double fatality of his unknown birth and his natural deformity, imprisoned from his infancy in that impassable double circle, the poor wretch had grown used to seeing nothing in this world beyond the religious walls which had received him under their shadow. Notre-Dame had been to him successively, as he grew up and developed, the egg, the nest, the house, the country, the universe.

There was certainly a sort of mysterious and pre-existing harmony between this creature and this church. When, still a little fellow, he had dragged himself tortuously and by jerks beneath the shadows of its vaults, he seemed, with his human face and his bestial limbs, the natural reptile of that humid and sombre pavement, upon which the shadow of the Romanesque capitals cast so many strange forms.

Later on, the first time that he caught hold, mechanically, of the ropes to the towers, and hung suspended from them, and set the bell to clanging, it produced upon his adopted father, Claude, the effect of a child whose tongue is unloosed and who begins to speak.

It is thus that, little by little, developing always in sympathy with the cathedral, living there, sleeping there, hardly ever leaving it, subject every hour to the mysterious impress, he came to resemble it, he incrusted himself in it, so to speak, and became an integral part of it. His salient angles fitted into the retreating angles of the cathedral (if we may be allowed this figure of speech), and he seemed not only its inhabitant but more than that, its natural tenant. One might almost say that he had assumed its form, as the snail takes on the form of its shell. It was his dwelling, his hole, his envelope. There existed between him and the old church so profound an instinctive sympathy, so many magnetic affinities, so many material affinities, that he adhered to it somewhat as a tortoise adheres to its shell. The rough and wrinkled cathedral was his shell.

It is useless to warn the reader not to take literally all the similes which we are obliged to employ here to express the singular, symmetrical, direct, almost consubstantial union of a man and an edifice. It is equally unnecessary to state to what a degree that whole cathedral was familiar to him, after so long and so intimate a cohabitation. That dwelling was peculiar to him. It had no depths to which Quasimodo had not penetrated, no height which he had not scaled. He often climbed many stones up the front, aided solely by the uneven points of the carving. The towers, on whose exterior surface he was frequently seen clambering, like a lizard gliding along a perpendicular wall, those two gigantic twins, so lofty, so menacing, so formidable, possessed for him neither vertigo, nor terror, nor shocks of amazement.

To see them so gentle under his hand, so easy to scale, one would have said that he had tamed them. By dint of leaping, climbing, gambolling amid the abysses of the gigantic cathedral he had become, in some sort, a monkey and a goat, like the Calabrian child who swims before he walks, and plays with the sea while still a babe.

Moreover, it was not his body alone which seemed fashioned after the Cathedral, but his mind also. In what condition was that mind? What bent had it contracted, what form had it assumed beneath that knotted envelope, in that savage life? This it would be hard to determine. Quasimodo had been born one-eyed, hunchbacked, lame. It was with great difficulty, and by dint of great patience that Claude Frollo had succeeded in teaching him to talk. But a fatality was attached to the poor foundling. Bellringer of Notre-Dame at the age of fourteen, a new infirmity had come to complete his misfortunes: the bells had broken the drums of his ears; he had become deaf. The only gate which nature had left wide open for him had been abruptly closed, and forever.

In closing, it had cut off the only ray of joy and of light which still made its way into the soul of Quasimodo. His soul fell into profound night. The wretched being's misery became as incurable and as complete as his deformity. Let us add that his deafness rendered him to some extent dumb. For, in order not to make others laugh, the very moment that he found himself to be deaf, he resolved upon a silence which he only broke when he was alone. He voluntarily tied that tongue which Claude Frollo had taken so much pains to unloose. Hence, it came about, that when necessity constrained him to speak, his tongue was torpid, awkward, and like a door whose hinges have grown rusty.

If now we were to try to penetrate to the soul of Quasimodo through that thick, hard rind; if we could sound the depths of that badly constructed organism; if it were granted to us to look with a torch behind those non-transparent organs to explore the shadowy interior of that opaque creature, to elucidate his obscure corners, his absurd no-thoroughfares, and suddenly to cast a vivid light upon the soul enchained at the extremity of that cave, we should, no doubt, find the unhappy Psyche in some poor, cramped, and ricketty attitude, like those prisoners beneath the Leads of Venice, who grew old bent double in a stone box which was both too low and too short for them.

It is certain that the mind becomes atrophied in a defective body. Quasimodo was barely conscious of a soul cast in his own image, moving blindly within him. The impressions of objects underwent a considerable refraction before reaching his mind. His brain was a peculiar medium; the ideas which passed through it issued forth completely distorted. The reflection which resulted from this refraction was, necessarily, divergent and perverted.

Hence a thousand optical illusions, a thousand aberrations of judgment, a thousand deviations, in which his thought strayed, now mad, now idiotic.

The first effect of this fatal organization was to trouble the glance which he cast upon things. He received hardly any immediate perception of them. The external world seemed much farther away to him than it does to us.

The second effect of his misfortune was to render him malicious.

He was malicious, in fact, because he was savage; he was savage because he was ugly. There was logic in his nature, as there is in ours.

His strength, so extraordinarily developed, was a cause of still greater malevolence: "**Malus puer robustus**," says Hobbes.

This justice must, however be rendered to him. Malevolence was not, perhaps, innate in him. From his very first steps among men, he had felt himself, later on he had seen himself, spewed out, blasted, rejected. Human words were, for him, always a raillery or a malediction. As he grew up, he had found nothing but hatred around him. He had caught the general malevolence. He had picked up the weapon with which he had been wounded.

After all, he turned his face towards men only with reluctance; his cathedral was sufficient for him. It was peopled with marble figures,–kings, saints, bishops,–who at least did not burst out laughing in his face, and who gazed upon him only with tranquillity and kindliness. The other statues, those of the monsters and demons, cherished no hatred for him, Quasimodo. He resembled them too much for that. They seemed rather, to be scoffing at other men. The saints were his friends, and blessed him; the monsters were his friends and guarded him. So he held long communion with them. He sometimes passed whole hours crouching before one of these statues, in solitary conversation with it. If any one came, he fled like a lover surprised in his serenade.

And the cathedral was not only society for him, but the universe, and all nature beside. He dreamed of no other hedgerows than the painted windows, always in flower; no other shade than that of the foliage of stone which spread out, loaded with birds, in the tufts of the Saxon capitals; of no other mountains than the colossal towers of the church; of no other ocean than Paris, roaring at their bases.

What he loved above all else in the maternal edifice, that which aroused his soul, and made it open its poor wings, which it kept so miserably folded in its cavern, that which sometimes rendered him even happy, was the bells. He loved them, fondled them, talked to them, understood them. From the chime in the spire, over the intersection of the aisles and nave, to the great bell of the front, he cherished a tenderness for them all. The central spire and the two towers were to him as three great cages, whose birds, reared by himself, sang for him alone. Yet it was these very bells which had made him deaf; but mothers often love best that child which has caused them the most suffering.

It is true that their voice was the only one which he could still hear. On this score, the big bell was his beloved. It was she whom he preferred out of all that family of noisy girls which bustled above him, on festival days. This bell was named Marie. She was alone in the southern tower, with her sister Jacqueline, a bell of lesser size, shut up in a smaller cage beside hers. This

Jacqueline was so called from the name of the wife of Jean Montagu, who had given it to the church, which had not prevented his going and figuring without his head at Montfaucon. In the second tower there were six other bells, and, finally, six smaller ones inhabited the belfry over the crossing, with the wooden bell, which rang only between after dinner on Good Friday and the morning of the day before Easter. So Quasimodo had fifteen bells in his seraglio; but big Marie was his favorite.

No idea can be formed of his delight on days when the grand peal was sounded. At the moment when the archdeacon dismissed him, and said, "Go!" he mounted the spiral staircase of the clock tower faster than any one else could have descended it. He entered perfectly breathless into the aerial chamber of the great bell; he gazed at her a moment, devoutly and lovingly; then he gently addressed her and patted her with his hand, like a good horse, which is about to set out on a long journey. He pitied her for the trouble that she was about to suffer. After these first caresses, he shouted to his assistants, placed in the lower story of the tower, to begin. They grasped the ropes, the wheel creaked, the enormous capsule of metal started slowly into motion. Quasimodo followed it with his glance and trembled. The first shock of the clapper and the brazen wall made the framework upon which it was mounted quiver. Quasimodo vibrated with the bell.

"Vah!" he cried, with a senseless burst of laughter. However, the movement of the bass was accelerated, and, in proportion as it described a wider angle, Quasimodo's eye opened also more and more widely, phosphoric and flaming. At length the grand peal began; the whole tower trembled; woodwork, leads, cut stones, all groaned at once, from the piles of the foundation to the trefoils of its summit. Then Quasimodo boiled and frothed; he went and came; he trembled from head to foot with the tower. The bell, furious, running riot, presented to the two walls of the tower alternately its brazen throat, whence escaped that tempestuous breath, which is audible leagues away. Quasimodo stationed himself in front of this open throat; he crouched and rose with the oscillations of the bell, breathed in this overwhelming breath, gazed by turns at the deep place, which swarmed with people, two hundred feet below him, and at that enormous, brazen tongue which came, second after second, to howl in his ear.

It was the only speech which he understood, the only sound which broke for him the universal silence. He swelled out in it as a bird does in the sun. All of a sudden, the frenzy of the bell seized upon him; his look became extraordinary; he lay in wait for the great bell as it passed, as a spider lies in wait for a fly, and flung himself abruptly upon it, with might and main. Then, suspended above the abyss, borne to and fro by the formidable swinging of the bell, he seized the brazen monster by the ear-laps, pressed it between both knees, spurred it on with his heels, and redoubled the fury of the peal with the whole shock and weight of his body. Meanwhile, the tower trembled; he shrieked and gnashed his teeth, his red hair rose erect, his breast heaving like a bellows, his eye flashed flames, the monstrous bell neighed, panting, beneath him; and then it was no longer the great bell of Notre-Dame nor Quasimodo: it was a dream, a whirlwind, a tempest, dizziness mounted astride of noise; a spirit clinging to a flying crupper, a strange centaur, half man, half bell; a sort of horrible Astolphus, borne away upon a prodigious hippogriff of living bronze.

The presence of this extraordinary being caused, as it were, a breath of life to circulate throughout the entire cathedral. It seemed as though there escaped from him, at least according to the growing superstitions of the crowd, a mysterious emanation which animated all the stones of Notre-Dame, and made the deep bowels of the ancient church to palpitate. It sufficed for people to know that he was there, to make them believe that they beheld the thousand statues of the galleries and the fronts in motion. And the cathedral did indeed seem a docile and obedient creature beneath his hand; it waited on his will to raise its great voice; it was possessed and filled with Quasimodo, as with a familiar spirit. One would have said that he made the immense edifice breathe. He was everywhere about it; in fact, he multiplied himself on all points of the structure. Now one perceived with affright at the very top of one of the towers, a fantastic dwarf climbing, writhing, crawling on all fours, descending outside above the abyss, leaping from projection to projection, and going to ransack the belly of some sculptured gorgon; it was Quasimodo dislodging the crows. Again, in some obscure corner of the church one came in contact with a sort of living chimera, crouching and scowling; it was Quasimodo engaged in thought. Sometimes one caught sight, upon a bell tower, of an enormous head and a bundle of disordered limbs swinging furiously at the end of a rope; it was Quasimodo ringing vespers or the Angelus. Often at night a hideous form was seen wandering along the frail balustrade of carved lacework, which crowns the towers and borders the circumference of the apse; again it was the hunchback of Notre-Dame. Then, said the women of the neighborhood, the whole church took on something fantastic, supernatural, horrible; eyes and mouths were opened, here and there; one heard the dogs, the monsters, and the gargoyles of stone, which keep watch night and day, with outstretched neck and open jaws, around the monstrous cathedral, barking. And, if it was a Christmas Eve, while the great bell, which seemed to emit the death rattle, summoned the faithful to the midnight mass, such an air was spread over the sombre façade that one would have declared that the grand portal was devouring the throng, and that the rose window was watching it. And all this came from Quasimodo. Egypt would have taken him for the god of this temple; the Middle Ages believed him to be its demon: he was in fact its soul.

To such an extent was this disease that for those who know that Quasimodo has existed, Notre-Dame is to-day deserted, inanimate, dead. One feels that something has disappeared from it. That immense body is empty; it is a skeleton; the spirit has quitted it, one sees its place and that is all. It is like a skull which still has holes for the eyes, but no longer sight.

CHAPTER FOUR

The Dog and his Master

NEVERTHELESS, THERE WAS one human creature whom Quasimodo excepted from his malice and from his hatred for others, and whom he loved even more, perhaps, than his cathedral: this was Claude Frollo.

The matter was simple; Claude Frollo had taken him in, had adopted him, had nourished him, had reared him. When a little lad, it was between Claude Frollo's legs that he was accustomed to seek refuge, when the dogs and the children barked after him. Claude Frollo had taught him to talk, to read, to write. Claude Frollo had finally made him the bellringer. Now, to give the big bell in marriage to Quasimodo was to give Juliet to Romeo.

Hence Quasimodo's gratitude was profound, passionate, boundless; and although the visage of his adopted father was often clouded or severe, although his speech was habitually curt, harsh, imperious, that gratitude never wavered for a single moment. The archdeacon had in Quasimodo the most submissive slave, the most docile lackey, the most vigilant of dogs. When the poor bellringer became deaf, there had been established between him and Claude Frollo, a language of signs, mysterious and understood by themselves alone. In this manner the archdeacon was the sole human being with whom Quasimodo had preserved communication. He was in sympathy with but two things in this world: Notre-Dame and Claude Frollo.

There is nothing which can be compared with the empire of the archdeacon over the bellringer; with the attachment of the bellringer for the archdeacon. A sign from Claude and the idea of giving him pleasure would have sufficed to make Quasimodo hurl himself headlong from the summit of Notre-Dame. It was a remarkable thing–all that physical strength which had reached in Quasimodo such an extraordinary development, and which was placed by him blindly at the disposition of another. There was in it, no doubt, filial devotion, domestic attachment; there was also the fascination of one spirit by another spirit. It was a poor, awkward, and clumsy organization, which stood with lowered head and supplicating eyes before a lofty and profound, a powerful and superior intellect. Lastly, and above all, it was gratitude. Gratitude so pushed to its extremest limit, that we do not know to what to compare it. This virtue is not one of those of which the finest examples are to be met with among men. We will say then, that Quasimodo loved the archdeacon as never a dog, never a horse, never an elephant loved his master.

CHAPTER FIVE

More About Claude Frollo

IN 1482, QUASIMODO WAS about twenty years of age; Claude Frollo, about thirty-six. One had grown up, the other had grown old.

Claude Frollo was no longer the simple scholar of the college of Torchi, the tender protector of a little child, the young and dreamy philosopher who knew many things and was ignorant of many. He was a priest, austere, grave, morose; one charged with souls; monsieur the archdeacon of Josas, the bishop's second acolyte, having charge of the two deaneries of Montlhéry, and Châteaufort, and one hundred and seventy-four country curacies. He was an imposing and sombre personage, before whom the choir boys in alb and in jacket trembled, as well as the machicots[25], and the brothers of Saint-Augustine and the matutinal clerks of Notre-Dame, when he passed slowly beneath the lofty arches of the choir, majestic, thoughtful, with arms folded and his head so bent upon his breast that all one saw of his face was his large, bald brow.

Dom Claude Frollo had, however, abandoned neither science nor the education of his young brother, those two occupations of his life. But as time went on, some bitterness had been mingled with these

25 An official of Notre-Dame, lower than a beneficed clergyman, higher than simple paid chanters.

things which were so sweet. In the long run, says Paul Diacre, the best lard turns rancid. Little Jehan Frollo, surnamed (**du Moulin**) "of the Mill" because of the place where he had been reared, had not grown up in the direction which Claude would have liked to impose upon him. The big brother counted upon a pious, docile, learned, and honorable pupil. But the little brother, like those young trees which deceive the gardener's hopes and turn obstinately to the quarter whence they receive sun and air, the little brother did not grow and did not multiply, but only put forth fine bushy and luxuriant branches on the side of laziness, ignorance, and debauchery. He was a regular devil, and a very disorderly one, who made Dom Claude scowl; but very droll and very subtle, which made the big brother smile.

Claude had confided him to that same college of Torchi where he had passed his early years in study and meditation; and it was a grief to him that this sanctuary, formerly edified by the name of Frollo, should to-day be scandalized by it. He sometimes preached Jehan very long and severe sermons, which the latter intrepidly endured. After all, the young scapegrace had a good heart, as can be seen in all comedies. But the sermon over, he none the less tranquilly resumed his course of seditions and enormities. Now it was a **béjaune** or yellow beak (as they called the new arrivals at the university), whom he had been mauling by way of welcome; a precious tradition which has been carefully preserved to our own day. Again, he had set in movement a band of scholars, who had flung themselves upon a wine-shop in classic fashion, **quasi classico excitati**, had then beaten the tavern-keeper "with offensive cudgels," and joyously pillaged the tavern, even to smashing in the hogsheads of wine in the cellar. And then it was a fine report in Latin, which the sub-monitor of Torchi carried piteously to Dom Claude with this dolorous marginal comment,–**Rixa; prima**

causa vinum optimum potatum. Finally, it was said, a thing quite horrible in a boy of sixteen, that his debauchery often extended as far as the Rue de Glatigny.

Claude, saddened and discouraged in his human affections, by all this, had flung himself eagerly into the arms of learning, that sister which, at least does not laugh in your face, and which always pays you, though in money that is sometimes a little hollow, for the attention which you have paid to her. Hence, he became more and more learned, and, at the same time, as a natural consequence, more and more rigid as a priest, more and more sad as a man. There are for each of us several parallelisms between our intelligence, our habits, and our character, which develop without a break, and break only in the great disturbances of life.

As Claude Frollo had passed through nearly the entire circle of human learning–positive, exterior, and permissible–since his youth, he was obliged, unless he came to a halt, **ubi defuit orbis**, to proceed further and seek other aliments for the insatiable activity of his intelligence. The antique symbol of the serpent biting its tail is, above all, applicable to science. It would appear that Claude Frollo had experienced this. Many grave persons affirm that, after having exhausted the **fas** of human learning, he had dared to penetrate into the **nefas**. He had, they said, tasted in succession all the apples of the tree of knowledge, and, whether from hunger or disgust, had ended by tasting the forbidden fruit. He had taken his place by turns, as the reader has seen, in the conferences of the theologians in Sorbonne,–in the assemblies of the doctors of art, after the manner of Saint-Hilaire,–in the disputes of the decretalists, after the manner of Saint-Martin,–in the congregations of physicians at the holy water font of Notre-Dame, **ad cupam Nostræ-Dominæ**. All the dishes permitted and approved, which those four great kitchens called the four faculties could elaborate and serve to the understanding, he had devoured, and had been satiated with them before his hunger was appeased. Then he had penetrated further, lower, beneath all that finished, material, limited knowledge; he had, perhaps, risked his soul, and had seated himself in the cavern at that mysterious table of the alchemists, of the astrologers, of the hermetics, of which Averroès, Guillaume de Paris, and Nicolas Flamel hold the end in the Middle Ages; and which extends in the East, by the light of the seven-branched candlestick, to Solomon, Pythagoras, and Zoroaster.

That is, at least, what was supposed, whether rightly or not. It is certain that the archdeacon often visited the cemetery of the Saints-Innocents, where, it is true, his father and mother had been buried, with other victims of the plague of 1466; but that he appeared far less devout before the cross of their grave than before the strange figures with which the tomb of Nicolas Flamel and Claude Pernelle, erected just beside it, was loaded.

It is certain that he had frequently been seen to pass along the Rue des Lombards, and furtively enter a little house which formed the corner of the Rue des Ecrivans and the Rue Marivault. It was the house which Nicolas Flamel had built, where he had died about 1417, and which, constantly deserted since that time, had already begun to fall in ruins,–so greatly had the hermetics and the alchemists of all countries wasted away the walls, merely by carving their names upon them. Some neighbors even affirm that they had once seen, through an air-hole, Archdeacon Claude excavating, turning over, digging up the earth in the two cellars, whose supports had been daubed with numberless couplets and hieroglyphics by Nicolas Flamel himself. It was supposed that Flamel had buried the philosopher's stone in the cellar; and the alchemists, for the space of two centuries, from Magistri to Father Pacifique, never ceased to worry the soil until the house, so cruelly ransacked and turned over, ended by falling into dust beneath their feet.

Again, it is certain that the archdeacon had been seized with a singular passion for the symbolical door of Notre-Dame, that page of a conjuring book written in stone, by Bishop Guillaume de Paris, who has, no doubt, been damned for having affixed so infernal a frontispiece to the sacred poem chanted by the rest of the edifice. Archdeacon Claude had the credit also of having fathomed the mystery of the colossus of Saint Christopher, and of that lofty, enigmatical statue which then stood at the entrance of the vestibule, and which the people, in derision, called “Monsieur Legris.” But, what every one might have noticed was the interminable hours which he often employed, seated upon the parapet of the area in front of the church, in contemplating the sculptures of the front; examining now the foolish virgins with their lamps reversed, now the wise virgins with their lamps upright; again, calculating the angle of vision of that raven which belongs to the left front, and which is looking at a mysterious point inside the church, where is concealed the philosopher's stone, if it be not in the cellar of Nicolas Flamel.

It was, let us remark in passing, a singular fate for the Church of Notre-Dame at that epoch to be so beloved, in two different degrees, and with so much devotion, by two beings so dissimilar as Claude and Quasimodo. Beloved by one, a sort of instinctive and savage half-man, for its beauty, for its stature, for the harmonies which emanated from its magnificent ensemble; beloved by the other, a learned and passionate imagination, for its myth, for the sense which it contains, for the symbolism scattered beneath the sculptures of its front,–like the first text underneath the second in a palimpsest,–in a word, for the enigma which it is eternally propounding to the understanding.

Furthermore, it is certain that the archdeacon had established himself in that one of the two towers which looks upon the Grève, just beside the frame for the bells, a very secret little cell, into which no one, not even the bishop, entered without his leave, it was said. This tiny cell had formerly been made almost at the summit of the tower, among the ravens' nests, by Bishop Hugo de Besançon[26] who had wrought sorcery there in his day. What that cell contained, no one knew; but from the strand of the Terrain, at night, there was often seen to appear, disappear, and reappear at brief and regular intervals, at a little dormer window opening upon the back of the tower, a certain red, intermittent, singular light which seemed to follow the panting breaths of a bellows, and to proceed from a flame, rather than from a light. In the darkness, at that

---

26 Hugo II. de Bisuncio, 1326-1332.

height, it produced a singular effect; and the goodwives said: “There’s the archdeacon blowing! hell is sparkling up yonder!”

There were no great proofs of sorcery in that, after all, but there was still enough smoke to warrant a surmise of fire, and the archdeacon bore a tolerably formidable reputation. We ought to mention however, that the sciences of Egypt, that necromancy and magic, even the whitest, even the most innocent, had no more envenomed enemy, no more pitiless denunciator before the gentlemen of the officialty of Notre-Dame. Whether this was sincere horror, or the game played by the thief who shouts, “stop thief!” at all events, it did not prevent the archdeacon from being considered by the learned heads of the chapter, as a soul who had ventured into the vestibule of hell, who was lost in the caves of the cabal, groping amid the shadows of the occult sciences. Neither were the people deceived thereby; with any one who possessed any sagacity,

Quasimodo passed for the demon; Claude Frollo, for the sorcerer. It was evident that the bellringer was to serve the archdeacon for a given time, at the end of which he would carry away the latter's soul, by way of payment. Thus the archdeacon, in spite of the excessive austerity of his life, was in bad odor among all pious souls; and there was no devout nose so inexperienced that it could not smell him out to be a magician.

And if, as he grew older, abysses had formed in his science, they had also formed in his heart. That at least, is what one had grounds for believing on scrutinizing that face upon which the soul was only seen to shine through a sombre cloud. Whence that large, bald brow? that head forever bent? that breast always heaving with sighs? What secret thought caused his mouth to smile with so much bitterness, at the same moment that his scowling brows approached each other like two bulls on the point of fighting? Why was what hair he had left already gray? What was that internal fire which sometimes broke forth in his glance, to such a degree that his eye resembled a hole pierced in the wall of a furnace?

These symptoms of a violent moral preoccupation, had acquired an especially high degree of intensity at the epoch when this story takes place. More than once a choir-boy had fled in terror at finding him alone in the church, so strange and dazzling was his look. More than once, in the choir, at the hour of the offices, his neighbor in the stalls had heard him mingle with the plain song, **ad omnem tonum**, unintelligible parentheses. More than once the laundress of the Terrain charged “with washing the chapter” had observed, not without affright, the marks of nails and clenched fingers on the surplice of monsieur the archdeacon of Josas.

However, he redoubled his severity, and had never been more exemplary. By profession as well as by character, he had always held himself aloof from women; he seemed to hate them more than ever. The mere rustling of a silken petticoat caused his hood to fall over his eyes. Upon this score he was so jealous of austerity and reserve, that when the Dame de Beaujeu, the king's daughter, came to visit the cloister of Notre-Dame, in the month of December, 1481, he gravely opposed her entrance, reminding the bishop of the statute of the Black Book, dating from the vigil of Saint-Barthélemy, 1334, which interdicts access to the cloister to "any woman whatever, old or young, mistress or maid." Upon which the bishop had been constrained to recite to him the ordinance of Legate Odo, which excepts certain great dames, **aliquæ magnates mulieres, quæ sine scandalo vitari non possunt**. And again the archdeacon had protested, objecting that the ordinance of the legate, which dated back to 1207, was anterior by a hundred and twenty-seven years to the Black Book, and consequently was abrogated in fact by it. And he had refused to appear before the princess.

It was also noticed that his horror for Bohemian women and gypsies had seemed to redouble for some time past. He had petitioned the bishop for an edict which expressly forbade the Bohemian women to come and dance and beat their tambourines on the place of the Parvis; and for about the same length of time, he had been ransacking the mouldy placards of the officialty, in order to collect the cases of sorcerers and witches condemned to fire or the rope, for complicity in crimes with rams, sows, or goats.

CHAPTER SIX

Unpopularity

THE ARCHDEACON AND THE bellringer, as we have already said, were but little loved by the populace great and small, in the vicinity of the cathedral. When Claude and Quasimodo went out together, which frequently happened, and when they were seen traversing in company, the valet behind the master, the cold, narrow, and gloomy streets of the block of Notre-Dame, more than one evil word, more than one ironical quaver, more than one insulting jest greeted them on their way, unless Claude Frollo, which was rarely the case, walked with head upright and raised, showing his severe and almost august brow to the dumbfounded jeerers.

Both were in their quarter like "the poets" of whom Régnier speaks,–

"All sorts of persons run after poets,
As warblers fly shrieking after owls."

Sometimes a mischievous child risked his skin and bones for the ineffable pleasure of driving a pin into Quasimodo's hump. Again, a young girl, more bold and saucy than was fitting, brushed the priest's black robe, singing in his face the sardonic ditty, "**niche, niche**, the devil is caught." Sometimes a group of squalid old crones, squatting in a file under the shadow of the steps to a porch, scolded noisily as the archdeacon and the bellringer passed, and tossed them this encouraging welcome, with a curse: "Hum!

there's a fellow whose soul is made like the other one's body!" Or a band of schoolboys and street urchins, playing hop-scotch, rose in a body and saluted him classically, with some cry in Latin: "**Eia! eia! Claudius cum claudo**!"

But the insult generally passed unnoticed both by the priest and the bellringer. Quasimodo was too deaf to hear all these gracious things, and Claude was too dreamy.

VOLUME ONE

BOOK FIFTH

CHAPTER ONE

Abbas Beati Martini

DOM CLAUDE'S FAME HAD spread far and wide. It procured for him, at about the epoch when he refused to see Madame de Beaujeu, a visit which he long remembered.

It was in the evening. He had just retired, after the office, to his canon's cell in the cloister of Notre-Dame. This cell, with the exception, possibly, of some glass phials, relegated to a corner, and filled with a decidedly equivocal powder, which strongly resembled the alchemist's "powder of projection," presented nothing strange or mysterious. There were, indeed, here and there, some inscriptions on the walls, but they were pure sentences of learning and piety, extracted from good authors. The archdeacon had just seated himself, by the light of a three-jetted copper lamp, before a vast coffer crammed with manuscripts. He had rested his elbow upon the open volume of Honorius d'Autun, **De predestinatione et libero arbitrio**, and he was turning over, in deep meditation, the leaves of a printed folio which he had just brought, the sole product of the press which his cell contained. In the midst of his revery there came a knock at his door. "Who's there?" cried the learned man, in the gracious tone of a famished dog, disturbed over his bone.

A voice without replied, "Your friend,

Jacques Coictier." He went to open the door.

It was, in fact, the king's physician; a person about fifty years of age, whose harsh physiognomy was modified only by a crafty eye. Another man accompanied him. Both wore long slate-colored robes, furred with minever, girded and closed, with caps of the same stuff and hue. Their hands were concealed by their sleeves, their feet by their robes, their eyes by their caps.

"God help me, messieurs!" said the archdeacon, showing them in; "I was not expecting distinguished visitors at such an hour." And while speaking in this courteous fashion he cast an uneasy and scrutinizing glance from the physician to his companion.

"'Tis never too late to come and pay a visit to so considerable a learned man as Dom Claude Frollo de Tirechappe," replied Doctor Coictier, whose Franche-Comté accent made all his phrases drag along with the majesty of a train-robe.

Therethenensuedbetweenthephysicianand the archdeacon one of those congratulatory prologues which, in accordance with custom, at that epoch preceded all conversations between learned men, and which did not prevent them from detesting each other in the most cordial manner in the world. However, it is the same nowadays; every wise man's mouth complimenting another wise man is a vase of honeyed gall.

Claude Frollo's felicitations to Jacques Coictier bore reference principally to the temporal advantages which the worthy physician had found means to extract, in the course of his much envied career, from each malady of the king, an operation of alchemy much better and more certain than the pursuit of the philosopher's stone.

"In truth, Monsieur le Docteur Coictier, I felt great joy on learning of the bishopric given your nephew, my reverend seigneur Pierre Versé. Is he not Bishop of Amiens?"

"Yes, monsieur Archdeacon; it is a grace

and mercy of God."

"Do you know that you made a great figure on Christmas Day at the head of your company of the chamber of accounts, Monsieur President?"

"Vice-President, Dom Claude. Alas! nothing more."

"How is your superb house in the Rue Saint-André des Arcs coming on? 'Tis a Louvre. I love greatly the apricot tree which is carved on the door, with this play of words: 'A L'ABRICOTIER–Sheltered from reefs.'"

"Alas! Master Claude, all that masonry costeth me dear. In proportion as the house is erected, I am ruined."

"Ho! have you not your revenues from the jail, and the bailiwick of the Palais, and the rents of all the houses, sheds, stalls, and booths of the enclosure? 'Tis a fine breast to suck."

"My castellany of Poissy has brought me in nothing this year."

"But your tolls of Triel, of Saint-James, of

Saint-Germain-en-Laye are always good."

"Six score livres, and not even Parisian livres at that."

"You have your office of counsellor to the king. That is fixed."

"Yes, brother Claude; but that accursed seigneury of Poligny, which people make so much noise about, is worth not sixty gold crowns, year out and year in."

In the compliments which Dom Claude addressed to Jacques Coictier, there was that sardonical, biting, and covertly mocking accent, and the sad cruel smile of a superior and unhappy man who toys for a moment, by way of distraction, with the dense prosperity of a vulgar man. The other did not perceive it.

"Upon my soul," said Claude at length, pressing his hand, "I am glad to see you and in such good health."

"Thanks, Master Claude."

"By the way," exclaimed Dom Claude, "how is your royal patient?"

"He payeth not sufficiently his physician," replied the doctor, casting a side glance at his companion.

"Think you so, Gossip Coictier," said the latter.

These words, uttered in a tone of surprise and reproach, drew upon this unknown personage the attention of the archdeacon which, to tell the truth, had not been diverted from him a single moment since the stranger had set foot across the threshold of his cell. It had even required all the thousand reasons which he had for handling tenderly Doctor Jacques Coictier, the all-powerful physician of King Louis XI., to induce him to receive the latter thus accompanied. Hence, there was nothing very cordial in his manner when Jacques Coictier said to him,–

"By the way, Dom Claude, I bring you a colleague who has desired to see you on account of your reputation."

"Monsieur belongs to science?" asked the

archdeacon, fixing his piercing eye upon Coictier's companion. He found beneath the brows of the stranger a glance no less piercing or less distrustful than his own.

He was, so far as the feeble light of the lamp permitted one to judge, an old man about sixty years of age and of medium stature, who appeared somewhat sickly and broken in health. His profile, although of a very ordinary outline, had something powerful and severe about it; his eyes sparkled beneath a very deep superciliary arch, like a light in the depths of a cave; and beneath his cap which was well drawn down and fell upon his nose, one recognized the broad expanse of a brow of genius.

He took it upon himself to reply to the archdeacon's question,–

"Reverend master," he said in a grave tone, "your renown has reached my ears, and I wish to consult you. I am but a poor provincial gentleman, who removeth his shoes before entering the dwellings of the learned. You must know my name. I am called Gossip Tourangeau."

"Strange name for a gentleman," said the archdeacon to himself.

Nevertheless, he had a feeling that he was in the presence of a strong and earnest character. The instinct of his own lofty intellect made him recognize an intellect no less lofty under Gossip Tourangeau's furred cap, and as he gazed at the solemn face, the ironical smile which Jacques Coictier's presence called forth on his gloomy face, gradually disappeared as twilight fades on the horizon of night. Stern and silent, he had resumed his seat in his great armchair; his elbow rested as usual, on the table, and his brow on his hand. After a few moments of reflection, he motioned his visitors to be seated, and, turning to Gossip Tourangeau he said,–

"You come to consult me, master, and upon what science?"

"Your reverence," replied Tourangeau,

"I am ill, very ill. You are said to be great Æsculapius, and I am come to ask your advice in medicine."

"Medicine!" said the archdeacon, tossing his head. He seemed to meditate for a moment, and then resumed: "Gossip Tourangeau, since that is your name, turn your head, you will find my reply already written on the wall."

Gossip Tourangeau obeyed, and read this inscription engraved above his head: "**Medicine is the daughter of dreams**.– JAMBLIQUE."

Meanwhile, Doctor Jacques Coictier had heard his companion's question with a displeasure which Dom Claude's response had but redoubled. He bent down to the ear of Gossip Tourangeau, and said to him, softly enough not to be heard by the archdeacon: "I warned you that he was mad. You insisted on seeing him."

"'Tis very possible that he is right, madman as he is, Doctor Jacques," replied his comrade in the same low tone, and with a bitter smile.

"As you please," replied Coictier dryly. Then, addressing the archdeacon: "You are clever at your trade, Dom Claude, and you are no more at a loss over Hippocrates than a monkey is over a nut. Medicine a dream! I suspect that the pharmacopolists and the master physicians would insist upon stoning you if they were here. So you deny the influence of philtres upon the blood, and unguents on the skin! You deny that eternal pharmacy of flowers and metals, which is called the world, made expressly for that eternal invalid called man!"

"I deny," said Dom Claude coldly, "neither pharmacy nor the invalid. I reject the physician."

"Then it is not true," resumed Coictier hotly, "that gout is an internal eruption; that a wound caused by artillery is to be cured by the application of a young mouse roasted; that young blood, properly injected, restores youth to aged veins; it is not true that two and two make four, and that emprostathonos follows opistathonos."

The archdeacon replied without perturbation: "There are certain things of which I think in a certain fashion."

Coictier became crimson with anger.

"There, there, my good Coictier, let us not get angry," said Gossip Tourangeau. "Monsieur the archdeacon is our friend."

Coictier calmed down, muttering in a low tone,–

"After all, he's mad."

"**Pasque-dieu**, Master Claude," resumed Gossip Tourangeau, after a silence, "You embarrass me greatly. I had two things to consult you upon, one touching my health and the other touching my star."

"Monsieur," returned the archdeacon, "if that be your motive, you would have done as well not to put yourself out of breath climbing my staircase. I do not believe in Medicine. I do not believe in Astrology."

"Indeed!" said the man, with surprise.

Coictier gave a forced laugh.

"You see that he is mad," he said, in a low tone, to Gossip Tourangeau. "He does not believe in astrology."

"The idea of imagining," pursued Dom Claude, "that every ray of a star is a thread which is fastened to the head of a man!"

"And what then, do you believe in?" exclaimed Gossip Tourangeau.

The archdeacon hesitated for a moment, then he allowed a gloomy smile to escape, which seemed to give the lie to his response: "**Credo in Deum**."

"**Dominum nostrum**," added Gossip Tourangeau, making the sign of the cross.

"Amen," said Coictier.

"Reverend master," resumed Tourangeau, "I am charmed in soul to see you in such a religious frame of mind. But have you reached the point, great savant as you are, of no longer believing in science?"

"No," said the archdeacon, grasping the arm of Gossip Tourangeau, and a ray of enthusiasm lighted up his gloomy eyes, “no, I do not reject science. I have not crawled so long, flat on my belly, with my nails in the earth, through the innumerable ramifications of its caverns, without perceiving far in front of me, at the end of the obscure gallery, a light, a flame, a something, the reflection, no doubt, of the dazzling central laboratory where the patient and the wise have found out God.”

“And in short,” interrupted Tourangeau, “what do you hold to be true and certain?”

“Alchemy.”

Coictier exclaimed, “Pardieu, Dom Claude, alchemy has its use, no doubt, but why blaspheme medicine and astrology?”

“Naught is your science of man, naught is your science of the stars,” said the archdeacon, commandingly.

“That’s driving Epidaurus and Chaldea very fast,” replied the physician with a grin.

“Listen, Messire Jacques. This is said in good faith. I am not the king’s physician, and his majesty has not given me the Garden of Dædalus in which to observe the constellations. Don't get angry, but listen to me. What truth have you deduced, I will not say from medicine, which is too foolish a thing, but from astrology? Cite to me the virtues of the vertical boustrophedon, the treasures of the number ziruph and those of the number zephirod!"

"Will you deny," said Coictier, "the sympathetic force of the collar bone, and the cabalistics which are derived from it?"

"An error, Messire Jacques! None of your formulas end in reality. Alchemy on the other hand has its discoveries. Will you contest results like this? Ice confined beneath the earth for a thousand years is transformed into rock crystals. Lead is the ancestor of all metals. For gold is not a metal, gold is light. Lead requires only four periods of two hundred years each, to pass in succession from the state of lead, to the state of red arsenic, from red arsenic to tin, from tin to silver. Are not these facts? But to believe in the collar bone, in the full line and in the stars, is as ridiculous as to believe with the inhabitants of Grand-Cathay that the golden oriole turns into a mole, and that grains of wheat turn into fish of the carp species."

"I have studied hermetic science!" exclaimed Coictier, "and I affirm–"

The fiery archdeacon did not allow him to finish: "And I have studied medicine, astrology, and hermetics. Here alone is the truth." (As he spoke thus, he took from the top of the coffer a phial filled with the powder which we have mentioned above), "here alone is light! Hippocrates is a dream; Urania is a dream; Hermes, a thought. Gold is the sun; to make gold is to be God. Herein lies the one and only science. I have sounded the depths of medicine and astrology, I tell you! Naught, nothingness! The human body, shadows! the planets, shadows!"

And he fell back in his armchair in a commanding and inspired attitude. Gossip

Touraugeau watched him in silence. Coictier tried to grin, shrugged his shoulders imperceptibly, and repeated in a low voice,–

"A madman!"

"And," said Tourangeau suddenly, "the wondrous result,–have you attained it, have you made gold?"

"If I had made it," replied the archdeacon, articulating his words slowly, like a man who is reflecting, "the king of France would be named Claude and not Louis."

The stranger frowned.

"What am I saying?" resumed Dom Claude, with a smile of disdain. "What would the throne of France be to me when I could rebuild the empire of the Orient?"

"Very good!" said the stranger.

"Oh, the poor fool!" murmured Coictier.

The archdeacon went on, appearing to reply now only to his thoughts,–

"But no, I am still crawling; I am scratching my face and knees against the pebbles of the subterranean pathway. I catch a glimpse,

I do not contemplate! I do not read, I spell out!"

"And when you know how to read!" demanded the stranger, "will you make gold?"

"Who doubts it?" said the archdeacon.

"In that case Our Lady knows that I am greatly in need of money, and I should much desire to read in your books. Tell me, reverend master, is your science inimical or displeasing to Our Lady?"

"Whose archdeacon I am?" Dom Claude contented himself with replying, with tranquil hauteur.

"That is true, my master. Well! will it please you to initiate me? Let me spell with you."

Claude assumed the majestic and pontifical attitude of a Samuel.

"Old man, it requires longer years than remain to you, to undertake this voyage across mysterious things. Your head is very gray! One comes forth from the cavern only with white hair, but only those with dark hair enter it. Science alone knows well how to hollow, wither, and dry up human faces; she needs not to have old age bring her faces already furrowed. Nevertheless, if the desire possesses you of putting yourself under discipline at your age, and of deciphering the formidable alphabet of the sages, come to me; 'tis well, I will make the effort. I will not tell you, poor old man, to go and visit the sepulchral chambers of the pyramids, of which ancient Herodotus speaks, nor the brick tower of Babylon, nor the immense white marble sanctuary of the Indian temple of Eklinga. I, no more than yourself, have seen the Chaldean masonry works constructed according to the sacred form of the Sikra, nor the temple of Solomon, which is destroyed, nor the stone doors of the sepulchre of the kings of Israel, which are broken. We will content ourselves with the fragments of the book of Hermes which we have here. I will explain to you the statue of Saint Christopher, the symbol of the sower, and that of the two angels which are on the front of the Sainte-Chapelle, and one of which holds in his hands a vase, the other, a cloud–"

Here Jacques Coictier, who had been unhorsed by the archdeacon's impetuous replies, regained his saddle, and interrupted him with the triumphant tone of one learned man correcting another,–"**Erras amice Claudi**. The symbol is not the number. You take Orpheus for Hermes."

"'Tis you who are in error," replied the archdeacon, gravely. "Dædalus is the base; Orpheus is the wall; Hermes is the edifice,–that is all. You shall come when you will," he continued, turning to Tourangeau, "I will show you the little parcels of gold which remained at the bottom of Nicholas Flamel's alembic, and you shall compare them with the gold of Guillaume de Paris. I will teach you the secret virtues of the Greek word, **peristera**. But, first of all, I will make you read, one after the other, the marble letters of the alphabet, the granite pages of the book. We shall go to the portal of Bishop Guillaume and of Saint-Jean le Rond at the Sainte-Chapelle, then to the house of Nicholas Flamel, Rue Manvault, to his tomb, which is at the Saints-Innocents, to his two hospitals, Rue de Montmorency. I will make you read the hieroglyphics which cover the four great iron cramps on the portal of the hospital Saint-Gervais, and of the Rue de la Ferronnerie. We will spell out in company, also, the façade of Saint-Côme, of Sainte-Geneviève-des-Ardents, of Saint Martin, of Saint-Jacques de la Boucherie–."

For a long time, Gossip Tourangeau, intelligent as was his glance, had appeared not to understand Dom Claude. He interrupted.

"**Pasque-dieu**! what are your books, then?"

"Here is one of them," said the archdeacon.

And opening the window of his cell he

pointed out with his finger the immense church of Notre-Dame, which, outlining against the starry sky the black silhouette of its two towers, its stone flanks, its monstrous haunches, seemed an enormous two-headed sphinx, seated in the middle of the city.

The archdeacon gazed at the gigantic edifice for some time in silence, then extending his right hand, with a sigh, towards the printed book which lay open on the table, and his left towards Notre-Dame, and turning a sad glance from the book to the church,–"Alas," he said, "this will kill that."

Coictier, who had eagerly approached the book, could not repress an exclamation. "Hé, but now, what is there so formidable in this: 'GLOSSA IN EPISTOLAS D. PAULI, **Norimbergæ, Antonius Koburger**, 1474.' This is not new. 'Tis a book of Pierre Lombard, the Master of Sentences. Is it because it is printed?"

"You have said it," replied Claude, who seemed absorbed in a profound meditation, and stood resting, his forefinger bent backward on the folio which had come from the famous press of Nuremberg. Then he added these mysterious words: "Alas! alas! small things come at the end of great things; a tooth triumphs over a mass. The Nile rat kills the crocodile, the swordfish kills the whale, the book will kill the edifice."

The curfew of the cloister sounded at the moment when Master Jacques was repeating to his companion in low tones, his eternal refrain, "**He is mad!**" To which his companion this time replied, "I believe that he is."

It was the hour when no stranger could remain in the cloister. The two visitors withdrew. "Master," said Gossip Tourangeau, as he took leave of the archdeacon, "I love wise men and great minds, and I hold you in singular esteem. Come to-morrow to the Palace des Tournelles, and inquire for the

Abbé de Sainte-Martin, of Tours."

The archdeacon returned to his chamber dumbfounded, comprehending at last who Gossip Tourangeau was, and recalling that passage of the register of Sainte-Martin, of Tours:–**Abbas beati Martini, SCILICET REX FRANCIÆ, est canonicus de consuetudine et habet parvam præbendam quam habet sanctus Venantius, et debet sedere in sede thesaurarii**.

It is asserted that after that epoch the archdeacon had frequent conferences with Louis XI., when his majesty came to Paris, and that Dom Claude's influence quite overshadowed that of Olivier le Daim and Jacques Coictier, who, as was his habit, rudely took the king to task on that account.

CHAPTER TWO

This will Kill That

OUR LADY READERS WILL pardon us if we pause for a moment to seek what could have been the thought concealed beneath those enigmatic words of the archdeacon: "This will kill that. The book will kill the edifice."

To our mind, this thought had two faces. In the first place, it was a priestly thought. It was the affright of the priest in the presence of a new agent, the printing press. It was the terror and dazzled amazement of the men of the sanctuary, in the presence of the luminous press of Gutenberg. It was the pulpit and the manuscript taking the alarm at the printed word: something similar to the stupor of a sparrow which should behold the angel Legion unfold his six million wings. It was the cry of the prophet who already hears emancipated humanity roaring and swarming; who beholds in the future, intelligence sapping faith, opinion dethroning belief, the world shaking off Rome. It was the prognostication of the philosopher who sees human thought, volatilized by the press, evaporating from the theocratic recipient. It was the terror of the soldier who examines the brazen battering ram, and says:–"The tower will crumble." It signified that one power was about to succeed another power. It meant, "The press will kill the church."

But underlying this thought, the first and most simple one, no doubt, there was in our opinion another, newer one, a corollary of the first, less easy to perceive and more easy to contest, a view as philosophical and belonging no longer to the priest alone but to the savant and the artist. It was a presentiment that human thought, in changing its form, was about to change its mode of expression; that the dominant idea of each generation would no longer be written with the same matter, and in the same manner; that the book of stone, so solid and so durable, was about to make way for the book of paper, more solid and still more durable. In this connection the archdeacon's vague formula had a second sense. It meant, "Printing will kill architecture."

In fact, from the origin of things down to the fifteenth century of the Christian era, inclusive, architecture is the great book of humanity, the principal expression of man in his different stages of development, either as a force or as an intelligence.

When the memory of the first races

felt itself overloaded, when the mass of reminiscences of the human race became so heavy and so confused that speech naked and flying, ran the risk of losing them on the way, men transcribed them on the soil in a manner which was at once the most visible, most durable, and most natural. They sealed each tradition beneath a monument.

The first monuments were simple masses of rock, “which the iron had not touched,” as Moses says. Architecture began like all writing. It was first an alphabet. Men planted a stone upright, it was a letter, and each letter was a hieroglyph, and upon each hieroglyph rested a group of ideas, like the capital on the column. This is what the earliest races did everywhere, at the same moment, on the surface of the entire world. We find the “standing stones” of the Celts in Asian Siberia; in the pampas of America.

Later on, they made words; they placed stone

upon stone, they coupled those syllables of granite, and attempted some combinations. The Celtic dolmen and cromlech, the Etruscan tumulus, the Hebrew galgal, are words. Some, especially the tumulus, are proper names. Sometimes even, when men had a great deal of stone, and a vast plain, they wrote a phrase. The immense pile of Karnac is a complete sentence.

At last they made books. Traditions had brought forth symbols, beneath which they disappeared like the trunk of a tree beneath its foliage; all these symbols in which humanity placed faith continued to grow, to multiply, to intersect, to become more and more complicated; the first monuments no longer sufficed to contain them, they were overflowing in every part; these monuments hardly expressed now the primitive tradition, simple like themselves, naked and prone upon the earth. The symbol felt the need of expansion in the edifice. Then architecture was developed in proportion with human thought; it became a giant with a thousand heads and a thousand arms, and fixed all this floating symbolism in an eternal, visible, palpable form. While Dædalus, who is force, measured; while Orpheus, who is intelligence, sang;–the pillar, which is a letter; the arcade, which is a syllable; the pyramid, which is a word,–all set in movement at once by a law of geometry and by a law of poetry, grouped themselves, combined, amalgamated, descended, ascended, placed themselves side by side on the soil, ranged themselves in stories in the sky, until they had written under the dictation of the general idea of an epoch, those marvellous books which were also marvellous edifices: the Pagoda of Eklinga, the Rhamseion of Egypt, the Temple of Solomon.

The generating idea, the word, was not only at the foundation of all these edifices, but also in the form. The temple of Solomon, for example, was not alone the binding of the holy book; it was the holy book itself. On each one of its concentric walls, the priests could read the word translated and manifested to the eye, and thus they followed its transformations from sanctuary to sanctuary, until they seized it in its last tabernacle, under its most concrete form, which still belonged to architecture: the arch. Thus the word was enclosed in an edifice, but its image was upon its envelope, like the human form on the coffin of a mummy.

And not only the form of edifices, but the sites selected for them, revealed the thought which they represented, according as the symbol to be expressed was graceful or grave. Greece crowned her mountains with a temple harmonious to the eye; India disembowelled hers, to chisel therein those monstrous subterranean pagodas, borne up by gigantic rows of granite elephants.

Thus, during the first six thousand years of the world, from the most immemorial pagoda of Hindustan, to the cathedral of Cologne, architecture was the great handwriting of the human race. And this is so true, that not only every religious symbol, but every human thought, has its page and its monument in that immense book.

All civilization begins in theocracy and ends in democracy. This law of liberty following unity is written in architecture. For, let us insist upon this point, masonry must not be thought to be powerful only in erecting the temple and in expressing the myth and sacerdotal symbolism; in inscribing in hieroglyphs upon its pages of stone the mysterious tables of the law. If it were thus,–as there comes in all human society a moment when the sacred symbol is worn out and becomes obliterated under freedom of thought, when man escapes from the priest, when the excrescence of philosophies and systems devour the face of religion,–architecture could not reproduce this new state of human thought; its leaves, so crowded on the face, would be empty on the back; its work would be mutilated; its book would be incomplete. But no.

Let us take as an example the Middle Ages, where we see more clearly because it is nearer to us. During its first period, while theocracy is organizing Europe, while the Vatican is rallying and reclassing about itself the elements of a Rome made from the Rome which lies in ruins around the Capitol, while Christianity is seeking all the stages of society amid the rubbish of anterior civilization, and rebuilding with its ruins a new hierarchic universe, the keystone to whose vault is the priest–one first hears a dull echo from that chaos, and then, little by little, one sees, arising from beneath the breath of Christianity, from beneath the hand of the barbarians, from the fragments of the dead Greek and Roman architectures, that mysterious Romanesque architecture, sister of the theocratic masonry of Egypt and of India, inalterable emblem of pure catholicism, unchangeable hieroglyph of the papal unity. All the thought of that day is written, in fact, in this sombre, Romanesque style. One feels everywhere in it authority, unity, the impenetrable, the absolute, Gregory VII.; always the priest, never the man; everywhere caste, never the people.

But the Crusades arrive. They are a great popular movement, and every great popular movement, whatever may be its cause and object, always sets free the spirit of liberty from its final precipitate. New things spring into life every day. Here opens the stormy period of the Jacqueries, Pragueries, and Leagues. Authority wavers, unity is divided. Feudalism demands to share with theocracy, while awaiting the inevitable arrival of the people, who will assume the part of the lion: **Quia nominor leo**. Seignory pierces through sacerdotalism; the commonality, through seignory. The face of Europe is changed. Well! the face of architecture is changed also. Like civilization, it has turned a page, and the new spirit of the time finds her ready to write at its dictation. It returns from the crusades with the pointed arch, like the nations with liberty.

Then, while Rome is undergoing gradual dismemberment, Romanesque architecture dies. The hieroglyph deserts the cathedral, and betakes itself to blazoning the donjon keep, in order to lend prestige to feudalism. The cathedral itself, that edifice formerly so dogmatic, invaded henceforth by the **bourgeoisie**, by the community, by liberty, escapes the priest and falls into the power of the artist. The artist builds it after his own fashion. Farewell to mystery, myth, law. Fancy and caprice, welcome. Provided the priest has his basilica and his altar, he has nothing to say. The four walls belong to the artist. The architectural book belongs no longer to the priest, to religion, to Rome; it is the property of poetry, of imagination, of the people. Hence the rapid and innumerable transformations of that architecture which owns but three centuries, so striking after the stagnant immobility of the Romanesque architecture, which owns six or seven. Nevertheless, art marches on with giant strides. Popular genius amid originality accomplish the task which the bishops formerly fulfilled. Each race writes its line upon the book, as it passes; it erases the ancient Romanesque hieroglyphs on the frontispieces of cathedrals, and at the most one only sees dogma cropping out here and there, beneath the new symbol which it has deposited. The popular drapery hardly permits the religious skeleton to be suspected. One cannot even form an idea of the liberties which the architects then take, even toward the Church. There are capitals knitted of nuns and monks, shamelessly coupled, as on the hall of chimney pieces in the Palais de Justice, in Paris. There is Noah's adventure carved to the last detail, as under the great portal of Bourges. There is a bacchanalian monk, with ass's ears and glass in hand, laughing in the face of a whole community, as on the lavatory of the Abbey of Bocherville. There exists at that epoch, for thought written in stone, a privilege exactly comparable to our present liberty of the press. It is the liberty of architecture.

This liberty goes very far. Sometimes a portal, a façade, an entire church, presents a symbolical sense absolutely foreign to worship, or even hostile to the Church. In the thirteenth century, Guillaume de Paris, and Nicholas Flamel, in the fifteenth, wrote such seditious pages. Saint-Jacques de la Boucherie was a whole church of the opposition.

Thought was then free only in this manner; hence it never wrote itself out completely except on the books called edifices. Thought, under the form of edifice, could have beheld itself burned in the public square by the hands of the executioner, in its manuscript form, if it had been sufficiently imprudent to risk itself thus; thought, as the door of a church, would have been a spectator of the punishment of thought as a book. Having thus only this resource, masonry, in order to make its way to the light, flung itself upon it from all quarters. Hence the immense quantity of cathedrals which have covered Europe–a number so prodigious that one can hardly believe it even after having verified it. All the material forces, all the intellectual forces of society converged towards the same point: architecture. In this manner, under the pretext of building churches to God, art was developed in its magnificent proportions.

Then whoever was born a poet became an architect. Genius, scattered in the masses, repressed in every quarter under feudalism as under a **testudo** of brazen bucklers, finding no issue except in the direction of architecture,–gushed forth through that art, and its Iliads assumed the form of cathedrals. All other arts obeyed, and placed themselves under the discipline of architecture. They were the workmen of the great work. The architect, the poet, the master, summed up in his person the sculpture which carved his façades, painting which illuminated his windows, music which set his bells to pealing, and breathed into his organs. There was nothing down to poor poetry,–properly speaking, that which persisted in vegetating in manuscripts,–which was not forced, in order to make something of itself, to come and frame itself in the edifice in the shape of a hymn or of prose; the same part, after all, which the tragedies of Æschylus had played in the sacerdotal festivals of Greece; Genesis, in the temple of Solomon.

Thus, down to the time of Gutenberg, architecture is the principal writing, the universal writing. In that granite book, begun by the Orient, continued by Greek and Roman antiquity, the Middle Ages wrote the last page. Moreover, this phenomenon of an architecture of the people following an architecture of caste, which we have just been observing in the Middle Ages, is reproduced with every analogous movement in the human intelligence at the other great epochs of history. Thus, in order to enunciate here only summarily, a law which it would require volumes to develop: in the high Orient, the cradle of primitive times, after Hindoo architecture came Phœnician architecture, that opulent mother of Arabian architecture; in antiquity, after Egyptian architecture, of which Etruscan style and cyclopean monuments are but one variety, came Greek architecture (of which the Roman style is only a continuation), surcharged with the Carthaginian dome; in modern times, after Romanesque architecture came Gothic architecture. And by separating there three series into their component parts, we shall find in the three eldest sisters, Hindoo architecture, Egyptian architecture, Romanesque architecture, the same symbol; that is to say, theocracy, caste, unity, dogma, myth, God: and for the three younger sisters, Phœnician architecture, Greek architecture, Gothic architecture, whatever, nevertheless, may be the diversity of form inherent in their nature, the same signification also; that is to say, liberty, the people, man.

In the Hindu, Egyptian, or Romanesque architecture, one feels the priest, nothing but the priest, whether he calls himself Brahmin, Magian, or Pope. It is not the same in the architectures of the people. They are richer and less sacred. In the Phœnician, one feels the merchant; in the Greek, the republican; in the Gothic, the citizen.

The general characteristics of all theocratic architecture are immutability, horror of progress, the preservation of traditional lines, the consecration of the primitive types, the constant bending of all the forms of men and of nature to the incomprehensible caprices of the symbol. These are dark books, which the initiated alone understand how to decipher. Moreover, every form, every deformity even, has there a sense which renders it inviolable. Do not ask of Hindoo, Egyptian, Romanesque masonry to reform their design, or to improve their statuary. Every attempt at perfecting is an impiety to them. In these architectures it seems as though the rigidity of the dogma had spread over the stone like a sort of second petrifaction. The general characteristics of popular masonry, on the contrary, are progress, originality, opulence, perpetual movement. They are already sufficiently detached from religion to think of their beauty, to take care of it, to correct without relaxation their parure of statues or arabesques. They are of the age. They have something human, which they mingle incessantly with the divine symbol under which they still produce. Hence, edifices comprehensible to every soul, to every intelligence, to every imagination, symbolical still, but as easy to understand as nature. Between theocratic architecture and this there is the difference that lies between a sacred language and a vulgar language, between hieroglyphics and art, between Solomon and Phidias.

If the reader will sum up what we have hitherto briefly, very briefly, indicated, neglecting a thousand proofs and also a thousand objections of detail, he will be led to this: that architecture was, down to the fifteenth century, the chief register of humanity; that in that interval not a thought which is in any degree complicated made its appearance in the world, which has not been worked into an edifice; that every popular idea, and every religious law, has had its monumental records; that the human race has, in short, had no important thought which it has not written in stone. And why? Because every thought, either philosophical or religious, is interested in perpetuating itself; because the idea which has moved one generation wishes to move others also, and leave a trace. Now, what a precarious immortality is that of the manuscript! How much more solid, durable, unyielding, is a book of stone! In order to destroy the written word, a torch and a Turk are sufficient. To demolish the constructed word, a social revolution, a terrestrial revolution are required. The barbarians passed over the Coliseum; the deluge, perhaps, passed over the Pyramids.

In the fifteenth century everything changes.

Human thought discovers a mode of perpetuating itself, not only more durable and more resisting than architecture, but still more simple and easy. Architecture is dethroned. Gutenberg's letters of lead are about to supersede Orpheus's letters of stone.

The book is about to kill the edifice.

The invention of printing is the greatest event in history. It is the mother of revolution. It is the mode of expression of humanity which is totally renewed; it is human thought stripping off one form and donning another; it is the complete and definitive change of skin of that symbolical serpent which since the days of Adam has represented intelligence.

In its printed form, thought is more imperishable than ever; it is volatile, irresistible, indestructible. It is mingled with the air. In the days of architecture it made a mountain of itself, and took powerful possession of a century and a place. Now it converts itself into a flock of birds, scatters itself to the four winds, and occupies all points of air and space at once.

We repeat, who does not perceive that in this form it is far more indelible? It was solid, it has become alive. It passes from duration in time to immortality. One can demolish a mass; how can one extirpate ubiquity? If a flood comes, the mountains will have long disappeared beneath the waves, while the birds will still be flying about; and if a single ark floats on the surface of the cataclysm, they will alight upon it, will float with it, will be present with it at the ebbing of the waters; and the new world which emerges from this chaos will behold, on its awakening, the thought of the world which has been submerged soaring above it, winged and living.

And when one observes that this mode of expression is not only the most conservative, but also the most simple, the most convenient, the most practicable for all; when one reflects that it does not drag after it bulky baggage, and does not set in motion a heavy apparatus; when one compares thought forced, in order to transform itself into an edifice, to put in motion four or five other arts and tons of gold, a whole mountain of stones, a whole forest of timber-work, a whole nation of workmen; when one compares it to the thought which becomes a book, and for which a little paper, a little ink, and a pen suffice,–how can one be surprised that human intelligence should have quitted architecture for printing? Cut the primitive bed of a river abruptly with a canal hollowed out below its level, and the river will desert its bed.

Behold how, beginning with the discovery of printing, architecture withers away little by little, becomes lifeless and bare. How one feels the water sinking, the sap departing, the thought of the times and of the people withdrawing from it! The chill is almost imperceptible in the fifteenth century; the press is, as yet, too weak, and, at the most, draws from powerful architecture a superabundance of life. But practically beginning with the sixteenth century, the malady of architecture is visible; it is no longer the expression of society; it becomes classic art in a miserable manner; from being Gallic, European, indigenous, it becomes Greek and Roman; from being true and modern, it becomes pseudo-classic. It is this decadence which is called the Renaissance. A magnificent decadence, however, for the ancient Gothic genius, that sun which sets behind the gigantic press of

Mayence, still penetrates for a while longer with its rays that whole hybrid pile of Latin arcades and Corinthian columns.

It is that setting sun which we mistake for the dawn.

Nevertheless, from the moment when architecture is no longer anything but an art like any other; as soon as it is no longer the total art, the sovereign art, the tyrant art,–it has no longer the power to retain the other arts. So they emancipate themselves, break the yoke of the architect, and take themselves off, each one in its own direction. Each one of them gains by this divorce. Isolation aggrandizes everything. Sculpture becomes statuary, the image trade becomes painting, the canon becomes music. One would pronounce it an empire dismembered at the death of its Alexander, and whose provinces become kingdoms.

Hence Raphael, Michael Angelo, Jean Goujon, Palestrina, those splendors of the dazzling sixteenth century.

Thought emancipates itself in all directions at the same time as the arts. The arch-heretics of the Middle Ages had already made large incisions into Catholicism. The sixteenth century breaks religious unity. Before the invention of printing, reform would have been merely a schism; printing converted it into a revolution. Take away the press; heresy is enervated. Whether it be Providence or Fate, Gutenburg is the precursor of Luther.

Nevertheless, when the sun of the Middle Ages is completely set, when the Gothic genius is forever extinct upon the horizon, architecture grows dim, loses its color, becomes more and more effaced. The printed book, the gnawing worm of the edifice, sucks and devours it. It becomes bare, denuded of its foliage, and grows visibly emaciated. It is petty, it is poor, it is nothing. It no longer expresses anything, not even the memory of the art of another time.

Reduced to itself, abandoned by the other arts, because human thought is abandoning it, it summons bunglers in place of artists. Glass replaces the painted windows. The stone-cutter succeeds the sculptor. Farewell all sap, all originality, all life, all intelligence. It drags along, a lamentable workshop mendicant, from copy to copy. Michael Angelo, who, no doubt, felt even in the sixteenth century that it was dying, had a last idea, an idea of despair. That Titan of art piled the Pantheon on the Parthenon, and made Saint-Peter's at Rome. A great work, which deserved to remain unique, the last originality of architecture, the signature of a giant artist at the bottom of the colossal register of stone which was closed forever. With Michael Angelo dead, what does this miserable architecture, which survived itself in the state of a spectre, do? It takes Saint-Peter in Rome, copies it and parodies it. It is a mania. It is a pity. Each century has its Saint-Peter's of Rome; in the seventeenth century, the Val-de-Grâce; in the eighteenth, Sainte-Geneviève. Each country has its Saint-Peter's of Rome. London has one; Petersburg has another; Paris has two or three. The insignificant testament, the last dotage of a decrepit grand art falling back into infancy before it dies.

If, in place of the characteristic monuments which we have just described, we examine the general aspect of art from the sixteenth to the eighteenth century, we notice the same phenomena of decay and phthisis. Beginning with François II., the architectural form of the edifice effaces itself more and more, and allows the geometrical form, like the bony structure of an emaciated invalid, to become prominent. The fine lines of art give way to the cold and inexorable lines of geometry. An edifice is no longer an edifice; it is a polyhedron. Meanwhile, architecture is tormented in her struggles to conceal this nudity. Look at the Greek pediment inscribed upon the Roman pediment, and vice versâ. It is still the Pantheon on the Parthenon: Saint-Peter's of Rome. Here are the brick houses of Henri IV., with their stone corners; the Place Royale, the Place Dauphine. Here are the churches of Louis XIII., heavy, squat, thickset, crowded together, loaded with a dome like a hump. Here is the Mazarin architecture, the wretched Italian pasticcio of the Four Nations. Here are the palaces of Louis XIV., long barracks for courtiers, stiff, cold, tiresome. Here, finally, is Louis XV., with chiccory leaves and vermicelli, and all the warts, and all the fungi, which disfigure that decrepit, toothless, and coquettish old architecture. From François II. to Louis XV., the evil has increased in geometrical progression. Art has no longer anything but skin upon its bones. It is miserably perishing.

Meanwhile what becomes of printing? All the life which is leaving architecture comes to it. In proportion as architecture ebbs, printing swells and grows. That capital of forces which human thought had been expending in edifices, it henceforth expends in books. Thus, from the sixteenth century onward, the press, raised to the level of decaying architecture, contends with it and kills it. In the seventeenth century it is already sufficiently the sovereign, sufficiently triumphant, sufficiently established in its victory, to give to the world the feast of a great literary century. In the eighteenth, having reposed for a long time at the Court of Louis XIV., it seizes again the old sword of Luther, puts it into the hand of Voltaire, and rushes impetuously to the attack of that ancient Europe, whose architectural expression it has already killed. At the moment when the eighteenth century comes to an end, it has destroyed everything. In the nineteenth, it begins to reconstruct.

Now, we ask, which of the three arts has really represented human thought for the last three centuries? which translates it? which expresses not only its literary and scholastic vagaries, but its vast, profound, universal movement? which constantly superposes itself, without a break, without a gap, upon the human race, which walks a monster with a thousand legs?–Architecture or printing?

It is printing. Let the reader make no mistake; architecture is dead; irretrievably slain by the printed book,–slain because it endures for a shorter time,–slain because it costs more. Every cathedral represents millions. Let the reader now imagine what an investment of funds it would require to rewrite the architectural book; to cause thousands of edifices to swarm once more upon the soil; to return to those epochs when the throng of monuments was such, according to the statement of an eye witness, "that one would have said that the world in shaking itself, had cast off its old garments in order to cover itself with a white vesture of churches." **Erat enim ut si mundus, ipse excutiendo semet, rejecta vetustate, candidam**

ecclesiarum vestem indueret. (GLABER RADOLPHUS.)

A book is so soon made, costs so little, and can go so far! How can it surprise us that all human thought flows in this channel? This does not mean that architecture will not still have a fine monument, an isolated masterpiece, here and there. We may still have from time to time, under the reign of printing, a column made I suppose, by a whole army from melted cannon, as we had under the reign of architecture, Iliads and Romanceros, Mahabâhrata, and Nibelungen Lieds, made by a whole people, with rhapsodies piled up and melted together. The great accident of an architect of genius may happen in the twentieth century, like that of Dante in the thirteenth. But architecture will no longer be the social art, the collective art, the dominating art. The grand poem, the grand edifice, the grand work of humanity will no longer be built: it will be printed.

And henceforth, if architecture should arise again accidentally, it will no longer be mistress. It will be subservient to the law of literature, which formerly received the law from it. The respective positions of the two arts will be inverted. It is certain that in architectural epochs, the poems, rare it is true, resemble the monuments. In India, Vyasa is branching, strange, impenetrable as a pagoda. In Egyptian Orient, poetry has like the edifices, grandeur and tranquillity of line; in antique Greece, beauty, serenity, calm; in Christian Europe, the Catholic majesty, the popular naïvete, the rich and luxuriant vegetation of an epoch of renewal. The Bible resembles the Pyramids; the Iliad, the Parthenon; Homer, Phidias. Dante in the thirteenth century is the last Romanesque church; Shakespeare in the sixteenth, the last Gothic cathedral.

Thus, to sum up what we have hitherto said, in a fashion which is necessarily incomplete and mutilated, the human race has two books, two registers, two testaments: masonry and printing; the Bible of stone and the Bible of paper. No doubt, when one contemplates these two Bibles, laid so broadly open in the centuries, it is permissible to regret the visible majesty of the writing of granite, those gigantic alphabets formulated in colonnades, in pylons, in obelisks, those sorts of human mountains which cover the world and the past, from the pyramid to the bell tower, from Cheops to Strasbourg. The past must be reread upon these pages of marble. This book, written by architecture, must be admired and perused incessantly; but the grandeur of the edifice which printing erects in its turn must not be denied.

That edifice is colossal. Some compiler of statistics has calculated, that if all the volumes which have issued from the press since Gutenberg's day were to be piled one upon another, they would fill the space between the earth and the moon; but it is not that sort of grandeur of which we wished to speak.

Nevertheless, when one tries to collect in one's mind a comprehensive image of the total products of printing down to our own days, does not that total appear to us like an immense construction, resting upon the entire world, at which humanity toils without relaxation, and whose monstrous crest is lost in the profound mists of the future? It is the anthill of intelligence. It is the hive whither come all imaginations, those golden bees, with their honey.

The edifice has a thousand stories. Here and there one beholds on its staircases the gloomy caverns of science which pierce its interior. Everywhere upon its surface, art causes its arabesques, rosettes, and laces to thrive luxuriantly before the eyes. There, every individual work, however capricious and isolated it may seem, has its place and its projection. Harmony results from the whole. From the cathedral of Shakespeare to the mosque of Byron, a thousand tiny bell towers are piled pell-mell above this metropolis of universal thought. At its base are written some ancient titles of humanity which architecture had not registered. To the left of the entrance has been fixed the ancient bas-relief, in white marble, of Homer; to the right, the polyglot Bible rears its seven heads. The hydra of the Romancero and some other hybrid forms, the Vedas and the Nibelungen bristle further on.

Nevertheless, the prodigious edifice still remains incomplete. The press, that giant machine, which incessantly pumps all the intellectual sap of society, belches forth without pause fresh materials for its work. The whole human race is on the scaffoldings. Each mind is a mason. The humblest fills his hole, or places his stone. Rétif de La Bretonne brings his hod of plaster. Every day a new course rises. Independently of the original and individual contribution of each writer, there are collective contingents. The eighteenth century gives the **Encyclopedia**, the revolution gives the **Moniteur**. Assuredly, it is a construction which increases and piles up in endless spirals; there also are confusion of tongues, incessant activity, indefatigable labor, eager competition of all humanity, refuge promised to intelligence, a new Flood against an overflow of barbarians. It is the second tower of Babel of the human race.

VOLUME ONE

BOOK SIXTH

CHAPTER ONE

An Impartial Glance at the Ancient Magistracy

A VERY HAPPY PERSONAGE in the year of grace 1482, was the noble gentleman Robert d'Estouteville, chevalier, Sieur de Beyne, Baron d'Ivry and Saint Andry en la Marche, counsellor and chamberlain to the king, and guard of the provostship of Paris. It was already nearly seventeen years since he had received from the king, on November 7, 1465, the comet year,[27] that fine charge of the provostship of Paris, which was reputed rather a seigneury than an office. **Dignitas**, says Joannes Lœmnœus, **quæ cum non exigua potestate politiam concernente, atque prærogativis multis et juribus conjuncta est**. A marvellous thing in '82 was a gentleman bearing the king's commission, and whose letters of institution ran back to the epoch of the marriage of the natural daughter of Louis XI. with Monsieur the Bastard of Bourbon.

The same day on which Robert d'Estouteville took the place of Jacques de Villiers in the provostship of Paris, Master Jehan Dauvet replaced Messire Helye de Thorrettes in the first presidency of the

27 This comet against which Pope Calixtus, uncle of Borgia, ordered public prayers, is the same which reappeared in 1835.

Court of Parliament, Jehan Jouvenel des Ursins supplanted Pierre de Morvilliers in the office of chancellor of France, Regnault des Dormans ousted Pierre Puy from the charge of master of requests in ordinary of the king's household. Now, upon how many heads had the presidency, the chancellorship, the mastership passed since Robert d'Estouteville had held the provostship of Paris. It had been "granted to him for safekeeping," as the letters patent said; and certainly he kept it well. He had clung to it, he had incorporated himself with it, he had so identified himself with it that he had escaped that fury for change which possessed Louis XI., a tormenting and industrious king, whose policy it was to maintain the elasticity of his power by frequent appointments and revocations. More than this; the brave chevalier had obtained the reversion of the office for his son, and for two years already, the name of the noble man Jacques d'Estouteville, equerry, had figured beside his at the head of the register of the salary list of the provostship of Paris. A rare and notable favor indeed! It is true that Robert d'Estouteville was a good soldier, that he had loyally raised his pennon against "the league of public good," and that he had presented to the queen a very marvellous stag in confectionery on the day of her entrance to Paris in 14.... Moreover, he possessed the good friendship of Messire Tristan l'Hermite, provost of the marshals of the king's household. Hence a very sweet and pleasant existence was that of Messire Robert. In the first place, very good wages, to which were attached, and from which hung, like extra bunches of grapes on his vine, the revenues of the civil and criminal registries of the provostship, plus the civil and criminal revenues of the tribunals of Embas of the Châtelet, without reckoning some little toll from the bridges of Mantes and of Corbeil, and the profits on the craft of Shagreen-makers of Paris, on the corders of firewood and the measurers of salt. Add to this the pleasure of displaying himself in rides about the city, and of making his fine military costume, which you may still admire sculptured on his tomb in the abbey of Valmont in Normandy, and his morion, all embossed at Montlhéry, stand out a contrast against the parti-colored red and tawny robes of the aldermen and police. And then, was it nothing to wield absolute supremacy over the sergeants of the police, the porter and watch of the Châtelet, the two auditors of the Châtelet, **auditores castelleti**, the sixteen commissioners of the sixteen quarters, the jailer of the Châtelet, the four enfeoffed sergeants, the hundred and twenty mounted sergeants, with maces, the chevalier of the watch with his watch, his sub-watch, his counter-watch and his rear-watch? Was it nothing to exercise high and low justice, the right to interrogate, to hang and to draw, without reckoning petty jurisdiction in the first resort (**in prima instantia**, as the charters say), on that viscomty of Paris, so nobly appanaged with seven noble bailiwicks? Can anything sweeter be imagined than rendering judgments and decisions, as Messire Robert d'Estouteville daily did in the Grand Châtelet, under the large and flattened arches of Philip Augustus? and going, as he was wont to do every evening, to that charming house situated in the Rue Galilée, in the enclosure of the royal palace, which he held in right of his wife, Madame Ambroise de Loré, to repose after the fatigue of having sent some poor wretch to pass the night in "that little cell of the Rue de Escorcherie, which the provosts and aldermen of Paris used to make their prison; the same being eleven feet long, seven feet and four inches wide, and eleven feet high?"[28]

And not only had Messire Robert

---

28 Comptes du domaine, 1383.

d'Estouteville his special court as provost and vicomte of Paris; but in addition he had a share, both for eye and tooth, in the grand court of the king. There was no head in the least elevated which had not passed through his hands before it came to the headsman. It was he who went to seek M. de Nemours at the Bastille Saint Antoine, in order to conduct him to the Halles; and to conduct to the Grève M. de Saint-Pol, who clamored and resisted, to the great joy of the provost, who did not love monsieur the constable.

Here, assuredly, is more than sufficient to render a life happy and illustrious, and to deserve some day a notable page in that interesting history of the provosts of Paris, where one learns that Oudard de Villeneuve had a house in the Rue des Boucheries, that Guillaume de Hangest purchased the great and the little Savoy, that Guillaume Thiboust gave the nuns of Sainte-Geneviève his houses in the Rue

Clopin, that Hugues Aubriot lived in the Hôtel du Porc-Épic, and other domestic facts.

Nevertheless, with so many reasons for taking life patiently and joyously, Messire Robert d'Estouteville woke up on the morning of the seventh of January, 1482, in a very surly and peevish mood. Whence came this ill temper? He could not have told himself. Was it because the sky was gray? or was the buckle of his old belt of Montlhéry badly fastened, so that it confined his provostal portliness too closely? had he beheld ribald fellows, marching in bands of four, beneath his window, and setting him at defiance, in doublets but no shirts, hats without crowns, with wallet and bottle at their side? Was it a vague presentiment of the three hundred and seventy livres, sixteen sous, eight farthings, which the future King Charles VII. was to cut off from the provostship in the following year? The reader can take his choice; we, for our part, are much inclined to believe that he was in a bad humor, simply because he was in a bad humor.

Moreover, it was the day after a festival, a tiresome day for every one, and above all for the magistrate who is charged with sweeping away all the filth, properly and figuratively speaking, which a festival day produces in Paris. And then he had to hold a sitting at the Grand Châtelet. Now, we have noticed that judges in general so arrange matters that their day of audience shall also be their day of bad humor, so that they may always have some one upon whom to vent it conveniently, in the name of the king, law, and justice.

However, the audience had begun without him. His lieutenants, civil, criminal, and private, were doing his work, according to usage; and from eight o'clock in the morning, some scores of **bourgeois** and **bourgeoises**, heaped and crowded into an obscure corner of the audience chamber of

Embas du Châtelet, between a stout oaken barrier and the wall, had been gazing blissfully at the varied and cheerful spectacle of civil and criminal justice dispensed by Master Florian Barbedienne, auditor of the Châtelet, lieutenant of monsieur the provost, in a somewhat confused and utterly haphazard manner.

The hall was small, low, vaulted. A table studded with fleurs-de-lis stood at one end, with a large arm-chair of carved oak, which belonged to the provost and was empty, and a stool on the left for the auditor, Master Florian. Below sat the clerk of the court, scribbling; opposite was the populace; and in front of the door, and in front of the table were many sergeants of the provostship in sleeveless jackets of violet camlet, with white crosses. Two sergeants of the Parloir-aux-Bourgeois, clothed in their jackets of Toussaint, half red, half blue, were posted as sentinels before a low, closed door, which was visible at the extremity of the hall, behind the table. A single pointed window, narrowly encased in the thick wall, illuminated with a pale ray of January sun two grotesque figures,–the capricious demon of stone carved as a tail-piece in the keystone of the vaulted ceiling, and the judge seated at the end of the hall on the fleurs-de-lis.

Imagine, in fact, at the provost's table, leaning upon his elbows between two bundles of documents of cases, with his foot on the train of his robe of plain brown cloth, his face buried in his hood of white lamb's skin, of which his brows seemed to be of a piece, red, crabbed, winking, bearing majestically the load of fat on his cheeks which met under his chin, Master Florian Barbedienne, auditor of the Châtelet.

Now, the auditor was deaf. A slight defect in an auditor. Master Florian delivered judgment, none the less, without appeal and very suitably. It is certainly quite sufficient for a judge to have the air of listening; and the venerable auditor fulfilled this condition, the sole one in justice, all the better because his attention could not be distracted by any noise.

Moreover, he had in the audience, a pitiless censor of his deeds and gestures, in the person of our friend Jehan Frollo du Moulin, that little student of yesterday, that "stroller," whom one was sure of encountering all over Paris, anywhere except before the rostrums of the professors.

"Stay," he said in a low tone to his companion, Robin Poussepain, who was grinning at his side, while he was making his comments on the scenes which were being unfolded before his eyes, "yonder is Jehanneton du Buisson. The beautiful daughter of the lazy dog at the Marché-Neuf!–Upon my soul, he is condemning her, the old rascal! he has no more eyes than ears. Fifteen sous, four farthings, parisian, for having worn two rosaries! 'Tis somewhat dear. **Lex duri carminis**. Who's that? Robin Chief-de-Ville, hauberkmaker. For having been passed and received master of the said trade! That's his entrance money. He! two gentlemen among these knaves! Aiglet de Soins, Hutin de Mailly Two equerries, **Corpus Christi!** Ah! they have been playing at dice. When shall I see our rector here? A hundred livres parisian, fine to the king! That Barbedienne strikes like a deaf man,–as he is! I'll be my brother the archdeacon, if that keeps me from gaming; gaming by day, gaming by night, living at play, dying at play, and gaming away my soul after my shirt. Holy Virgin, what damsels! One after the other my lambs. Ambroise Lécuyère, Isabeau la Paynette, Bérarde Gironin! I know them all, by Heavens! A fine! a fine! That's what will teach you to wear gilded girdles! ten sous parisis! you coquettes! Oh! the old snout of a judge! deaf and imbecile! Oh! Florian the dolt! Oh! Barbedienne the blockhead! There he is at the table! He's eating the plaintiff, he's eating the suits, he eats, he chews, he crams, he fills himself. Fines, lost goods, taxes, expenses, loyal charges, salaries, damages, and interests, gehenna, prison, and jail, and fetters with expenses are Christmas spice cake and marchpanes of Saint-John to him! Look at him, the pig!–Come! Good! Another amorous woman! Thibaud-la-Thibaude, neither more nor less! For having come from the Rue Glatigny! What fellow is this? Gieffroy Mabonne, gendarme bearing the crossbow. He has cursed the name of the Father. A fine for la Thibaude! A fine for Gieffroy! A fine for them both! The deaf old fool! he must have mixed up the two cases! Ten to one that he makes the wench pay for the oath and the gendarme for the amour! Attention, Robin Poussepain! What are they going to bring in? Here are many sergeants! By Jupiter! all the bloodhounds of the pack are there. It must be the great beast of the hunt–a wild boar. And 'tis one, Robin, 'tis one. And a fine one too! **Hercle!**

’tis our prince of yesterday, our Pope of the Fools, our bellringer, our one-eyed man, our hunchback, our grimace! ’Tis Quasimodo!”

It was he indeed.

It was Quasimodo, bound, encircled, roped, pinioned, and under good guard. The squad of policemen who surrounded him was assisted by the chevalier of the watch in person, wearing the arms of France embroidered on his breast, and the arms of the city on his back. There was nothing, however, about Quasimodo, except his deformity, which could justify the display of halberds and arquebuses; he was gloomy, silent, and tranquil. Only now and then did his single eye cast a sly and wrathful glance upon the bonds with which he was loaded.

He cast the same glance about him, but it was so dull and sleepy that the women only pointed him out to each other in derision.

Meanwhile Master Florian, the auditor, turned over attentively the document in the complaint entered against Quasimodo, which the clerk handed him, and, having thus glanced at it, appeared to reflect for a moment. Thanks to this precaution, which he always was careful to take at the moment when on the point of beginning an examination, he knew beforehand the names, titles, and misdeeds of the accused, made cut and dried responses to questions foreseen, and succeeded in extricating himself from all the windings of the interrogation without allowing his deafness to be too apparent. The written charges were to him what the dog is to the blind man. If his deafness did happen to betray him here and there, by some incoherent apostrophe or some unintelligible question, it passed for profundity with some, and for imbecility with others. In neither case did the honor of the magistracy sustain any injury; for it is far better that a judge should be reputed imbecile or profound than deaf. Hence he took great care to conceal his deafness from the eyes of all, and he generally succeeded so well that he had reached the point of deluding himself, which is, by the way, easier than is supposed. All hunchbacks walk with their heads held high, all stutterers harangue, all deaf people speak low. As for him, he believed, at the most, that his ear was a little refractory. It was the sole concession which he made on this point to public opinion, in his moments of frankness and examination of his conscience.

Having, then, thoroughly ruminated Quasimodo's affair, he threw back his head and half closed his eyes, for the sake of more majesty and impartiality, so that, at that moment, he was both deaf and blind. A double condition, without which no judge is perfect. It was in this magisterial attitude that he began the examination.

"Your name?"

Now this was a case which had not been "provided for by law," where a deaf man should be obliged to question a deaf man.

Quasimodo, whom nothing warned that

a question had been addressed to him, continued to stare intently at the judge, and made no reply. The judge, being deaf, and being in no way warned of the deafness of the accused, thought that the latter had answered, as all accused do in general, and therefore he pursued, with his mechanical and stupid self-possession,–

"Very well. And your age?"

Again Quasimodo made no reply to this question. The judge supposed that it had been replied to, and continued,–

"Now, your profession?"

Still the same silence. The spectators had begun, meanwhile, to whisper together, and to exchange glances.

"That will do," went on the imperturbable auditor, when he supposed that the accused had finished his third reply. "You are accused before us, **primo**, of nocturnal disturbance; **secundo**, of a dishonorable act of violence upon the person of a foolish woman, **in præjudicium meretricis; tertio**, of rebellion and disloyalty towards the archers of the police of our lord, the king. Explain yourself upon all these points.–Clerk, have you written down what the prisoner has said thus far?"

At this unlucky question, a burst of laughter rose from the clerk's table caught by the audience, so violent, so wild, so contagious, so universal, that the two deaf men were forced to perceive it. Quasimodo turned round, shrugging his hump with disdain, while Master Florian, equally astonished, and supposing that the laughter of the spectators had been provoked by some irreverent reply from the accused, rendered visible to him by that shrug of the shoulders, apostrophized him indignantly,–

"You have uttered a reply, knave, which deserves the halter. Do you know to whom you are speaking?"

This sally was not fitted to arrest the explosion of general merriment. It struck all as so whimsical, and so ridiculous, that the wild laughter even attacked the sergeants of the Parloi-aux-Bourgeois, a sort of pikemen, whose stupidity was part of their uniform. Quasimodo alone preserved his seriousness, for the good reason that he understood nothing of what was going on around him. The judge, more and more irritated, thought it his duty to continue in the same tone, hoping thereby to strike the accused with a terror which should react upon the audience, and bring it back to respect.

"So this is as much as to say, perverse and thieving knave that you are, that you permit yourself to be lacking in respect towards the Auditor of the Châtelet, to the magistrate committed to the popular police of Paris, charged with searching out crimes, delinquencies, and evil conduct; with controlling all trades, and interdicting monopoly; with maintaining the pavements; with debarring the hucksters of chickens, poultry, and water-fowl; of superintending the measuring of fagots and other sorts of wood; of purging the city of mud, and the air of contagious maladies; in a word, with attending continually to public affairs, without wages or hope of salary! Do you know that I am called Florian Barbedienne, actual lieutenant to monsieur the provost, and, moreover, commissioner, inquisitor, **controller**, and examiner, with equal power in provostship, bailiwick, preservation, and inferior court of judicature?–"

There is no reason why a deaf man talking to a deaf man should stop. God knows where and when Master Florian would have landed, when thus launched at full speed in lofty eloquence, if the low door at the extreme end of the room had not suddenly opened, and given entrance to the provost in person. At his entrance Master Florian did not stop short, but, making a half-turn on his heels, and aiming at the provost the harangue with which he had been withering Quasimodo a moment before,–

"Monseigneur," said he, "I demand such penalty as you shall deem fitting against the prisoner here present, for grave and aggravated offence against the court."

And he seated himself, utterly breathless, wiping away the great drops of sweat which fell from his brow and drenched, like tears, the parchments spread out before him. Messire Robert d'Estouteville frowned and made a gesture so imperious and significant to Quasimodo, that the deaf man in some measure understood it.

The provost addressed him with severity, "What have you done that you have been brought hither, knave?"

The poor fellow, supposing that the provost was asking his name, broke the silence which he habitually preserved, and replied, in a harsh and guttural voice, "Quasimodo."

The reply matched the question so little that the wild laugh began to circulate once more, and Messire Robert exclaimed, red with wrath,–

"Are you mocking me also, you arrant knave?"

"Bellringer of Notre-Dame," replied Quasimodo, supposing that what was required of him was to explain to the judge who he was.

"Bellringer!" interpolated the provost, who had waked up early enough to be in a sufficiently bad temper, as we have said, not to require to have his fury inflamed by such strange responses. "Bellringer! I'll play you a chime of rods on your back through the squares of Paris! Do you hear, knave?"

"If it is my age that you wish to know," said Quasimodo, "I think that I shall be twenty at Saint Martin's day."

This was too much; the provost could no longer restrain himself.

"Ah! you are scoffing at the provostship, wretch! Messieurs the sergeants of the mace, you will take me this knave to the pillory of the Grève, you will flog him, and turn him for an hour. He shall pay me for it, **tête Dieu!** And I order that the present judgment shall be cried, with the assistance of four sworn trumpeters, in the seven castellanies of the viscomty of Paris."

The clerk set to work incontinently to draw up the account of the sentence.

"**Ventre Dieu!** 'tis well adjudged!" cried the little scholar, Jehan Frollo du Moulin, from his corner.

The provost turned and fixed his flashing eyes once more on Quasimodo. "I believe the knave said '**Ventre Dieu!**' Clerk, add twelve deniers Parisian for the oath, and let the vestry of Saint Eustache have the half of it; I have a particular devotion for Saint Eustache."

In a few minutes the sentence was drawn up. Its tenor was simple and brief. The customs of the provostship and the viscomty had not yet been worked over by President Thibaut Baillet, and by Roger Barmne, the king's advocate; they had not been obstructed, at that time, by that lofty hedge of quibbles and procedures, which the two jurisconsults planted there at the beginning of the sixteenth century. All was clear, expeditious, explicit. One went straight to the point then, and at the end of every path there was immediately visible, without thickets and without turnings; the wheel, the gibbet, or the pillory. One at least knew whither one was going.

The clerk presented the sentence to the provost, who affixed his seal to it, and departed to pursue his round of the audience hall, in a frame of mind which seemed destined to fill all the jails in Paris that day. Jehan Frollo and Robin Poussepain laughed in their sleeves. Quasimodo gazed on the whole with an indifferent and astonished air.

However, at the moment when Master Florian Barbedienne was reading the sentence in his turn, before signing it, the clerk felt himself moved with pity for the poor wretch of a prisoner, and, in the hope of obtaining some mitigation of the penalty, he approached as near the auditor's ear as possible, and said, pointing to Quasimodo, "That man is deaf."

He hoped that this community of infirmity would awaken Master Florian's interest in behalf of the condemned man. But, in the first place, we have already observed that Master Florian did not care to have his deafness noticed. In the next place, he was so hard of hearing that he did not catch a single word of what the clerk said to him; nevertheless, he wished to have the appearance of hearing, and replied, "Ah! ah! that is different; I did not know that. An hour more of the pillory, in that case."

And he signed the sentence thus modified.

"'Tis well done," said Robin Poussepain, who cherished a grudge against Quasimodo. "That will teach him to handle people roughly."

CHAPTER TWO

The Rat-Hole

THE READER MUST PERMIT us to take him back to the Place de Grève, which we quitted yesterday with Gringoire, in order to follow la Eseralda.

It is ten o'clock in the morning; everything is indicative of the day after a festival. The pavement is covered with rubbish; ribbons, rags, feathers from tufts of plumes, drops of wax from the torches, crumbs of the public feast. A goodly number of **bourgeois** are "sauntering," as we say, here and there, turning over with their feet the extinct brands of the bonfire, going into raptures in front of the Pillar House, over the memory of the fine hangings of the day before, and to-day staring at the nails that secured them a last pleasure. The venders of cider and beer are rolling their barrels among the groups. Some busy passers-by come and go. The merchants converse and call to each other from the thresholds of their shops. The festival, the ambassadors, Coppenole, the Pope of the Fools, are in all mouths; they vie with each other, each trying to criticise it best and laugh the most. And, meanwhile, four mounted sergeants, who have just posted themselves at the four sides of the pillory, have already concentrated around themselves a goodly proportion of the populace scattered on the Place, who condemn themselves to immobility and fatigue in the hope of a small execution.

If the reader, after having contemplated this lively and noisy scene which is being enacted in all parts of the Place, will now transfer his gaze towards that ancient demi-Gothic, demi-Romanesque house of the Tour-Roland, which forms the corner on the quay to the west, he will observe, at the angle of the façade, a large public breviary, with rich illuminations, protected from the rain by a little penthouse, and from thieves by a small grating, which, however, permits of the leaves being turned. Beside this breviary is a narrow, arched window, closed by two iron bars in the form of a cross, and looking on the square; the only opening which admits a small quantity of light and air to a little cell without a door, constructed on the ground-floor, in the thickness of the walls of the old house, and filled with a peace all the more profound, with a silence all the more gloomy, because a public place, the most populous and most noisy in Paris swarms and shrieks around it.

This little cell had been celebrated in Paris for nearly three centuries, ever since Madame Rolande de la Tour-Roland, in mourning for her father who died in the Crusades, had caused it to be hollowed out in the wall of her own house, in order to immure herself there forever, keeping of all her palace only this lodging whose door was walled up, and whose window stood open, winter and summer, giving all the rest to the poor and to God. The afflicted damsel had, in fact, waited twenty years for death in this premature tomb, praying night and day for the soul of her father, sleeping in ashes, without even a stone for a pillow, clothed in a black sack, and subsisting on the bread and water which the compassion of the passers-by led them to deposit on the ledge of her window, thus receiving charity after having bestowed it. At her death, at the moment when she was passing to the other sepulchre, she had bequeathed this one in perpetuity to afflicted women, mothers, widows, or maidens, who should wish to pray much for others or for themselves, and who should desire to inter themselves alive in a great grief or a great penance. The poor of her day had made her a fine funeral, with tears and benedictions; but, to their great regret, the pious maid had not been canonized, for lack of influence. Those among them who were a little inclined to impiety, had hoped that the matter might be accomplished in Paradise more easily than at Rome, and had frankly besought God, instead of the pope, in behalf of the deceased. The majority had contented themselves with holding the memory of Rolande sacred, and converting her rags into relics. The city, on its side, had founded in honor of the damoiselle, a public breviary, which had been fastened near the window of the cell, in order that passers-by might halt there from time to time, were it only to pray; that prayer might remind them of alms, and that the poor recluses, heiresses of Madame Rolande's vault, might not die outright of hunger and forgetfulness.

Moreover, this sort of tomb was not so very rare a thing in the cities of the Middle Ages. One often encountered in the most frequented street, in the most crowded and noisy market, in the very middle, under the feet of the horses, under the wheels of the carts, as it were, a cellar, a well, a tiny walled and grated cabin, at the bottom of which a human being prayed night and day, voluntarily devoted to some eternal lamentation, to some great expiation. And all the reflections which that strange spectacle would awaken in us to-day; that horrible cell, a sort of intermediary link between a house and the tomb, the cemetery and the city; that living being cut off from the human community, and thenceforth reckoned among the dead; that lamp consuming its last drop of oil in the darkness; that remnant of life flickering in the grave; that breath, that voice, that eternal prayer in a box of stone; that face forever turned towards the other world; that eye already illuminated with another sun; that ear pressed to the walls of a tomb; that soul a prisoner in that body; that body a prisoner in that dungeon cell, and beneath that double envelope of flesh and granite, the murmur of that soul in pain;–nothing of all this was perceived by the crowd. The piety of that age, not very subtle nor much given to reasoning, did not see so many facets in an act of religion. It took the thing in the block, honored, venerated, hallowed the sacrifice at need, but did not analyze the sufferings, and felt but moderate pity for them. It brought some pittance to the miserable penitent from time to time, looked through the hole to see whether he were still living, forgot his name, hardly knew how many years ago he had begun to die, and to the stranger, who questioned them about the living skeleton who was perishing in that cellar, the neighbors replied simply, "It is the recluse."

Everything was then viewed without metaphysics, without exaggeration, without magnifying glass, with the naked eye. The microscope had not yet been invented, either for things of matter or for things of the mind.

Moreover, although people were but little surprised by it, the examples of this sort of cloistration in the hearts of cities were in truth frequent, as we have just said. There were in Paris a considerable number of these cells, for praying to God and doing penance; they were nearly all occupied. It is true that the clergy did not like to have them empty, since that implied lukewarmness in believers, and that lepers were put into them when there were no penitents on hand. Besides the cell on the Grève, there was one at Montfaucon, one at the Charnier des Innocents, another I hardly know where,–at the Clichon House, I think; others still at many spots where traces of them are found in traditions, in default of memorials. The University had also its own. On Mount Sainte-Geneviève a sort of Job of the Middle Ages, for the space of thirty years, chanted the seven penitential psalms on a dunghill at the bottom of a cistern, beginning anew when he had finished, singing loudest at night, **magna voce per umbras**, and to-day, the antiquary fancies that he hears his voice as he enters the Rue du Puits-qui-parle–the street of the "Speaking Well."

To confine ourselves to the cell in the Tour-Roland, we must say that it had never lacked recluses. After the death of Madame Roland, it had stood vacant for a year or two, though rarely. Many women had come thither to mourn, until their death, for relatives, lovers, faults. Parisian malice, which thrusts its finger into everything, even into things which concern it the least, affirmed that it had beheld but few widows there.

In accordance with the fashion of the epoch, a Latin inscription on the wall indicated to the learned passer-by the pious purpose of this cell. The custom was retained until the middle of the sixteenth century of explaining an edifice by a brief device inscribed above the door. Thus, one still reads in France, above the wicket of the prison in the seignorial mansion of Tourville, **Sileto et spera**; in Ireland, beneath the armorial bearings which surmount the grand door to Fortescue Castle, **Forte scutum, salus ducum**; in England, over the principal entrance to the hospitable mansion of the Earls Cowper: **Tuum est**. At that time every edifice was a thought.

As there was no door to the walled cell of the Tour-Roland, these two words had been carved in large Roman capitals over the window,–

TU, ORA.

And this caused the people, whose good sense does not perceive so much refinement in things, and likes to translate **Ludovico Magno** by **Porte Saint-Denis**, to give to this dark, gloomy, damp cavity, the name of “The Rat-Hole.” An explanation less sublime, perhaps, than the other; but, on the other hand, more picturesque.

CHAPTER THREE

History of a Leavened Cake of Maize

AT THE EPOCH OF this history, the cell in the Tour-Roland was occupied. If the reader desires to know by whom, he has only to lend an ear to the conversation of three worthy gossips, who, at the moment when we have directed his attention to the Rat-Hole, were directing their steps towards the same spot, coming up along the water's edge from the Châtelet, towards the Grève.

Two of these women were dressed like good **bourgeoises** of Paris. Their fine white ruffs; their petticoats of linsey-woolsey, striped red and blue; their white knitted stockings, with clocks embroidered in colors, well drawn upon their legs; the square-toed shoes of tawny leather with black soles, and, above all, their headgear, that sort of tinsel horn, loaded down with ribbons and laces, which the women of Champagne still wear, in company with the grenadiers of the imperial guard of Russia, announced that they belonged to that class wives which holds the middle ground between what the lackeys call a woman and what they term a lady. They wore neither rings nor gold crosses, and it was easy to see that, in their ease, this did not proceed from poverty, but simply from fear of being fined. Their companion was attired in very much the same manner; but there was that indescribable something about her dress and bearing which suggested the wife of a provincial notary. One could see, by the way in which her girdle rose above her hips, that she had not been long in Paris. Add to this a plaited tucker, knots of ribbon on her shoes–and that the stripes of her petticoat ran horizontally instead of vertically, and a thousand other enormities which shocked good taste.

The two first walked with that step peculiar to Parisian ladies, showing Paris to women from the country. The provincial held by the hand a big boy, who held in his a large, flat cake.

We regret to be obliged to add, that, owing to the rigor of the season, he was using his tongue as a handkerchief.

The child was making them drag him along, **non passibus æquis**, as Virgil says, and stumbling at every moment, to the great indignation of his mother. It is true that he was looking at his cake more than at the pavement. Some serious motive, no doubt, prevented his biting it (the cake), for he contented himself with gazing tenderly at it. But the mother should have rather taken charge of the cake. It was cruel to make a Tantalus of the chubby-cheeked boy.

Meanwhile, the three demoiselles (for the name of **dames** was then reserved for noble women) were all talking at once.

"Let us make haste, Demoiselle Mahiette," said the youngest of the three, who was also the largest, to the provincial, "I greatly fear that we shall arrive too late; they told us at the Châtelet that they were going to take him directly to the pillory."

"Ah, bah! what are you saying, Demoiselle Oudarde Musnier?" interposed the other Parisienne. "There are two hours yet to the pillory. We have time enough. Have you ever seen any one pilloried, my dear Mahiette?"

"Yes," said the provincial, "at Reims."

"Ah, bah! What is your pillory at Reims?

A miserable cage into which only peasants are turned. A great affair, truly!"

"Only peasants!" said Mahiette, "at the cloth market in Reims! We have seen very fine criminals there, who have killed their father and mother! Peasants! For what do you take us, Gervaise?"

It is certain that the provincial was on the point of taking offence, for the honor of her pillory. Fortunately, that discreet damoiselle, Oudarde Musnier, turned the conversation in time.

"By the way, Damoiselle Mahiette, what say you to our Flemish Ambassadors? Have you as fine ones at Reims?"

"I admit," replied Mahiette, "that it is only in Paris that such Flemings can be seen."

"Did you see among the embassy, that big ambassador who is a hosier?" asked Oudarde.

"Yes," said Mahiette. "He has the eye of a Saturn."

"And the big fellow whose face resembles

a bare belly?" resumed Gervaise. "And the little one, with small eyes framed in red eyelids, pared down and slashed up like a thistle head?"

"'Tis their horses that are worth seeing," said Oudarde, "caparisoned as they are after the fashion of their country!"

"Ah my dear," interrupted provincial Mahiette, assuming in her turn an air of superiority, "what would you say then, if you had seen in '61, at the consecration at Reims, eighteen years ago, the horses of the princes and of the king's company? Housings and caparisons of all sorts; some of damask cloth, of fine cloth of gold, furred with sables; others of velvet, furred with ermine; others all embellished with goldsmith's work and large bells of gold and silver! And what money that had cost! And what handsome boy pages rode upon them!"

"That," replied Oudarde dryly, "does not prevent the Flemings having very fine horses, and having had a superb supper yesterday with monsieur, the provost of the merchants, at the Hôtel-de-Ville, where they were served with comfits and hippocras, and spices, and other singularities."

"What are you saying, neighbor!" exclaimed Gervaise. "It was with monsieur the cardinal, at the Petit Bourbon that they supped."

"Not at all. At the Hôtel-de-Ville.

"Yes, indeed. At the Petit Bourbon!"

"It was at the Hôtel-de-Ville," retorted Oudarde sharply, "and Dr. Scourable addressed them a harangue in Latin, which pleased them greatly. My husband, who is sworn bookseller told me so."

"It was at the Petit Bourbon," replied Gervaise, with no less spirit, "and this is what monsieur the cardinal's procurator presented to them: twelve double quarts of hippocras, white, claret, and red; twenty-four boxes of double Lyons marchpane, gilded; as many torches, worth two livres a piece; and six demi-queues[29] of Beaune wine, white and claret, the best that could be found. I have it from my husband, who is a cinquantenier[30], at the Parloir-aux Bourgeois, and who was this morning comparing the Flemish ambassadors with those of Prester John and the Emperor of Trebizond, who came from Mesopotamia to Paris, under the last king, and who wore rings in their ears."

"So true is it that they supped at the Hôtel-de-Ville," replied Oudarde but little affected by this catalogue, "that such a triumph of viands and comfits has never been seen."

"I tell you that they were served by Le Sec, sergeant of the city, at the Hôtel du Petit-Bourbon, and that that is where you are mistaken."

"At the Hôtel-de-Ville, I tell you!"

"At the Petit-Bourbon, my dear! and they

---

29 A Queue was a cask which held a hogshead and a half.

30 A captain of fifty men.

had illuminated with magic glasses the word **Hope**, which is written on the grand portal."

"At the Hôtel-de-Ville! At the Hôtel-de-Ville! And Husson-le-Voir played the flute!"

"I tell you, no!"

"I tell you, yes!"

"I say, no!"

Plump and worthy Oudarde was preparing to retort, and the quarrel might, perhaps, have proceeded to a pulling of caps, had not Mahiette suddenly exclaimed,–"Look at those people assembled yonder at the end of the bridge! There is something in their midst that they are looking at!"

"In sooth," said Gervaise, "I hear the sounds of a tambourine. I believe 'tis the little Esmeralda, who plays her mummeries with her goat. Eh, be quick, Mahiette! redouble your pace and drag along your boy. You are come hither to visit the curiosities of Paris. You saw the Flemings yesterday; you must see the gypsy to-day."

"The gypsy!" said Mahiette, suddenly

retracing her steps, and clasping her son's arm forcibly. "God preserve me from it! She would steal my child from me! Come, Eustache!"

And she set out on a run along the quay towards the Grève, until she had left the bridge far behind her. In the meanwhile, the child whom she was dragging after her fell upon his knees; she halted breathless. Oudarde and Gervaise rejoined her.

"That gypsy steal your child from you!" said Gervaise. "That's a singular freak of yours!"

Mahiette shook her head with a pensive air.

"The singular point is," observed Oudarde, "that **la sachette** has the same idea about the Egyptian woman."

"What is **la sachette**?" asked Mahiette.

"Hé!" said Oudarde, "Sister Gudule."

"And who is Sister Gudule?" persisted Mahiette.

"You are certainly ignorant of all but your

Reims, not to know that!" replied Oudarde. "'Tis the recluse of the Rat-Hole."

"What!" demanded Mahiette, "that poor woman to whom we are carrying this cake?"

Oudarde nodded affirmatively.

"Precisely. You will see her presently at her window on the Grève. She has the same opinion as yourself of these vagabonds of Egypt, who play the tambourine and tell fortunes to the public. No one knows whence comes her horror of the gypsies and Egyptians. But you, Mahiette–why do you run so at the mere sight of them?"

"Oh!" said Mahiette, seizing her child's round head in both hands, "I don't want that to happen to me which happened to Paquette la Chantefleurie."

"Oh! you must tell us that story, my good Mahiette," said Gervaise, taking her arm.

"Gladly," replied Mahiette, "but you must be ignorant of all but your Paris not to know that! I will tell you then (but 'tis not necessary for us to halt that I may tell you the tale), that Paquette la Chantefleurie was a pretty maid of eighteen when I was one myself, that is to say, eighteen years ago, and 'tis her own fault if she is not to-day, like me, a good, plump, fresh mother of six and thirty, with a husband and a son. However, after the age of fourteen, it was too late! Well, she was the daughter of Guybertant, minstrel of the barges at Reims, the same who had played before King Charles VII., at his coronation, when he descended our river Vesle from Sillery to Muison, when Madame the Maid of Orleans was also in the boat. The old father died when Paquette was still a mere child; she had then no one but her mother, the sister of M. Pradon, master-brazier and coppersmith in Paris, Rue Parin-Garlin, who died last year. You see she was of good family. The mother was a good simple woman, unfortunately, and she taught Paquette nothing but a bit of embroidery and toy-making which did not prevent the little one from growing very large and remaining very poor. They both dwelt at Reims, on the river front, Rue de Folle-Peine. Mark this: For I believe it was this which brought misfortune to Paquette. In '61, the year of the coronation of our King Louis XI. whom God preserve! Paquette was so gay and so pretty that she was called everywhere by no other name than **la Chantefleurie**–blossoming song. Poor girl! She had handsome teeth, she was fond of laughing and displaying them. Now, a maid who loves to laugh is on the road to weeping; handsome teeth ruin handsome eyes. So she was la Chantefleurie. She and her mother earned a precarious living; they had been very destitute since the death of the minstrel; their embroidery did not bring them in more than six farthings a week, which does not amount to quite two eagle liards. Where were the days when Father Guybertant had earned twelve sous parisian, in a single coronation, with a song? One winter (it was in that same year of '61), when the two women had neither fagots nor firewood, it was very cold, which gave la Chantefleurie such a fine color that the men called her Paquette![31] and many called her Pâquerette![32] and she was ruined.–Eustache, just let me see you bite that cake if you dare!–We immediately perceived that she was ruined, one Sunday when she came to church with a gold cross about her neck. At fourteen years of age! do you see? First it was the young Vicomte de Cormontreuil, who has his bell tower three leagues distant from Reims; then Messire Henri de Triancourt, equerry to the King; then less than that, Chiart de Beaulion, sergeant-at-arms; then, still descending, Guery Aubergeon, carver to the King; then, Macé de Frépus, barber to monsieur the dauphin; then, Thévenin le Moine, King's cook; then, the men growing continually younger and less noble, she fell

31 Ox-eye daisy.

32 Easter daisy.

to Guillaume Racine, minstrel of the hurdy-gurdy and to Thierry de Mer, lamplighter. Then, poor Chantefleurie, she belonged to every one: she had reached the last sou of her gold piece. What shall I say to you, my damoiselles? At the coronation, in the same year, '61, 'twas she who made the bed of the king of the debauchees! In the same year!"

Mahiette sighed, and wiped away a tear which trickled from her eyes.

"This is no very extraordinary history," said Gervaise, "and in the whole of it I see nothing of any Egyptian women or children."

"Patience!" resumed Mahiette, "you will see one child.–In '66, 'twill be sixteen years ago this month, at Sainte-Paule's day, Paquette was brought to bed of a little girl. The unhappy creature! it was a great joy to her; she had long wished for a child. Her mother, good woman, who had never known what to do except to shut her eyes, her mother was dead. Paquette had no longer any one to love in the world or any one to love her. La Chantefleurie had been a poor creature during the five years since her fall. She was alone, alone in this life, fingers were pointed at her, she was hooted at in the streets, beaten by the sergeants, jeered at by the little boys in rags. And then, twenty had arrived: and twenty is an old age for amorous women. Folly began to bring her in no more than her trade of embroidery in former days; for every wrinkle that came, a crown fled; winter became hard to her once more, wood became rare again in her brazier, and bread in her cupboard. She could no longer work because, in becoming voluptuous, she had grown lazy; and she suffered much more because, in growing lazy, she had become voluptuous. At least, that is the way in which monsieur the curé of Saint-Remy explains why these women are colder and hungrier than other poor women, when they are old."

"Yes," remarked Gervaise, "but the gypsies?"

"One moment, Gervaise!" said Oudarde, whose attention was less impatient. "What would be left for the end if all were in the beginning? Continue, Mahiette, I entreat you. That poor Chantefleurie!"

Mahiette went on.

"So she was very sad, very miserable, and furrowed her cheeks with tears. But in the midst of her shame, her folly, her debauchery, it seemed to her that she should be less wild, less shameful, less dissipated, if there were something or some one in the world whom she could love, and who could love her. It was necessary that it should be a child, because only a child could be sufficiently innocent for that. She had recognized this fact after having tried to love a thief, the only man who wanted her; but after a short time, she perceived that the thief despised her. Those women of love require either a lover or a child to fill their hearts. Otherwise, they are very unhappy. As she could not have a lover, she turned wholly towards a desire for a child, and as she had not ceased to be pious, she made her constant prayer to the good God for it. So the good God took pity on her, and gave her a little daughter. I will not speak to you of her joy; it was a fury of tears, and caresses, and kisses. She nursed her child herself, made swaddling-bands for it out of her coverlet, the only one which she had on her bed, and no longer felt either cold or hunger. She became beautiful once more, in consequence of it. An old maid makes a young mother. Gallantry claimed her once more; men came to see la Chantefleurie; she found customers again for her merchandise, and out of all these horrors she made baby clothes, caps and bibs, bodices with shoulder-straps of lace, and tiny bonnets of satin, without even thinking of buying herself another coverlet.–Master Eustache, I have already told you not to eat that cake.–It is certain that little Agnès, that was the child's name, a baptismal name, for it was a long time since la Chantefleurie had had any surname–it is certain that that little one was more swathed in ribbons and embroideries than a dauphiness of Dauphiny! Among other things, she had a pair of little shoes, the like of which King Louis XI. certainly never had! Her mother had stitched and embroidered them herself; she had lavished on them all the delicacies of her art of embroideress, and all the embellishments of a robe for the good Virgin. They certainly were the two prettiest little pink shoes that could be seen. They were no longer than my thumb, and one had to see the child's little feet come out of them, in order to believe that they had been able to get into them. 'Tis true that those little feet were so small, so pretty, so rosy! rosier than the satin of the shoes! When you have children, Oudarde, you will find that there is nothing prettier than those little hands and feet."

"I ask no better," said Oudarde with a sigh, "but I am waiting until it shall suit the good pleasure of M. Andry Musnier."

"However, Paquette's child had more that was pretty about it besides its feet. I saw her when she was only four months old; she was a love! She had eyes larger than her mouth, and the most charming black hair, which already curled. She would have been a magnificent brunette at the age of sixteen! Her mother became more crazy over her every day. She kissed her, caressed her, tickled her, washed her, decked her out, devoured her! She lost her head over her, she thanked God for her. Her pretty, little rosy feet above all were an endless source of wonderment, they were a delirium of joy! She was always pressing her lips to them, and she could never recover from her amazement at their smallness. She put them into the tiny shoes, took them out, admired them, marvelled at them, looked at the light through them, was curious to see them try to walk on her bed, and would gladly have passed her life on her knees, putting on and taking off the shoes from those feet, as though they had been those of an Infant Jesus."

"The tale is fair and good," said Gervaise in a low tone; "but where do gypsies come into all that?"

"Here," replied Mahiette. "One day there arrived in Reims a very queer sort of people. They were beggars and vagabonds who were roaming over the country, led by their duke and their counts. They were browned by exposure to the sun, they had closely curling hair, and silver rings in their ears. The women were still uglier than the men. They had blacker faces, which were always uncovered, a miserable frock on their bodies, an old cloth woven of cords bound upon their shoulder, and their hair hanging like the tail of a horse. The children who scrambled between their legs would have frightened as many monkeys. A band of excommunicates. All these persons came direct from lower Egypt to Reims through Poland. The Pope had confessed them, it was said, and had prescribed to them as penance to roam through the world for seven years, without sleeping in a bed; and so they were called penancers, and smelt horribly. It appears that they had formerly been Saracens, which was why they believed in Jupiter, and claimed ten livres of Tournay from all archbishops, bishops, and mitred abbots with croziers. A bull from the Pope empowered them to do that. They came to Reims to tell fortunes in the name of the King of Algiers, and the Emperor of Germany. You can readily imagine that no more was needed to cause the entrance to the town to be forbidden them. Then the whole band camped with good grace outside the gate of Braine, on that hill where stands a mill, beside the cavities of the ancient chalk pits. And everybody in Reims vied with his neighbor in going to see them. They looked at your hand, and told you marvellous prophecies; they were equal to predicting to Judas that he would become Pope. Nevertheless, ugly rumors were in circulation in regard to them; about children stolen, purses cut, and human flesh devoured. The wise people said to the foolish: “Don’t go there!” and then went themselves on the sly. It was an infatuation. The fact is, that they said things fit to astonish a cardinal. Mothers triumphed greatly over their little ones after the Egyptians had read in their hands all sorts of marvels written in pagan and in Turkish. One had an emperor; another, a pope; another, a captain. Poor Chantefleurie was seized with curiosity; she wished to know about herself, and whether her pretty little Agnès would not become some day Empress of Armenia, or something else. So she carried her to the

Egyptians; and the Egyptian women fell to admiring the child, and to caressing it, and to kissing it with their black mouths, and to marvelling over its little band, alas! to the great joy of the mother. They were especially enthusiastic over her pretty feet and shoes. The child was not yet a year old. She already lisped a little, laughed at her mother like a little mad thing, was plump and quite round, and possessed a thousand charming little gestures of the angels of paradise.

"She was very much frightened by the Egyptians, and wept. But her mother kissed her more warmly and went away enchanted with the good fortune which the soothsayers had foretold for her Agnès. She was to be a beauty, virtuous, a queen. So she returned to her attic in the Rue Folle-Peine, very proud of bearing with her a queen. The next day she took advantage of a moment when the child was asleep on her bed, (for they always slept together), gently left the door a little way open, and ran to tell a neighbor in the Rue de la Séchesserie, that the day would come when her daughter Agnès would be served at table by the King of England and the Archduke of Ethiopia, and a hundred other marvels. On her return, hearing no cries on the staircase, she said to herself: 'Good! the child is still asleep!' She found her door wider open than she had left it, but she entered, poor mother, and ran to the bed.–The child was no longer there, the place was empty. Nothing remained of the child, but one of her pretty little shoes. She flew out of the room, dashed down the stairs, and began to beat her head against the wall, crying: 'My child! who has my child? Who has taken my child?' The street was deserted, the house isolated; no one could tell her anything about it. She went about the town, searched all the streets, ran hither and thither the whole day long, wild, beside herself, terrible, snuffing at doors and windows like a wild beast which has lost its young. She was breathless, dishevelled, frightful to see, and there was a fire in her eyes which dried her tears. She stopped the passers-by and cried: 'My daughter! my daughter! my pretty little daughter! If any one will give me back my daughter, I will be his servant, the servant of his dog, and he shall eat my heart if he will.' She met M. le Curé of Saint-Remy, and said to him: 'Monsieur, I will till the earth with my finger-nails, but give me back my child!' It was heartrending, Oudarde; and I saw a very hard man, Master Ponce Lacabre, the procurator, weep. Ah! poor mother! In the evening she returned home. During her absence, a neighbor had seen two gypsies ascend up to it with a bundle in their arms, then descend again, after closing the door. After their departure, something like the cries of a child were heard in Paquette's room. The mother, burst into shrieks of laughter, ascended the stairs as though on wings, and entered.–A frightful thing to tell, Oudarde! Instead of her pretty little Agnès, so rosy and so fresh, who was a gift of the good God, a sort of hideous little monster, lame, one-eyed, deformed, was crawling and squalling over the floor. She hid her eyes in horror. 'Oh!' said she, 'have the witches transformed my daughter into this horrible animal?' They hastened to carry away the little club-foot; he would have driven her mad. It was the monstrous child of some gypsy woman, who had given herself to the devil. He appeared to be about four years old, and talked a language which was no human tongue; there were words in it which were impossible. La Chantefleurie flung herself upon the little shoe, all that remained to her of all that she loved. She remained so long motionless over it, mute, and without breath, that they thought she was dead. Suddenly she trembled all over, covered her relic with furious kisses, and burst out sobbing as though her heart were broken. I assure you that we were all weeping also. She said: ‘Oh, my little daughter! my pretty little daughter! where art thou?’–and it wrung your very heart. I weep still when I think of it. Our children are the marrow of our bones, you see.–My poor Eustache! thou art so fair!–If you only knew how nice he is! yesterday he said to me: ‘I want to be a gendarme, that I do.’ Oh! my Eustache! if I were to lose thee!–All at once la Chantefleurie rose, and set out to run through Reims, screaming: ‘To the gypsies’ camp! to the gypsies’ camp! Police, to burn the witches!’ The gypsies were gone. It was pitch dark. They could not be followed. On the morrow, two leagues from Reims, on a heath between Gueux and Tilloy, the remains of a large fire were found, some ribbons which had belonged to Paquette’s child, drops of blood, and the dung of a ram. The night just past had been a Saturday. There was no longer any doubt that the Egyptians had held their Sabbath on that heath, and that they had devoured the child in company with Beelzebub, as the practice is among the Mahometans. When La Chantefleurie learned these horrible things, she did not weep, she moved her lips as though to speak, but could not. On the morrow, her hair was gray. On the second day, she had disappeared.

"'Tis in truth, a frightful tale," said Oudarde, "and one which would make even a Burgundian weep."

"I am no longer surprised," added Gervaise, "that fear of the gypsies should spur you on so sharply."

"And you did all the better," resumed Oudarde, "to flee with your Eustache just now, since these also are gypsies from Poland."

"No," said Gervais, "'tis said that they come from Spain and Catalonia."

"Catalonia? 'tis possible," replied Oudarde. "Pologne, Catalogne, Valogne, I always confound those three provinces, One thing is certain, that they are gypsies."

"Who certainly," added Gervaise, "have teeth long enough to eat little children. I should not be surprised if la Smeralda ate a little of them also, though she pretends to be dainty. Her white goat knows tricks that are too malicious for there not to be some impiety underneath it all."

Mahiette walked on in silence. She was absorbed in that revery which is, in some sort, the continuation of a mournful tale, and which ends only after having communicated the emotion, from vibration to vibration, even to the very last fibres of the heart. Nevertheless, Gervaise addressed her, "And did they ever learn what became of la Chantefleurie?" Mahiette made no reply. Gervaise repeated her question, and shook her arm, calling her by name. Mahiette appeared to awaken from her thoughts.

"What became of la Chantefleurie?" she said, repeating mechanically the words whose impression was still fresh in her ear;

then, making an effort to recall her attention to the meaning of her words, "Ah!" she continued briskly, "no one ever found out."

She added, after a pause,–

"Some said that she had been seen to quit Reims at nightfall by the Fléchembault gate; others, at daybreak, by the old Basée gate. A poor man found her gold cross hanging on the stone cross in the field where the fair is held. It was that ornament which had wrought her ruin, in '61. It was a gift from the handsome Vicomte de Cormontreuil, her first lover. Paquette had never been willing to part with it, wretched as she had been. She had clung to it as to life itself. So, when we saw that cross abandoned, we all thought that she was dead. Nevertheless, there were people of the Cabaret les Vantes, who said that they had seen her pass along the road to Paris, walking on the pebbles with her bare feet. But, in that case, she must have gone out through the Porte de Vesle, and all this does not agree. Or, to speak more truly, I believe that she actually did depart by the Porte de Vesle, but departed from this world."

"I do not understand you," said Gervaise.

"La Vesle," replied Mahiette, with a melancholy smile, "is the river."

"Poor Chantefleurie!" said Oudarde, with a shiver,–"drowned!"

"Drowned!" resumed Mahiette, "who could have told good Father Guybertant, when he passed under the bridge of Tingueux with the current, singing in his barge, that one day his dear little Paquette would also pass beneath that bridge, but without song or boat.

"And the little shoe?" asked Gervaise.

"Disappeared with the mother," replied Mahiette.

"Poor little shoe!" said Oudarde.

Oudarde, a big and tender woman, would have been well pleased to sigh in company with Mahiette. But Gervaise, more curious, had not finished her questions.

"And the monster?" she said suddenly, to

Mahiette.

"What monster?" inquired the latter.

"The little gypsy monster left by the sorceresses in Chantefleurie's chamber, in exchange for her daughter. What did you do with it? I hope you drowned it also."

"No." replied Mahiette.

"What? You burned it then? In sooth, that is more just. A witch child!"

"Neither the one nor the other, Gervaise. Monseigneur the archbishop interested himself in the child of Egypt, exorcised it, blessed it, removed the devil carefully from its body, and sent it to Paris, to be exposed on the wooden bed at Notre-Dame, as a foundling."

"Those bishops!" grumbled Gervaise, "because they are learned, they do nothing like anybody else. I just put it to you, Oudarde, the idea of placing the devil among the foundlings! For that little monster was assuredly the devil. Well, Mahiette, what did they do with it in Paris? I am quite sure that no charitable person wanted it."

"I do not know," replied the Rémoise, "'twas just at that time that my husband bought the office of notary, at Beru, two leagues from the town, and we were no longer occupied with that story; besides, in front of Beru, stand the two hills of Cernay, which hide the towers of the cathedral in Reims from view."

While chatting thus, the three worthy **bourgeoises** had arrived at the Place de Grève. In their absorption, they had passed the public breviary of the Tour-Roland without stopping, and took their way mechanically towards the pillory around which the throng was growing more dense with every moment. It is probable that the spectacle which at that moment attracted all looks in that direction, would have made them forget completely the Rat-Hole, and the halt which they intended to make there, if big Eustache, six years of age, whom Mahiette was dragging along by the hand, had not abruptly recalled the object to them: "Mother," said he, as though some instinct warned him that the Rat-Hole was behind him, "can I eat the cake now?"

If Eustache had been more adroit, that is to say, less greedy, he would have continued to wait, and would only have hazarded that simple question, "Mother, can I eat the cake, now?" on their return to the University, to Master Andry Musnier's, Rue Madame la Valence, when he had the two arms of the Seine and the five bridges of the city between the Rat-Hole and the cake.

This question, highly imprudent at the moment when Eustache put it, aroused Mahiette's attention.

"By the way," she exclaimed, "we are forgetting the recluse! Show me the Rat-Hole, that I may carry her her cake."

"Immediately," said Oudarde, "'tis a charity."

But this did not suit Eustache.

"Stop! my cake!" said he, rubbing both ears alternatively with his shoulders, which, in such cases, is the supreme sign of discontent.

The three women retraced their steps, and, on arriving in the vicinity of the Tour-Roland, Oudarde said to the other two,–

"We must not all three gaze into the hole at once, for fear of alarming the recluse. Do you two pretend to read the **Dominus** in the breviary, while I thrust my nose into the aperture; the recluse knows me a little. I will give you warning when you can approach."

She proceeded alone to the window. At the moment when she looked in, a profound pity was depicted on all her features, and her frank, gay visage altered its expression and color as abruptly as though it had passed from a ray of sunlight to a ray of moonlight; her eye became humid; her mouth contracted, like that of a person on the point of weeping. A moment later, she laid her finger on her lips, and made a sign to Mahiette to draw near and look.

Mahiette, much touched, stepped up in silence, on tiptoe, as though approaching the bedside of a dying person.

It was, in fact, a melancholy spectacle which presented itself to the eyes of the two women, as they gazed through the grating of the Rat-Hole, neither stirring nor breathing.

The cell was small, broader than it was long, with an arched ceiling, and viewed from within, it bore a considerable resemblance to the interior of a huge bishop's mitre. On the bare flagstones which formed the floor, in one corner, a woman was sitting, or rather, crouching. Her chin rested on her knees, which her crossed arms pressed forcibly to her breast. Thus doubled up, clad in a brown sack, which enveloped her entirely in large folds, her long, gray hair pulled over in front, falling over her face and along her legs nearly to her feet, she presented, at the first glance, only a strange form outlined against the dark background of the cell, a sort of dusky triangle, which the ray of daylight falling through the opening, cut roughly into two shades, the one sombre, the other illuminated. It was one of those spectres, half light, half shadow, such as one beholds in dreams and in the extraordinary work of Goya, pale, motionless, sinister, crouching over a tomb, or leaning against the grating of a prison cell.

It was neither a woman, nor a man, nor a living being, nor a definite form; it was a figure, a sort of vision, in which the real and the fantastic intersected each other, like darkness and day. It was with difficulty that one distinguished, beneath her hair which spread to the ground, a gaunt and severe profile; her dress barely allowed the extremity of a bare foot to escape, which contracted on the hard, cold pavement. The little of human form of which one caught a sight beneath this envelope of mourning, caused a shudder.

That figure, which one might have supposed to be riveted to the flagstones, appeared to possess neither movement, nor thought, nor breath. Lying, in January, in that thin, linen sack, lying on a granite floor, without fire, in the gloom of a cell whose oblique air-hole allowed only the cold breeze, but never the sun, to enter from without, she did not appear to suffer or even to think. One would have said that she had turned to stone with the cell, ice with the season. Her hands were clasped, her eyes fixed. At first sight one took her for a spectre; at the second, for a statue.

Nevertheless, at intervals, her blue lips half opened to admit a breath, and trembled, but as dead and as mechanical as the leaves which the wind sweeps aside.

Nevertheless, from her dull eyes there escaped a look, an ineffable look, a profound, lugubrious, imperturbable look, incessantly fixed upon a corner of the cell which could not be seen from without; a gaze which seemed to fix all the sombre thoughts of that soul in distress upon some mysterious object.

Such was the creature who had received, from her habitation, the name of the "recluse"; and, from her garment, the name of "the sacked nun."

The three women, for Gervaise had rejoined Mahiette and Oudarde, gazed through the window. Their heads intercepted the feeble light in the cell, without the wretched being whom they thus deprived of it seeming to pay any attention to them. "Do not let us trouble her," said Oudarde, in a low voice, "she is in her ecstasy; she is praying."

Meanwhile, Mahiette was gazing with ever-increasing anxiety at that wan, withered, dishevelled head, and her eyes filled with tears. "This is very singular," she murmured.

She thrust her head through the bars, and succeeded in casting a glance at the corner where the gaze of the unhappy woman was immovably riveted.

When she withdrew her head from the window, her countenance was inundated with tears.

"What do you call that woman?" she asked Oudarde.

Oudarde replied,–

"We call her Sister Gudule."

"And I," returned Mahiette, "call her Paquette la Chantefleurie."

Then, laying her finger on her lips, she motioned to the astounded Oudarde to thrust her head through the window and look.

Oudarde looked and beheld, in the corner where the eyes of the recluse were fixed in that sombre ecstasy, a tiny shoe of pink satin, embroidered with a thousand fanciful designs in gold and silver.

Gervaise looked after Oudarde, and then the three women, gazing upon the unhappy mother, began to weep.

But neither their looks nor their tears disturbed the recluse. Her hands remained clasped; her lips mute; her eyes fixed; and that little shoe, thus gazed at, broke the heart of any one who knew her history.

The three women had not yet uttered a

single word; they dared not speak, even in a low voice. This deep silence, this deep grief, this profound oblivion in which everything had disappeared except one thing, produced upon them the effect of the grand altar at Christmas or Easter. They remained silent, they meditated, they were ready to kneel. It seemed to them that they were ready to enter a church on the day of Tenebræ.

At length Gervaise, the most curious of the three, and consequently the least sensitive, tried to make the recluse speak:

"Sister! Sister Gudule!"

She repeated this call three times, raising her voice each time. The recluse did not move; not a word, not a glance, not a sigh, not a sign of life.

Oudarde, in her turn, in a sweeter, more caressing voice,–"Sister!" said she, "Sister Sainte-Gudule!"

The same silence; the same immobility.

"A singular woman!" exclaimed Gervaise,

"and one not to be moved by a catapult!"

"Perchance she is deaf," said Oudarde.

"Perhaps she is blind," added Gervaise.

"Dead, perchance," returned Mahiette.

It is certain that if the soul had not already quitted this inert, sluggish, lethargic body, it had at least retreated and concealed itself in depths whither the perceptions of the exterior organs no longer penetrated.

"Then we must leave the cake on the window," said Oudarde; "some scamp will take it. What shall we do to rouse her?"

Eustache, who, up to that moment had been diverted by a little carriage drawn by a large dog, which had just passed, suddenly perceived that his three conductresses were gazing at something through the window, and, curiosity taking possession of him in his turn, he climbed upon a stone post, elevated himself on tiptoe, and applied his fat, red face to the opening, shouting, "Mother, let me see too!"

At the sound of this clear, fresh, ringing

child's voice, the recluse trembled; she turned her head with the sharp, abrupt movement of a steel spring, her long, fleshless hands cast aside the hair from her brow, and she fixed upon the child, bitter, astonished, desperate eyes. This glance was but a lightning flash.

"Oh my God!" she suddenly exclaimed, hiding her head on her knees, and it seemed as though her hoarse voice tore her chest as it passed from it, "do not show me those of others!"

"Good day, madam," said the child, gravely.

Nevertheless, this shock had, so to speak, awakened the recluse. A long shiver traversed her frame from head to foot; her teeth chattered; she half raised her head and said, pressing her elbows against her hips, and clasping her feet in her hands as though to warm them,–

"Oh, how cold it is!"

"Poor woman!" said Oudarde, with great compassion, "would you like a little fire?"

She shook her head in token of refusal.

"Well," resumed Oudarde, presenting her with a flagon; "here is some hippocras which will warm you; drink it."

Again she shook her head, looked at Oudarde fixedly and replied, "Water."

Oudarde persisted,–"No, sister, that is no beverage for January. You must drink a little hippocras and eat this leavened cake of maize, which we have baked for you."

She refused the cake which Mahiette offered to her, and said, "Black bread."

"Come," said Gervaise, seized in her turn with an impulse of charity, and unfastening her woolen cloak, "here is a cloak which is a little warmer than yours."

She refused the cloak as she had refused the flagon and the cake, and replied, "A sack."

"But," resumed the good Oudarde, "you must have perceived to some extent, that yesterday was a festival."

"I do perceive it," said the recluse; "'tis two days now since I have had any water in my crock."

She added, after a silence, "'Tis a festival, I am forgotten. People do well. Why should the world think of me, when I do not think of it? Cold charcoal makes cold ashes."

And as though fatigued with having said so much, she dropped her head on her knees again. The simple and charitable Oudarde, who fancied that she understood from her last words that she was complaining of the cold, replied innocently, "Then you would like a little fire?"

"Fire!" said the sacked nun, with a strange accent; "and will you also make a little for the poor little one who has been beneath the sod for these fifteen years?"

Every limb was trembling, her voice quivered, her eyes flashed, she had raised herself upon her knees; suddenly she extended her thin, white hand towards the child, who was regarding her with a look of astonishment. "Take away that child!" she cried. "The Egyptian woman is about to pass by."

Then she fell face downward on the earth, and her forehead struck the stone, with the sound of one stone against another stone. The three women thought her dead. A moment later, however, she moved, and they beheld her drag herself, on her knees and elbows, to the corner where the little shoe was. Then they dared not look; they no longer saw her; but they heard a thousand kisses and a thousand sighs, mingled with heartrending cries, and dull blows like those of a head in contact with a wall. Then, after one of these blows, so violent that all three of them staggered, they heard no more.

"Can she have killed herself?" said Gervaise, venturing to pass her head through the air-hole. "Sister! Sister Gudule!"

"Sister Gudule!" repeated Oudarde.

"Ah! good heavens! she no longer moves!" resumed Gervaise; "is she dead? Gudule! Gudule!"

Mahiette, choked to such a point that

she could not speak, made an effort. "Wait," said she. Then bending towards the window, "Paquette!" she said, "Paquette le Chantefleurie!"

A child who innocently blows upon the badly ignited fuse of a bomb, and makes it explode in his face, is no more terrified than was Mahiette at the effect of that name, abruptly launched into the cell of Sister Gudule.

The recluse trembled all over, rose erect on her bare feet, and leaped at the window with eyes so glaring that Mahiette and Oudarde, and the other woman and the child recoiled even to the parapet of the quay.

Meanwhile, the sinister face of the recluse appeared pressed to the grating of the air-hole. "Oh! oh!" she cried, with an appalling laugh; "'tis the Egyptian who is calling me!"

At that moment, a scene which was passing at the pillory caught her wild eye. Her brow contracted with horror, she stretched her two skeleton arms from her cell, and shrieked in a voice which resembled a death-rattle, “So ’tis thou once more, daughter of Egypt! ’Tis thou who callest me, stealer of children! Well! Be thou accursed! accursed! accursed! accursed!”

CHAPTER FOUR

A Tear for a Drop of Water

THESE WORDS WERE, so to speak, the point of union of two scenes, which had, up to that time, been developed in parallel lines at the same moment, each on its particular theatre; one, that which the reader has just perused, in the Rat-Hole; the other, which he is about to read, on the ladder of the pillory. The first had for witnesses only the three women with whom the reader has just made acquaintance; the second had for spectators all the public which we have seen above, collecting on the Place de Grève, around the pillory and the gibbet.

That crowd which the four sergeants posted at nine o'clock in the morning at the four corners of the pillory had inspired with the hope of some sort of an execution, no doubt, not a hanging, but a whipping, a cropping of ears, something, in short,–that crowd had increased so rapidly that the four policemen, too closely besieged, had had occasion to "press" it, as the expression then ran, more than once, by sound blows of their whips, and the haunches of their horses.

This populace, disciplined to waiting for public executions, did not manifest very much impatience. It amused itself with watching the pillory, a very simple sort of monument, composed of a cube of masonry about six feet high and hollow in the interior. A very steep staircase, of unhewn stone, which was called by distinction "the ladder," led to the upper platform, upon which was visible a horizontal wheel of solid oak. The victim was bound upon this wheel, on his knees, with his hands behind his back. A wooden shaft, which set in motion a capstan concealed in the interior of the little edifice, imparted a rotatory motion to the wheel, which always maintained its horizontal position, and in this manner presented the face of the condemned man to all quarters of the square in succession. This was what was called "turning" a criminal.

As the reader perceives, the pillory of the Grève was far from presenting all the recreations of the pillory of the Halles. Nothing architectural, nothing monumental. No roof to the iron cross, no octagonal lantern, no frail, slender columns spreading out on the edge of the roof into capitals of acanthus leaves and flowers, no waterspouts of chimeras and monsters, on carved woodwork, no fine sculpture, deeply sunk in the stone.

They were forced to content themselves

with those four stretches of rubble work, backed with sandstone, and a wretched stone gibbet, meagre and bare, on one side.

The entertainment would have been but a poor one for lovers of Gothic architecture. It is true that nothing was ever less curious on the score of architecture than the worthy gapers of the Middle Ages, and that they cared very little for the beauty of a pillory.

The victim finally arrived, bound to the tail of a cart, and when he had been hoisted upon the platform, where he could be seen from all points of the Place, bound with cords and straps upon the wheel of the pillory, a prodigious hoot, mingled with laughter and acclamations, burst forth upon the Place. They had recognized Quasimodo.

It was he, in fact. The change was singular. Pilloried on the very place where, on the day before, he had been saluted, acclaimed, and proclaimed Pope and Prince of Fools, in the cortège of the Duke of Egypt, the King of Thunes, and the Emperor of Galilee! One thing is certain, and that is, that there was not a soul in the crowd, not even himself, though in turn triumphant and the sufferer, who set forth this combination clearly in his thought. Gringoire and his philosophy were missing at this spectacle.

Soon Michel Noiret, sworn trumpeter to the king, our lord, imposed silence on the louts, and proclaimed the sentence, in accordance with the order and command of monsieur the provost. Then he withdrew behind the cart, with his men in livery surcoats.

Quasimodo, impassible, did not wince. All resistance had been rendered impossible to him by what was then called, in the style of the criminal chancellery, "the vehemence and firmness of the bonds" which means that the thongs and chains probably cut into his flesh; moreover, it is a tradition of jail and wardens, which has not been lost, and which the handcuffs still preciously preserve among us, a civilized, gentle, humane people (the galleys and the guillotine in parentheses).

He had allowed himself to be led, pushed, carried, lifted, bound, and bound again. Nothing was to be seen upon his countenance but the astonishment of a savage or an idiot. He was known to be deaf; one might have pronounced him to be blind.

They placed him on his knees on the circular plank; he made no resistance. They removed his shirt and doublet as far as his girdle; he allowed them to have their way. They entangled him under a fresh system of thongs and buckles; he allowed them to bind and buckle him. Only from time to time he snorted noisily, like a calf whose head is hanging and bumping over the edge of a butcher's cart.

"The dolt," said Jehan Frollo of the Mill, to his friend Robin Poussepain (for the two students had followed the culprit, as was to have been expected), "he understands no more than a cockchafer shut up in a box!"

There was wild laughter among the crowd when they beheld Quasimodo's hump, his camel's breast, his callous and hairy shoulders laid bare. During this gayety, a man in the livery of the city, short of stature and robust of mien, mounted the platform and placed himself near the victim. His name speedily circulated among the spectators. It was Master Pierrat Torterue, official torturer to the Châtelet.

He began by depositing on an angle of the pillory a black hour-glass, the upper lobe of which was filled with red sand, which it allowed to glide into the lower receptacle; then he removed his parti-colored surtout, and there became visible, suspended from his right hand, a thin and tapering whip of long, white, shining, knotted, plaited thongs, armed with metal nails. With his left hand, he negligently folded back his shirt around his right arm, to the very armpit.

In the meantime, Jehan Frollo, elevating

his curly blonde head above the crowd (he had mounted upon the shoulders of Robin Poussepain for the purpose), shouted: “Come and look, gentle ladies and men! they are going to peremptorily flagellate Master Quasimodo, the bellringer of my brother, monsieur the archdeacon of Josas, a knave of oriental architecture, who has a back like a dome, and legs like twisted columns!”

And the crowd burst into a laugh, especially the boys and young girls.

At length the torturer stamped his foot. The wheel began to turn. Quasimodo wavered beneath his bonds. The amazement which was suddenly depicted upon his deformed face caused the bursts of laughter to redouble around him.

All at once, at the moment when the wheel in its revolution presented to Master Pierrat, the humped back of Quasimodo, Master Pierrat raised his arm; the fine thongs whistled sharply through the air, like a handful of adders, and fell with fury upon the wretch’s shoulders.

Quasimodo leaped as though awakened with a start. He began to understand. He writhed in his bonds; a violent contraction of surprise and pain distorted the muscles of his face, but he uttered not a single sigh. He merely turned his head backward, to the right, then to the left, balancing it as a bull does who has been stung in the flanks by a gadfly.

A second blow followed the first, then a third, and another and another, and still others. The wheel did not cease to turn, nor the blows to rain down.

Soon the blood burst forth, and could be seen trickling in a thousand threads down the hunchback's black shoulders; and the slender thongs, in their rotatory motion which rent the air, sprinkled drops of it upon the crowd.

Quasimodo had resumed, to all appearance, his first imperturbability. He had at first tried, in a quiet way and without much outward movement, to break his bonds. His eye had been seen to light up, his muscles to stiffen, his members to concentrate their force, and the straps to stretch. The effort was powerful, prodigious, desperate; but the provost's seasoned bonds resisted. They cracked, and that was all. Quasimodo fell back exhausted. Amazement gave way, on his features, to a sentiment of profound and bitter discouragement. He closed his single eye, allowed his head to droop upon his breast, and feigned death.

From that moment forth, he stirred no more. Nothing could force a movement from him. Neither his blood, which did not cease to flow, nor the blows which redoubled in fury, nor the wrath of the torturer, who grew excited himself and intoxicated with the execution, nor the sound of the horrible thongs, more sharp and whistling than the claws of scorpions.

At length a bailiff from the Châtelet clad in black, mounted on a black horse, who had been stationed beside the ladder since the beginning of the execution, extended his ebony wand towards the hour-glass. The torturer stopped. The wheel stopped. Quasimodo's eye opened slowly.

The scourging was finished. Two lackeys of the official torturer bathed the bleeding shoulders of the patient, anointed them with some unguent which immediately closed all the wounds, and threw upon his back a sort of yellow vestment, in cut like a chasuble. In the meanwhile, Pierrat Torterue allowed the thongs, red and gorged with blood, to drip upon the pavement.

All was not over for Quasimodo. He had still to undergo that hour of pillory which Master Florian Barbedienne had so judiciously added to the sentence of Messire Robert d'Estouteville; all to the greater glory of the old physiological and psychological play upon words of Jean de Cumène, **Surdus absurdus**: a deaf man is absurd.

So the hour-glass was turned over once

more, and they left the hunchback fastened to the plank, in order that justice might be accomplished to the very end.

The populace, especially in the Middle Ages, is in society what the child is in the family. As long as it remains in its state of primitive ignorance, of moral and intellectual minority, it can be said of it as of the child,–

'Tis the pitiless age.

We have already shown that Quasimodo was generally hated, for more than one good reason, it is true. There was hardly a spectator in that crowd who had not or who did not believe that he had reason to complain of the malevolent hunchback of Notre-Dame. The joy at seeing him appear thus in the pillory had been universal; and the harsh punishment which he had just suffered, and the pitiful condition in which it had left him, far from softening the populace had rendered its hatred more malicious by arming it with a touch of mirth.

Hence, the "public prosecution" satisfied, as the bigwigs of the law still express it in their jargon, the turn came of a thousand private vengeances. Here, as in the Grand Hall, the women rendered themselves particularly prominent. All cherished some rancor against him, some for his malice, others for his ugliness. The latter were the most furious.

"Oh! mask of Antichrist!" said one.

"Rider on a broom handle!" cried another.

"What a fine tragic grimace," howled a third, "and who would make him Pope of the Fools if to-day were yesterday?"

"'Tis well," struck in an old woman. "This is the grimace of the pillory. When shall we have that of the gibbet?"

"When will you be coiffed with your big bell a hundred feet under ground, cursed bellringer?"

"But 'tis the devil who rings the Angelus!"

"Oh! the deaf man! the one-eyed creature! the hunch-back! the monster!"

"A face to make a woman miscarry better than all the drugs and medicines!"

And the two scholars, Jehan du Moulin, and Robin Poussepain, sang at the top of their lungs, the ancient refrain,–

"Une hart
Pour le pendard!
Un fagot
Pour le magot!"[33]

A thousand other insults rained down upon him, and hoots and imprecations, and laughter, and now and then, stones.

Quasimodo was deaf but his sight was clear, and the public fury was no less energetically depicted on their visages than in their words. Moreover, the blows from the stones explained the bursts of laughter.

At first he held his ground. But little by little that patience which had borne up under the lash of the torturer, yielded and gave way before all these stings of insects. The

33 A rope for the gallows bird! A fagot for the ape.

bull of the Asturias who has been but little moved by the attacks of the picador grows irritated with the dogs and banderilleras.

He first cast around a slow glance of hatred upon the crowd. But bound as he was, his glance was powerless to drive away those flies which were stinging his wound. Then he moved in his bonds, and his furious exertions made the ancient wheel of the pillory shriek on its axle. All this only increased the derision and hooting.

Then the wretched man, unable to break his collar, like that of a chained wild beast, became tranquil once more; only at intervals a sigh of rage heaved the hollows of his chest. There was neither shame nor redness on his face. He was too far from the state of society, and too near the state of nature to know what shame was. Moreover, with such a degree of deformity, is infamy a thing that can be felt? But wrath, hatred, despair, slowly lowered over that hideous visage a cloud which grew ever more and more sombre, ever more and more charged with electricity, which burst forth in a thousand lightning flashes from the eye of the cyclops.

Nevertheless, that cloud cleared away for a moment, at the passage of a mule which traversed the crowd, bearing a priest. As far away as he could see that mule and that priest, the poor victim's visage grew gentler. The fury which had contracted it was followed by a strange smile full of ineffable sweetness, gentleness, and tenderness. In proportion as the priest approached, that smile became more clear, more distinct, more radiant. It was like the arrival of a Saviour, which the unhappy man was greeting. But as soon as the mule was near enough to the pillory to allow of its rider recognizing the victim, the priest dropped his eyes, beat a hasty retreat, spurred on rigorously, as though in haste to rid himself of humiliating appeals, and not at all desirous of being saluted and recognized by a poor fellow in such a predicament.

This priest was Archdeacon Dom Claude Frollo.

The cloud descended more blackly than ever upon Quasimodo's brow. The smile was still mingled with it for a time, but was bitter, discouraged, profoundly sad.

Time passed on. He had been there at least an hour and a half, lacerated, maltreated, mocked incessantly, and almost stoned.

All at once he moved again in his chains with redoubled despair, which made the whole framework that bore him tremble, and, breaking the silence which he had obstinately preserved hitherto, he cried in a hoarse and furious voice, which resembled a bark rather than a human cry, and which was drowned in the noise of the hoots–"Drink!"

This exclamation of distress, far from exciting compassion, only added amusement to the good Parisian populace who surrounded the ladder, and who, it must be confessed, taken in the mass and as a multitude, was then no less cruel and brutal than that horrible tribe of robbers among whom we have already conducted the reader, and which was simply the lower stratum of the populace. Not a voice was raised around the unhappy victim, except to jeer at his thirst. It is certain that at that moment he was more grotesque and repulsive than pitiable, with his face purple and dripping, his eye wild, his mouth foaming with rage and pain, and his tongue lolling half out. It must also be stated that if a charitable soul of a **bourgeois** or **bourgeoise**, in the rabble, had attempted to carry a glass of water to that wretched creature in torment, there reigned around the infamous steps of the pillory such a prejudice of shame and ignominy, that it would have sufficed to repulse the good Samaritan.

At the expiration of a few moments, Quasimodo cast a desperate glance upon the crowd, and repeated in a voice still more heartrending: “Drink!”

And all began to laugh.

"Drink this!" cried Robin Poussepain, throwing in his face a sponge which had been soaked in the gutter. "There, you deaf villain, I'm your debtor."

A woman hurled a stone at his head,–

"That will teach you to wake us up at night with your peal of a dammed soul."

"He, good, my son!" howled a cripple, making an effort to reach him with his crutch, "will you cast any more spells on us from the top of the towers of Notre-Dame?"

"Here's a drinking cup!" chimed in a man, flinging a broken jug at his breast. "'Twas you that made my wife, simply because she passed near you, give birth to a child with two heads!"

"And my cat bring forth a kitten with six paws!" yelped an old crone, launching a brick at him.

"Drink!" repeated Quasimodo panting, and for the third time.

At that moment he beheld the crowd give

way. A young girl, fantastically dressed, emerged from the throng. She was accompanied by a little white goat with gilded horns, and carried a tambourine in her hand.

Quasimodo's eyes sparkled. It was the gypsy whom he had attempted to carry off on the preceding night, a misdeed for which he was dimly conscious that he was being punished at that very moment; which was not in the least the case, since he was being chastised only for the misfortune of being deaf, and of having been judged by a deaf man. He doubted not that she had come to wreak her vengeance also, and to deal her blow like the rest.

He beheld her, in fact, mount the ladder rapidly. Wrath and spite suffocate him. He would have liked to make the pillory crumble into ruins, and if the lightning of his eye could have dealt death, the gypsy would have been reduced to powder before she reached the platform.

She approached, without uttering a syllable, the victim who writhed in a vain effort to escape her, and detaching a gourd from her girdle, she raised it gently to the parched lips of the miserable man.

Then, from that eye which had been, up to that moment, so dry and burning, a big tear was seen to fall, and roll slowly down that deformed visage so long contracted with despair. It was the first, in all probability, that the unfortunate man had ever shed.

Meanwhile, he had forgotten to drink. The gypsy made her little pout, from impatience, and pressed the spout to the tusked month of Quasimodo, with a smile.

He drank with deep draughts. His thirst was burning.

When he had finished, the wretch protruded his black lips, no doubt, with the object of kissing the beautiful hand which had just succoured him. But the young girl, who was, perhaps, somewhat distrustful, and who remembered the violent attempt of the night, withdrew her hand with the frightened gesture of a child who is afraid of being bitten by a beast.

Then the poor deaf man fixed on her a look full of reproach and inexpressible sadness.

It would have been a touching spectacle anywhere,–this beautiful, fresh, pure, and charming girl, who was at the same time so weak, thus hastening to the relief of so much misery, deformity, and malevolence. On the pillory, the spectacle was sublime.

The very populace were captivated by it, and began to clap their hands, crying,–

"Noël! Noël!"

It was at that moment that the recluse caught sight, from the window of her bole, of the gypsy on the pillory, and hurled at her her sinister imprecation,–

"Accursed be thou, daughter of Egypt! Accursed! accursed!"

CHAPTER FIVE

End of the Story of the Cake

LA ESMERALDA TURNED PALE and descended from the pillory, staggering as she went. The voice of the recluse still pursued her,–

"Descend! descend! Thief of Egypt! thou shalt ascend it once more!"

"The sacked nun is in one of her tantrums," muttered the populace; and that was the end of it. For that sort of woman was feared;

which rendered them sacred. People did not then willingly attack one who prayed day and night.

The hour had arrived for removing Quasimodo. He was unbound, the crowd dispersed.

Near the Grand Pont, Mahiette, who was returning with her two companions, suddenly halted,–

"By the way, Eustache! what did you do with that cake?"

"Mother," said the child, "while you were talking with that lady in the bole, a big dog took a bite of my cake, and then I bit it also."

"What, sir, did you eat the whole of it?" she went on.

"Mother, it was the dog. I told him, but he would not listen to me. Then I bit into it, also."

"'Tis a terrible child!" said the mother, smiling and scolding at one and the same time. "Do you see, Oudarde? He already eats all the fruit from the cherry-tree in our orchard of Charlerange. So his grandfather says that he will be a captain. Just let me catch you at it again, Master Eustache. Come along, you greedy fellow!"

CONTINUES IN VOLUME TWO

www.ingramcontent.com/pod-product-compliance
Lightning Source LLC
Chambersburg PA
CBHW020919310726
48980CB00011B/952/J

* 9 7 8 1 8 3 4 1 2 3 9 1 2 *